FOOL HEARTS

PLUM VALLEY COWBOYS BOOK ONE

EMMY SANDERS

Beta Reading by A.F., C.J. Banks, Lauren, Reppy Andrews, and Sadie Jay

Editing by LesCourt Author Services

Proofreading by Ky

Cover Design by Cate Ashwood

ISBN: 9798986448305

Content Warning: This book contains homophobia and the off-page traumatic death of an adult side character due to medical complications. Please take caution if this subject matter may be triggering for you.

For all the tender hearts who know what it's like to love big.
May you get back what you give.

CONTENTS

Prologue

Wyatt

In Plum Valley, Texas, where the cattle count is higher than the population, everybody knows every-dang-body. Smack-dab in the center of the Texas Hill Country, Plum Valley boasts some of the state's finest beef, a fact Plum Vallians are prouder than punch about. It's even on the sign. Not that you'd bother to visit, but if you *did* brave the one-and-a-half lane road that swerves and curves up the mountain Plum Valley sits atop, you'd see it. There, at the final turn, is our town's welcoming committee in the form of one large bovine-shaped piece of wood, declaring, "*Plum Valley, occupancy 596, best beef in all of Texas.*"

Contrary to its name, Plum Valley is *not* known for its plums. Not anymore. Most of the orchards were razed in the mid-1900s to make room for more grazing. After all, Plum Vallians were, and still are, serious about their beef.

When I was young, I thought I'd live and die in Plum Valley. It was what I knew. The rolling hills dotted with Longhorn and Hereford cattle, Main Street with its dozen or so brick-faced shopfronts, the combination elementary-middle-high school that butted up against one of the town's largest processing plants. It was a simple life, but a good one.

The rose-colored glasses fell off around the time I entered the double digits and realized somebody like me wasn't going to be accepted in a small, southern town like ours, with its conservative views and gay population of one.

If it wasn't clear, that *one* was me.

Leaving Plum Valley was simultaneously one of the hardest and easiest decisions I ever made. I didn't think I'd be back here after that, and I sure didn't think I'd be a thirty-four-year-old bachelor, living with his best friend. The very same friend responsible for my going in the first place. Yet here I am, back in the place I grew up, living that life I dreamed about when I was a young boy. With one very complicated detail.

The fact that I'm in love with that friend.

My tragically-straight, but oh-so-swoon-worthy—if I were the type of guy to swoon—friend. The one I live with. The one I moved away and back for. The one who's oblivious to my feelings.

Mhm, sure is a long story.

I didn't see this coming when I was eight, swinging on the porch swing with Easton, making a pact to be together forever. It was kid stuff, thinking the world would stay as it was: easy and fun and free. Best friends forever, that's what we said.

If only I knew what that meant. *Best friends forever.* Because now, everything is different.

Now, with each one of those passing years on the long way to forever, little pieces of me get carved out and left empty. Unrequited love, that's what they call it. And I'm the fool who's willingly putting himself in front of the knife to be cut over and over again.

And perhaps most foolish of all? I don't regret it. I never will.

But there *is* a piece of me, a very tiny piece, that's been getting louder these days. A voice inside that's telling me it's time. Time to move on. Move out. Time to sow my own life with somebody who's capable of loving me back.

So, I guess I lied.

Leaving Plum Valley isn't the hardest decision I've faced. Letting Easton go will be.

But I'm getting ahead of myself here. I should probably start at the beginning.

Part I: The Beginning

CHAPTER 1

1991

Wyatt, age 11

"Blue or red?" Easton asks, like he doesn't already know. I answer anyway.

"Red."

Easton hands over the red ice pop, and we dig in. Ice pops are my favorite, and Easton knows that, just like he knows red is my *very* favorite. My parents don't keep ice pops in the freezer, but Easton's mama does.

"What do you think middle school will be like?" I ask, kicking at the tall grass around the fence we're sitting on. We'll be in sixth grade after summer is over. I don't know what to think about that.

"The same," Easton replies, and I laugh.

"Yeah, prob'ly." It is in the same school, after all. Same folk, same place, just a new number. "Do you think Layla will ask you out again?"

Layla will be in sixth, like us. She's been asking Easton to go steady since first grade, before we understood what any of it meant. Holding hands and all that. Maybe kissing. I don't know how I feel about that, either.

Easton just shrugs. "Dunno."

"Well, do you want her to?"

"Dunno."

That's Easton, short and to the point. Maybe he really doesn't know what to make of it, like me.

"I don't think I like girls," I admit.

I'm not sure what made me say it. I haven't told anyone else yet. Definitely not my parents. They wouldn't like it. Pa is always going on about good ol' fashioned values. I guess I just trust Easton most.

Easton looks my way for real this time and holds my gaze. "That's all right," he says, and I believe him. After a minute, he adds, "I ain't gonna tell."

He doesn't need to say it—I know he won't—but I appreciate it all the same.

Being different around here isn't good. I don't think it's like that everywhere, but in Plum Valley, girls like boys, and boys like girls, and that's just the way of it.

We're quiet for a bit, just listening to the sound of cattle mooing, a soundtrack you can hear just about everywhere in these parts.

"I don't think I wanna be a rancher," Easton says, looking out over the herd.

"What'll you be?" I ask.

He shrugs. "Always liked horses."

I nod. I can see that. Easton is good at riding, and horses like him, too.

"Would your dad let you?"

Easton's dad owns this cattle ranch. It's one of the biggest in town, and there are a lot of them. He likes Longhorn the best, and he has a whole ton of fields that Easton and I can explore, so long as we leave the cattle alone.

Just like this field we're in now. It's the furthest away from Easton's house. So far out the ice pops were half slush by the time Easton arrived with them.

I keep eating mine, wondering if my mouth is as red as Easton's is blue.

It's a long while before Easton answers. He's like that sometimes, but I don't mind.

"Don't think he'll get a say when I'm old enough."

That's a good point. Adults can do whatever they want, like eat dessert first. Easton's mama told me that once.

I like Easton's mama. She's warm and hugs me lots, and she never seems to mind me being around, not like Easton's dad does.

Easton has two brothers, too. One older and one younger. I don't have any siblings, but I always thought Easton was like my brother.

We finish our ice pops, hands and mouths sticky, and watch the cattle grazing, flicking their tails occasionally to chase off flies.

"I gotta go home," Easton says. "I'm feedin' the horses tonight."

"All right," I say, hopping down from the fence.

I climb onto my bike, kicking the stand in, and Easton does the same before turning back my way.

"Still comin' to the barbeque tomorrow?"

"'Course," I reply. I wouldn't miss it. Easton's dad is real good on the grill, and his mama makes delicious banana cream pie.

"Right," Easton says, nodding. He turns back around, biking east, which I chuckle about since it's like his name, and I go north.

When I get home, I can smell supper cooking in the kitchen. Pa is kicked back on the couch, muddy boots taking up space in front of the door. Ma will have to clean those later. I don't like that, but that's the rule around here. I bypass the living room and go straight for the kitchen. When Ma sees me, she tsks and grabs a washcloth, rubbing it harshly over my face and hands.

"You'll spoil your supper."

"Need any help?" I ask instead of talking about the ice pop.

Ma huffs and gives me a pat out the door. "That ain't your job."

I don't think it's hers, either, but I know better than to say that. Instead, I sneak my dad's boots into the mudroom and wash them before anyone can notice.

★

"I'm done with chores. I'm gonna head to Easton's now," I call out to my ma. She's picking herbs in the garden. It's a sunny day, so she's wearing a big, floppy hat on top of her head.

She looks in my direction when I call, squinting into the sun. "Check with your pa first," she reminds me, as if I would forget.

For some reason, I always have to run things by Pa, even if Ma already said it was all right. It doesn't make sense, but then again, I get a talking-to when I don't follow the rules.

I find Pa out in the old shed, grease covering his hands as he works on a lawn mower that's been on the fritz.

"Where you off to?" he asks, before I even have a chance to say anything.

"Easton's, sir. His mama invited me over for that barbeque."

Pa grunts, twisting the screwdriver in his hand. "You spend too much time with that boy."

"He's my friend," I defend. Seems pretty simple to me, but Pa is always telling me I should make other friends.

Why would I need other friends when I have Easton?

"Be off, then. Make sure you get back before dark."

"Yessir," I say, peeling away before he can change his mind.

I hop on my rusted red bike and pedal to Easton's fast as I can. I know a few shortcuts through ranching land, so it doesn't take me as long as going through the center of town would. Although it is more tiring going over grass, that's for sure.

The Moores are having a party to celebrate the Fourth of July. Mama Moore invited my parents, too, but they declined. They aren't much for celebrating.

A bunch of cars are parked down the driveway when I get there. I lean my bike against the porch, which is painted a real pretty white, and run around back. Everyone is congregated there already.

I find Easton right away, sitting in the treehouse with his brother.

Hawthorne is still practically a baby, only seven. That's four whole years younger than me and Easton. He has a gap between his front teeth that makes him look like a bunny rabbit.

"Want one?" Easton asks, holding out his plate. There are three hot dogs on top: two whole and one half-eaten. They all have ketchup, but no mustard because Easton doesn't like spicy food.

"Sure." I grab a whole one. Mouth full, I wonder aloud, "Do y'think they'll do any fireworks before it's dark?"

"Why would they do 'em before it's dark?"

"Well, I was just wonderin', 'cause I gotta be back before then," I explain.

"Oh," Easton says, scrunching his face up like he's thinking.

As I'm licking the ketchup off my fingers, Mama Moore's voice rings out over the yard. "Who wants ice cream?"

We all scramble out of the treehouse.

Later, when most everybody is playing a game of touch football in the backyard, Mama Moore comes over to me.

"Wyatt, baby, I talked to your pa over the phone, and he said you can stay for fireworks. Mr. Moore will drive you back home after, all right?"

I know my pa will probably give me a talking-to later about that, but I don't mind. It will be worth it to see the fireworks.

"Thank you, ma'am," I tell her earnestly. Although I have a feeling I really have Easton to thank. I bet he snuck off to get his mama's help while the rest of us were eating our ice cream.

She gives me a pat on the shoulder and smiles. Mama Moore is always plentiful with her smiles.

When the sky gets dark, the adults lay out blankets under the stars. There's a fire going for s'mores, and I eat four. When I'm done, my hands are sticky and my stomach is full.

Easton and I pick a blanket all to ourselves and lie down side by side. When the fireworks start, I can't stop staring. The explosions of red and blue and green and purple. They're so big, each one lighting up the night sky.

It seems odd to me, but also kinda beautiful, that a firework's purpose is to flash and then be gone. They don't last long, but they sure make people happy. I wonder what it'd feel like to be a firework. Would it hurt? Or would it be worth it to see all the smiling faces below?

"Where d'you think we go when we die?" Easton asks from beside me.

I look over at my friend, but he's still staring up at the sky.

"Heaven?"

"Think so?" he asks.

"Maybe." I don't really know. Pastor Nichols talks about Heaven and Hell sometimes, but it's hard to imagine either. I don't think a lot of what he teaches us in church could be true, so maybe he's wrong about Heaven, too.

"I think, maybe, we become stars."

"Yeah?" I like that idea, that we could stay up in the sky forever, able to watch down over our loved ones.

"Yeah," he says. "Hopefully, we'll be part of the same constellation."

I like that idea a lot, too.

CHAPTER 2

Easton, age 14

Today is the county fair, which means, like just about every other Plum Vallian, I'm here with my family, roasting under the midday sun. It's hot as heck today, a fact even the large iced soda in my hand doesn't fix. That's Texas for ya.

My brothers and I are exploring the grounds together. My dad said that was all right so long as we didn't split up. I'm to watch Hawthorne, and Clive is supposed to watch me. He doesn't do the best job, though, my older brother, seeing as he's a little more preoccupied with watching girls these days.

But I'm doing my part, watching Hawthorne. He wants to go look at the chickens, and we're headed that way when I notice a small foal lying on the ground, off to the side of everything else. A man and a woman are sitting behind it in the bed of their rusted, old truck, but my eyes snag on a sign beside that little horse, declaring it "FREE."

I peel off in that direction, drawn like a magnet, and Hawthorne automatically follows. As I get closer, I notice the horse's ears flicking around, but it doesn't turn its head to face us. And I'm guessing that has something to do with the fact that its eyes don't look quite right.

"Hey there," I say to the horse, squatting down but not trying to touch it. Its ears flick in my direction again.

"He's free," the woman in the truck says right away. "A real nice horse, wouldn't hurt a fly. Want him?"

I look up at her. "What's wrong with his eyes?" I ask, examining the horse.

"Blind," the man says while chewing on a piece of straw.

"We can't take care of 'im," the woman adds, "but he's a good horse."

"What's his name?" I hold my hand out, close enough for the horse to scent me. He snuffs against my palm.

"Monty."

My head pops up in surprise, and I know in an instant, deep down in my heart, that this is my horse.

Clive walks over then, having finally realized we weren't next to him. "What's goin' on?"

"Can you get Dad?" I ask.

He stares at me for a moment but nods and walks off. Hawthorne comes up next to me, sitting down and watching as I let the little foal examine my hand. The horse seems curious, if not a little wary.

The woman looks excited as my dad approaches several minutes later, sensing, I assume, that they've found someone to unload the blind horse on.

"What'd you need me for?" Dad asks. I see the moment it clicks, his eyes scanning the "FREE" sign near the horse. He looks over at me warily.

"Please?" I ask. "He don't cost nothin', and I'll use all my chore money for his upkeep. I'll take care of him myself, I promise."

My dad sets his jaw, ready to refuse. I've asked for a horse many times before, but his answer is always no. I even spend most of my free time helping out with the ranch horses, cleaning their stalls, brushing them down, anything to show my dad I'm serious and old enough for the responsibility now that I'm a teenager. But his answer is always still no.

I'm readying myself for the same reply this time, as well as thinking up what I can try to counter with, when Hawthorne speaks up.

"I like his color. What's that called?"

"Buckskin," I tell him. Monty is a light tan, kind of like the color of straw, with dark, nearly black points.

"It's real pretty," Hawthorne says. "Reminds me of Mama's hair."

My dad coughs from behind us as my own heart twinges, and when I look up, I can see the change in his eyes. Mama is a touchy subject for all of us still. She passed about two years ago, right near my twelfth birthday. Sudden and unexpected stroke. It hasn't gotten easier, her being gone, but I try to remember her in small ways when I can. And Hawthorne is right. Monty's color is just like Mama's hair.

"Please," I ask my dad again, quietly. Silently begging.

He clears his throat and nods, and I swear my heart lifts right up in happiness.

The couple who brought the horse is pleased to pass him on to us, and they drive off before we've even finished loading Monty into my dad's trailer. It's slow going, seeing as the foal needs extra reassurance to move through a world he can't see, but I'm able to lead him into the trailer and get him comfortable on a bed of straw.

My foot won't stop bouncing the entire way home, and as soon as my dad parks, I'm out the door and rounding the trailer to retrieve my new horse. Monty's ears flick when the door clanks open, and I talk to him gently as I approach so he knows

I'm coming. He doesn't budge until I clip a lead on his bridle and give him a gentle pull.

As I'm leading Monty into the horse barn, taking my time so as to not overwhelm him, Wyatt rides up. Monty's ear twitches toward the sound of Wyatt's bike treads kicking up stone, and I internally curse, wishing for once that my friend had a quiet setting.

"Shh," I whisper, soothing the young foal. I run my hand over his neck lightly to calm him.

"What's this?" Wyatt asks as he dismounts his bike. He drops it against the side of the barn, and the jarring sound makes Monty kick up his head.

"Quiet," I admonish him gently.

Wyatt tilts his head, but he doesn't question me. He comes up to us, quieter now, as he watches me lead the horse around the interior of his new home. I walk him around all four walls of the stall, out the door, back in, and around again. I show him his water trough and food, although he doesn't eat. Then I close the door, myself inside, and unclip his lead.

The little horse doesn't move much from his spot, but he tilts his head this way and that, tracking our sounds.

"New horse?" Wyatt asks softly, letting his arms rest through the bars of the stall, close to my head.

I nod, keeping my eyes on Monty to make sure he doesn't spook. He flicks his ears toward Wyatt, but is otherwise calm.

"He's mine."

"Oh," Wyatt says in interest. "Looks young."

"He is, just four months." That much, at least, I was able to learn from the couple at the fair.

The foal kicks at the ground a little before lying down, and I take that as my cue to walk out. He turns his head as I go, black tail twitching a bit.

"He's blind," I tell my friend.

Wyatt looks back in the stall with a narrowed, assessing gaze, likely taking note of the horse's cloudy eyes and the way he doesn't quite look at you, just cants his head in your general direction. I appreciate the fact that there's no pity there, in Wyatt's gaze. Just curiosity.

I give my friend a tap on the shoulder and motion for him to follow me out of the barn so that Monty can have some peace. We step out into the relatively cool night air and walk over to the house, taking seats beside one another on the porch swing outside the front door. The crickets are already chirping.

"All right, so you gonna tell me how you got a blind baby horse?" Wyatt asks, kicking the swing into motion.

"We were at the fair today, and these folks were there, tryin' to get rid of him."

"'Cause he's blind?" Wyatt asks.

I nod, thinking back to that moment when I first set eyes on the buckskin foal. I don't know for sure what called me to the little horse, other than I've always had a soft spot for them.

"They were givin' him away for free." I pause, smiling. "Name's Monty."

"You're shittin' me." He gapes, making me chuckle under my breath.

"Nope."

"Well, damn, Easton." Wyatt slaps me on the shoulder as he kicks the swing into motion again. "Your best friend and your best horse have the same name. Seems like fate to me."

Wyatt James Montgomery. Monty.

Maybe it is fate.

The thought makes me smile.

★

I click my tongue at Monty, and he comes toward me slowly. He's about eight months old now and a good bit bigger than when I first got him. He's looking healthier, too. His ribs aren't so pronounced.

When Monty's muzzle bumps into my arm, I bring my hand up and run it over the smooth, cool surface of his nose. His nostrils flare against my hand as he sniffs me in greeting. I jog a little bit away and give Monty the cue for *left*, which is not the direction I'm in. He rotates his body counterclockwise a bit and stops.

"Good." I praise him softly.

I'm working with him in the paddock, like I do every day, and today, I specifically set out a few soft obstacles and rewards. Monty is near a block I wrapped in foam, in case he decides to try his hand at running and hits it full speed. As I give him cues we've been working on for months, he makes his way around the obstacle, feeling it out occasionally with his nose, without my direct help. This is a big step.

My goal is to be able to direct Monty verbally so that if he were in trouble, he could better navigate out. I'll get him used to being ridden once he's old enough, too, and he already trusts me implicitly to lead him with a rope, but this is a way for Monty to have more independence. Sure, I would still need to be present to give him his cues, but Monty doesn't have the advantage of sight, and I want him to feel a little less alone in the world.

It doesn't take long for Monty to get past the obstacle and find the apple waiting for him. He chomps it up happily, and I praise him over and over.

"You're doin' good with him."

I look up, surprised to see my dad standing outside the paddock.

"Thanks," I say with a nod.

He doesn't say anything else, just watches as I lead Monty by hand to another obstacle, this time working on a couple of his newer cues, *slow* and *stop*.

As I'm letting Monty bump his nose into the obstacle to get a feel for where it is, I hear the clinking of a bike chain. I look up in time to catch sight of Wyatt practically screeching around the corner into our driveway, and I chuckle as he wobbles a little and rights himself.

"Still friends with that boy," my dad says, not quite a question.

I frown over at him. Why wouldn't I be? "Uh-huh."

He grunts. "What about that Layla? She was comin' 'round here for a bit."

"We're not friends," I answer, a little confused. "She moved, anyhow."

What is my dad getting at? Sure, Layla did stop by maybe twice. Once when she asked me to join her for a picnic, which I thought was kinda strange. And then another time when she dropped off a pie, saying her and her mama baked extras. I wasn't going to complain about pie.

But that doesn't make us friends.

My dad just grunts again before walking off toward the house. Part of me is disappointed he won't keep watching, but maybe it's for the best now that Wyatt is here.

"How's your best horse?" my best friend asks once he arrives, practically flinging gravel in his haste to dismount from his still-moving bike.

"Comin' along just fine," I answer.

Monty does well with the second obstacle, and I decide he's had enough work for the day.

"Gimme a hand," I tell Wyatt.

He hops into the paddock without question, making sure to greet Monty first with quiet words and a gentle touch. The horse knows Wyatt well at this point and returns his greeting, snuffling his outstretched hand.

Wyatt helps me move the blocks out of the paddock, and then he fetches an extra-long lead at my request. I've been working on giving Monty chances to really get moving. So far, he's only gone up to a trot, but I'm hoping I can get him going at a canter today.

Wyatt stands to the side as I start Monty off, clipping the long lead to his bridle and walking along his side. When I start jogging, Monty picks up his speed, too, pulling his head up high and looking regal. Once he has a good pace set, I let out his lead slowly, making sure to keep pressure taut. In no time at all, Monty is trotting around me in a good twenty-foot-wide circle while I stand in place.

I encourage him to go faster, but he keeps holding himself back.

After a few minutes, I give the command for Monty to slow and then stop and am pleased when he does as asked. Giving him a few carrots from my pocket, I motion Wyatt over.

"Switch with me? I wanna get him runnin'."

"Sure." Wyatt nods, taking the rope.

Monty starts up walking and then trotting, again. This time, I jog the same circle, between Wyatt and Monty, just behind the lead rope. I encourage him along, praising, and with one stutter step and a whip of his head, he speeds up, breaking into a canter at last. I give a quiet "Whoop" and slink out of the circle, watching Monty truly run for maybe the first time in his life.

He looks as happy as a horse can, his spindly legs kicking off the ground, tail trailing behind him. Wyatt looks just as happy, a huge grin on his face as he holds the rope, spinning in place and leading Monty through his circle.

Wyatt's brown eyes meet mine then, and I swear he grins wider, looking goofy as all get-out. I chuckle, and I can't help but internally scoff at my dad's earlier words. Why would I need other friends? Wyatt is the best.

Best horse. Best friend.

CHAPTER 3

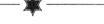

Wyatt, age 16

"Heya, Wyatt. You goin' to the bonfire tonight?"

I look up from the scoop of double mint I'm dropping into the junior cone for little Mary Watkins and lock eyes with Melinda Baker, a fellow tenth-grader, who's currently batting her overly large false lashes in my direction. Melinda blows a bubble of her bright pink gum, letting it pop obnoxiously before her tongue swoops it back behind her cherry-red lips. I assume this is supposed to be enticing in some form, but all I feel watching those lashes and painted lips is mild annoyance.

Because Melinda is blocking my view out front, where three shirtless Texan boys are repaving Main Street.

If there's anything better than a good ol' country boy, I have yet to find it.

Keeping my eye roll firmly on the inside, I offer Melinda a smile before passing Mary her cone. "Where else am I gonna be on a Friday night?"

This is Plum Valley, after all, not San Antonio. We don't even have a drive-in.

Mary walks out with her mom, and Melinda takes her place in front of the ice cream counter, giggling like what I said was the funniest joke. She props her elbows on the glass and kicks out a hip. I glance over her shoulder, but the only piece of Stanley Turbins I can see is his left arm. As such, I resign myself to helping Melinda, if nothing else than to get her on her way.

"What'll you have?" I ask, replacing the top on the double mint and stepping up to the register.

"How 'bout a dance?"

Melinda's friend, who's waiting over near a booth, giggles at that, her pigtails dancing around her shoulders as she ducks her head quickly.

I know what she means, but I decide to play dumb. It's worked for me thus far in avoiding girls my age. Easton is still the only one who knows I'm gay, and I plan to keep it that way. At least for now. It's not that I'm ashamed of my sexuality, not in the least. I don't *want* to hide who I am, but even in the nineties, being queer in Plum Valley is unheard of.

So, keeping my smile in place, I shrug and give my best *aw, shucks* expression.

"I'm workin' right now, Mel. You wanna try the cherry chocolate? Donna made it up fresh this mornin'."

Melinda turns back and forth, like she's presenting herself for best in show. All the while, her mouth keeps chewing. "No, silly. I mean tonight. Save a dance for me?"

"Sure, maybe." *Or not.* "Can I get your order, darlin'?"

That seems to appease the gum popper, who grins widely and finally looks down at the ice cream choices. She chooses the cherry chocolate, after all, and I ring her up and fill the order on autopilot, already contemplating the merits of skipping tonight's bonfire, simply to avoid Melinda's advances.

As Melinda's tongue rolls over top of the ice cream I gave her, her gaze staying brazenly on me all the while, I decide maybe I *will* sit this one out. I don't want that tongue any-where near me.

But then the bell over the door jingles, and I find myself looking up into the face of my best friend, and just that easily, I change my mind. Easton would spend every weekend avoid-ing the rest of the world if he could, and it's my job to drag him out.

"Welcome to Country Cones, home of the best dang ice cream in all of Plum Valley, Texas!" I exclaim loudly, spreading my arms wide.

The girls look confused at my outburst as they leave the shop. Easton just shakes his head, used to my antics.

"You're ridiculous," he claims.

"Psh, you love it," I say, dropping my arms. "We're goin' to the bonfire tonight. Don't argue."

I know he won't. "All right. Gonna share today?" he asks, gesturing toward the ice cream case.

I raise a brow. "Didn't Coach say he wanted you on some sorta high-protein diet?"

Easton grunts. "Y'know I don't actually give a darn about football. Besides, now that I'm workin' on the ranch, I'm buildin' muscle just fine. I don't need Coach's diet."

He says it completely matter-of-factly, my friend. There isn't a conceited bone in Easton's body. But, as he absent-mindedly rubs his stomach—which *has* gotten a lot more de-fined since his dad started letting him work the cattle instead of doing kiddy chores—I find my eyes dropping and have to take a gulp to clear my throat. Suddenly, it feels like I'm swallowing a lungful of wool.

Shit, am I checking out my friend again?

"No, you sure don't need a diet," I agree, averting my eyes. I scoop up a big helping of coconut ice cream and drop it into a cup before I hand the whole thing over to Easton. "Here. My treat."

Donna lets me have a scoop for free each shift. More often than not, that scoop goes to Easton.

He accepts it gladly, and as his tongue swirls around the spoon, my cock twitches. I can't help but think about Melinda and how her show did absolutely nothing for me. Yet, here is my friend—a guy, sure, but he's always just been my friend—and the sight of *his* tongue innocently dragging that sugary cream into his mouth is enough to make me concerned about popping a boner at work.

Yep, definitely still gay.

I turn around, determined not to think about Easton's tongue or his abs or any of his other fine assets, and instead busy myself with cleaning up the station while Easton eats.

It's not the first time I've gotten hard around my friend. I mean, can you blame me? I'm a horny sixteen-year-old, and Easton is the very definition of my dream guy. Solid and tall. Dark hair, those vibrant blue eyes. The goddamn cowboy boots and his worn, leather hat. It's not like that doesn't describe a handful of guys around our age, boots and hat especially. This *is* Texas, after all.

But Easton is just...Easton. With the low rumble of his voice and how he chooses his words carefully. And how he always has a little more to say to me than others. I can't help the fact that I find myself attracted to him, but I'll never let him know it.

He's aware I'm gay. If he were anything other than straight himself, he'd have let me know by now, surely. Which means all those thoughts and unfortunate boners stay hidden. For good.

It's not worth wrecking a friendship over. Easton is the most important person in my world. I wouldn't dare risk losing that.

"So, the bonfire, huh?" Easton drawls.

"Melinda wants in my britches," I say, waggling my eyebrows and attempting to distract myself from my current friend-focused thoughts.

Easton chuckles, shaking his head. "Too bad for her."

"Yep. Too bad for me, too. I just want in…" I look out front, saying the first name that comes to mind. "Stanley Turbin's britches."

Easton follows my gaze over his shoulder, scrunching up his face. "Really? Stanley?"

"What's wrong with Stanley?" I want to know.

My friend shrugs, shaking his head. "Not good enough for you."

"Oh, please." I laugh. "Like I can be choosy 'round here."

"Suppose not," Easton concedes, looking a little concerned about the matter. It warms my heart that my friend cares enough in the first place. "Think you'll ever leave?" he asks, and it's not the first time he has.

I shake my head. "Nah, nothin' better out there."

"What d'ya mean? Not that I want you to go, but dang, Wyatt. What is there for you here? We both know it's a small-minded town."

You.

I don't say that, don't even want to admit to myself how true it is.

"I can always go to San Antonio to meet somebody," I reply instead, hoping he drops it. I don't want to talk about leaving. Even thinking about leaving Plum Valley—and him—makes me nauseated.

Sure, it's a conservative town with plenty of folks set in their ways. But I like it here. The lifestyle, the wide open spaces and the ever-present smell of straw and animal dander coming off the breeze. It's my home. And sometimes I feel like times are changing, or they could be very soon. Maybe it'll get better. Maybe I can be myself here someday.

"I suppose," Easton says again. He looks like he wants to say more, so I cut him off.

"Anyways, I'm pickin' you up at nine, all right? Now, get outta here so I can watch Stanley in peace before my shift ends."

Easton shakes his head, but there's a smile on his face.

"Yeah, all right."

He leaves without another word, and I watch him go, ashamed to admit it's Easton's ass I'm watching instead of Stanley's.

CHAPTER 4

Easton

I hear Wyatt's old beater, clanking down the road that leads to my family's ranch, before I see it. I don't know how much longer that old thing will hold up, but it's all Wyatt has, and he won't let it go without a fight.

I admire that about my friend, his fighting attitude.

I grab my favorite hat and settle it in place on top of my head as I stomp down the porch stairs. I don't bother letting my dad know where I'm going tonight. He doesn't keep a very tight leash on us boys anymore. Maybe that's simply because we're getting older, but ever since Mama passed, he's been more aloof. Part of me wonders if he's just given up. On us. Or on family.

But I don't want to think about all that right now. I just want to hang out with my friend.

Wyatt leans over and pops the door open before I make it to the truck. "'Bout time," he teases, as if I'd ever keep him waiting.

"Mhm," I grumble.

Wyatt picks the conversation back up after we've pulled out of the driveway. "So when's your dad finally gonna let me work the ranch so I can quit scoopin' ice cream?"

Wyatt's parents aren't ranch folk, even though they live in a cattle town. His pa is a mechanic, and his ma stays at home. But for Wyatt, it's like ranching is in his bones in a way it never was for me. He's made no secret of the fact that he wants to work for our family, but my dad won't hear it. Now that I'm sixteen, Dad is letting me work real jobs on the ranch, and maybe Wyatt's hoping he'll let him, too.

"I'll ask him again," I say, although I don't want Wyatt getting his hopes up. My dad has never really taken to him, which doesn't make any sense to me, seeing as Wyatt is one of the best people I know.

Wyatt pulls up to Cindy Davenport's place, which is tonight's bonfire locale, courtesy of her out-of-town parents. Beat-up vehicles already litter the drive, and the roaring fire illuminates the form of a couple dozen teenagers walking around in front of the barn, red Solo cups in hand.

As soon as Wyatt and I step out of his truck, discomfort slithers down my spine. It's not that I don't like people, per se. I just don't relate to most. Wyatt has always been the exception. It feels like everybody else is on a different wavelength. At our age, especially, everything is about sex and hooking up, and that just doesn't appeal to me.

Well, in theory, sex appeals. I just haven't found someone I want to have it with.

So all these classmates getting together every week, trying to pair off, doesn't make sense to me. I'd rather hang out with Wyatt in the northeast pasture in that big oak tree with the low branch that's perfect for sitting on. We could talk, just the two of us, and watch the sky change.

But saying that out loud doesn't sound normal, not for a guy my age.

So I let Wyatt drag me to these things, where we usually just end up sitting and talking with one another anyhow.

"C'mon," Wyatt says, slapping my shoulder. "Let's get a beer."

The other teenage obsession. Alcohol. I don't really get that, either, but I'm not opposed to having one drink at these things.

Wyatt and I fill our cups at the keg that someone's older brother or sister likely bought, and then he leads us over to a fallen branch near the speakers that are blasting popular country tunes.

"So," Wyatt says, pointing out over the sparse crowd. "Anyone catchin' your eye?"

He asks me that every once in a while. Not in a pushy way like my dad does when he talks about settling down and good country values, just like he cares. Like he's invested in me, which I reckon he is. I'm invested in him, too.

"Same dozen girls who're always here. Why would my answer be any different?" I ask him.

He rolls his eyes. "Don't know, things change."

I shrug. "Slim pickin's, like you said."

Wyatt laughs. "Yeah."

It's not long before I notice Melinda eyeing Wyatt, like most of the girls do. I suppose he *is* an attractive guy, all floppy chestnut hair and big, brown eyes, with those lashes that make it look like he's wearing makeup. And he has a way of charming just about anybody if he wants to. I think a good part of that is just the way Wyatt is, but I can't help but wonder how much of it is a defense mechanism because there's so much he has to hide.

When it's clear Wyatt isn't picking up Melinda's hints, she makes her way over, stopping in front of us and twirling her hair. "Hey, Wyatt," she says, drawing out her syllables.

"Mel," he replies, tipping his hat.

"How 'bout that dance?" she asks, persistent as ever.

Wyatt wasn't kidding; Melinda really does fancy him. She's been playing this game for months now, even though Wyatt hasn't returned a shred of the same attention she's been giving him. I don't know how I feel about that, but it isn't good. Can't Melinda see he's not interested?

"Oh, I dunno, darlin'. Easton and I just got here," he starts to say, attempting to put her off, but she isn't having it.

She tugs playfully on his arm, causing him to slosh some of his drink over his boot. "C'mon," she urges. "One dance won't kill you."

I can see the moment Wyatt decides it's not worth the battle. He lets Melinda tug him to his feet, but before she can lead him to the trampled circle of grass that's been designated as the dance spot, a shadow falls over my shoulder.

"I'll dance with you, Mel," comes Shane Merchant's voice from behind me, "if Pretty Boy don't want to."

He says it, *pretty boy*, like some kind of insult. Like being good-looking is a bad thing. My hackles rise immediately. I've heard that phrase thrown at Wyatt for the past couple years by a few of the guys at school, always in the same sort of way. I don't get it, but Wyatt told me it isn't meant to be kind. Why would anyone have a problem with Wyatt?

Yet before I can do anything, like defend my friend some-how, Wyatt plays the whole thing off.

"There you go, Mel. I'll get the next one, all right? After I've finished my drink with my buddy. Thanks, Shane," he says, tipping his chin at our classmate before he sits back down next to me.

Melinda pouts, but she links her arm with Shane's and leads them off.

I look over at Wyatt, but he shakes his head, not wanting to talk about it, eyes downcast into his drink.

I don't know why he wants to stay here. Wyatt is meant for better than Plum Valley has to offer him. He deserves more. My friend has always been larger than life, but this place is like a cage, trapping him in the confines of what a good country boy *should* be. And Wyatt is more than that. He's something special. He shouldn't have to hide himself away just to fit in around here. Surely, there's someplace out there where he could be free.

Where guys like Shane wouldn't be rude for no good reason. Where he could join his peers on the dance floor, a man in his arms, if that's what he wanted to do.

But that's not going to happen here. Not until things change. And who knows when that's going to be. Wyatt shouldn't have to wait around for it.

I try to figure out a way to tell him that, without it sounding like I want him to go. I don't, not in the least, but I want him to be happy even more. I don't get the chance to say anything, however, because Becca Thompson chooses that moment to insert herself into our bubble, taking a seat in front of us on the grass, legs crossed in front of her.

"Shane is a dick," she says bluntly, "and not the good kind."

Wyatt lifts his head at that and laughs, and I'm glad for it.

"Yeah," he replies, "but what'cha gonna do?"

Becca shrugs. "Find a better one." She sends a wink my way, and I feel like I'm missing something.

"Not many 'round here," Wyatt says, reiterating our conversation from earlier.

"Eh," Becca hedges, "there are a couple good ones."

Becca and Wyatt start talking about our classmates and who they think might go to college in a couple years. It isn't a long list. But I tune them out. My mind is stuck on my friend. On the fact that he shouldn't have to measure each of his interactions just to make sure his secret stays safe. Why couldn't things be easier?

"You're being awfully quiet over there, Easton."

"Hm?" I say, realizing both Becca and Wyatt are watching me.

"He's always quiet," Wyatt teases. Although it's mostly true.

"What're your plans for after you graduate? Ranchin'?" Becca asks.

"Mm." I rub the back of my neck, shaking my head. "Don't think so."

"So then?" Becca laughs, reaching over to shove my leg gently.

"He wants to train horses," Wyatt puts in for me.

"Is that right?" Becca says, her eyes lighting up. "I *love* horses. I could help you."

Wyatt chuckles under his breath, although I'm not sure why. I just shrug at Becca. I don't think her offer is serious, and I also don't really want to talk about myself.

"You hear from Layla since she moved over to Austin?" Wyatt asks Becca. I appreciate the change of subject.

Becca ends up staying with us, and, much to my relief, neither Melinda nor Shane makes a reappearance. And even though Becca keeps asking me questions, I don't mind her company. Out of all the girls our age, Becca is maybe my favorite. In a way, she reminds me of Wyatt. Confident, carefree, a little more free-spirited than I'll ever be. It's easy being around her, and that's not something I can say often.

Eventually, Wyatt gets up to get himself and Becca another drink. When he comes back, he sits close enough for our thighs to touch. I don't think anything of it. I just knock my knee against his in greeting, but I notice Becca staring for a long moment at where we're touching. And even though I know I should probably move my leg, I can't bring myself to do it. Wyatt and I have always been close, and I don't want that to change.

When we finally leave at the end of the night, Becca hitches a ride in Wyatt's rusty, old truck. She sits between us on the bench seat, hands in her lap, humming along to the radio. Once Wyatt rolls to a stop in front of her house, she leans over and plants a kiss on his cheek. Then she scoots out of the truck, goes up on her tiptoes, and plants a kiss on my cheek, too.

"Easton," she says, looking up at me in a way that makes me feel like I'm under a spotlight. I resist the urge to squirm. "The fair is comin' through town this weekend. Would you go with me?"

It takes me a moment to find my tongue. "Like a date?" I ask, head swinging around to find Wyatt, for whatever reason. He's watching me with raised brows.

"Exactly like a date," Becca says, smiling.

"Oh, uh. I dunno, Becca," I say, looking down at my boots.

I can feel the weight of her gaze for a moment, but when I don't add anything else, she says, "All right, then. Let me know if you change your mind."

I nod, and Becca makes her way inside, shooting me one last smile before closing the door. Soon as I'm back in the truck, Wyatt chuckles at my uncomfortable expression.

"She's sweet on you," he says
I don't know how to feel about that.

CHAPTER 5

Wyatt, age 18

"Come on, stud, break's over."

Easton and I are in the High Hill pasture today, one of the only portions of the Moores' ranch that still has an active plum tree grove. We just finished eating our lunch after a morning spent checking the herd and mending fences. Maybe that's not how most teenagers would choose to spend a Saturday afternoon, but there's nowhere else I'd rather be.

Out here on the ranch, doing a good hard day's work with my best friend by my side, that's my idea of perfection. Days like this make it easy to ignore the rest of Plum Valley and feel like I'm in my own personal oasis.

It also doesn't hurt that I'm finally getting paid, seeing as Easton's dad, Miller, grudgingly agreed to hire me on for weekends at his son's insistence. And I'm determined to be the best goddamn employee he has. Hopefully, with a little time, he'll see that this is something I'm serious about and maybe even warm up to me because I don't want to be anywhere else.

Easton doesn't move as I clean up our lunch trash. Instead, he fiddles with the cap of his metal drinking flask.

"Somethin' wrong?" I ask.

"Nah, not really," he replies, his voice a low rumble. I like the deeper notes of it lately, the way Easton seems to be growing into a man. "Just..." He pauses. "Think I'm finally gonna say yes to Becca. Senior prom is comin' up."

My blood freezes, despite the heat radiating down on us. I knew this day would come. Of course it would. The day when Easton would finally set his sights on some girl, and I'd have to face the reality of my situation.

That I'm just a lonely gay boy in love with his straight best friend.

I don't even know how it happened. Or when. Maybe they've always been there, those feelings. Just morphing slowly over time, from love to, well, *love*.

I don't *want* to feel this way, knowing there's no happily ever after in store for Easton and me, but I also don't think we're really in control of our hearts.

As it is, every time Becca or somebody else flirts with Easton or asks him out, it's like a knife in my gut. It makes me feel physically ill, and who wants to feel like that?

I've been dreading the moment Easton would return the interest of one of his admirers, and I'm still not ready for it, even though that time has come. Maybe I was holding onto an impossibly small sliver of hope that Easton would look at *me* like that.

Well, hope is a dangerous thing.

Because now, it feels like that knife in my gut is twisting.

"Yeah? Becca?" I ask, trying, best as I can, to keep my voice neutral. I didn't expect it to be her. She's become a good friend and has asked Easton out a handful of times over the past two years, but he always said no.

"Mhm," Easton grunts.

"I didn't realize you liked her." I take a sip from my own water flask, just to give myself something to do.

"I didn't, either. It's kinda new."

"What d'you mean?" I ask.

"Well," he says, dragging the toe of his boot through the muddy ground. It's been raining on and off all morning, so the ground is pretty wet. It almost looks like Easton's spelling something, but each letter carves over the last, so it's impossible to tell what. "She's kinda the first girl I've thought about like that."

I tilt my head in confusion, when suddenly it clicks. He's truly never been attracted to anyone before Becca? Wait, he said *first girl*. Does that mean...

"You mean you're attracted to her, right?" I double check.

Easton nods.

"Like, you think she's hot, and you could see yourself fuckin' her?"

Easton blushes. "Well, sure, I suppose so."

Here goes. "Have you ever wanted to fuck a guy?"

He looks over at me, brows cinched. "No, I would've told you," he says, causing my hopeful little balloon to deflate. "I just never felt that before, for anyone, and I was startin' to think I just wasn't normal."

"First of all, I call bullshit on there bein' a *normal* when it comes to who we like or don't, or whether or not we do at all. Everybody is different. But all right then, so you like Becca now," I say, letting myself come to terms with that fact, hard as it is to do so.

"Sure do. Have you ever..." Easton trails off, and I watch him closely.

"Ever what?" I prompt.

"Had sex?"

Oh.

"Yeah. I told you 'bout the time I met that guy in San Antonio."

"Well, sure, but I guess I didn't know if you two...you know, or if it was just a date," Easton says, sounding so adorably nervous talking about sex that I want to say something filthy just to see him blush again. Over and over, really. But I decide to be good. At least, relatively.

"Oh, we definitely *you knowed*."

"What was it like?"

"Really?" I ask, chuckling a little uncomfortably. "You wanna do this?"

"Don't make me regret askin'. I'm freakin' out a bit over here, all right? I don't know how to *do* any of this. What if Becca wants to take things further after prom? I want to be prepared for that."

I knock my boot against the side of Easton's.

"All right, I'm done teasin'. It's different, obviously, for men and women. For me, it was good. Really good. The guy was a little older, and he knew what he was doin', so I followed his lead. He let me fuck him 'cause he liked it both ways and thought it'd be easier on me. Guess I really lucked out. I don't think all guys would've been so flexible about it."

Easton clears his throat. "So, what if neither of us knows what we're doin'?"

"Becca has had sex, Easton."

He stills. "How d'you know?"

I can't help but laugh. "She's *talked* about it right in front of you, I think more than once. The time I remember was when we were eatin' lunch outside near the football field, and you had a biology test comin' up, so all your notes were spread out in front of you. You punched me in the arm when I got mustard on one of your drawings."

"I remember that," he says.

"Yep, and Becca was laughin' about the anatomy of somethin'...what was it? Oh, right, ducks. 'Cause males have weird penises. And that got her talkin' about a guy she had sex with whose uncircumcised penis surprised her, 'cause she'd never seen one before."

"I definitely don't remember that part," Easton interjects.

"Clearly," I say, rolling my eyes. "So, there you go. I don't think you have anythin' to worry about, buddy. Just be honest with Becca. I'm sure she can help guide y'all. And you know she would never think less of you for not havin' experience."

Easton nods, and we go back to sitting in silence. Part of me can't believe I just gave Easton sex advice. It hurts, thinking about him with someone, but it's inevitable. The best thing I can do is support him.

"I think Becca suspects I'm gay," I muse out loud. She's not the only one, but the guys in our class aren't quite so nice about it. Apart from Easton, no one knows for sure, but that doesn't stop folks from speculating. I suppose it would've been easier to dispel the rumors if I'd tried dating a girl, even once, but I can't do it. To them, or to myself. It just doesn't feel right.

"Really?" Easton asks, looking concerned.

I nod. "But don't worry. She'd never say anythin'. She's too good of a person."

Although, at this point, I wonder if that wouldn't be the worst thing, folks finding out.

"Mm," Easton hums.

"C'mon," I say, brushing off my thoughts and smacking his arm. "We really gotta get back to work before your dad catches us slackin' and takes it outta my pay."

Easton snorts and shakes his head, but I'm not so convinced Miller Moore wouldn't really do that.

"We still need to wrangle that calf," Easton says as he picks up the bag with our trash.

"Yep, last one that needs taggin'."

Easton leads the way towards the herd. There are a few stragglers spread further out, but the calf we need to tag is with its mama, who's grazing in the sun right outside the plum grove. Our boots slip occasionally on the wet ground as we make our way towards them, making it slow going across the field. It doesn't help that we're also going uphill, and when I say hill, I actually mean a pretty darn steep incline. High Hill pasture is named so for a reason.

Most of the cattle don't pay us much mind as we get close. They're used to folks moving about. But as soon as the calf spots Easton approaching its flank, that little bugger takes off so fast I don't even have time to react. Easton makes a valiant attempt to grab its hind legs, but the only thing he succeeds at is slipping and taking a dive into the mud.

He looks so surprised at that turn of events, eyes wide and mouth slack as he lies in a pile of muck, that I just lose it. I laugh my head off, bent at the waist as Easton glares at me indignantly.

"Real helpful," he complains, pushing himself up. Unfortunately, that reveals just how much of him is now colored a muddy brown, which, in turn, makes me laugh even harder, despite Easton's scowl.

"Christ," I wheeze between breaths, waving my hand. "Oh, God. You shoulda seen yourself. Just *whoop*, splat. That might be the best thing I've ever seen. You sure you ain't a pig wrangler, cowboy?"

"Hilarious," he grumbles, uselessly wiping at some of the mud. "Let's see you have a go, then."

I clear the tears from my face, attempting to get myself under control. "Oh, no, that's all right. You've got this."

Easton sends me another glare, even as one corner of his mouth pulls up in amusement. I help corral the calf back in his direction, and after two more attempts, Easton manages to grab it. He keeps a firm grasp on the wiggly thing, and I tag its ear.

"There we go," I say as Easton lets go and the calf trots off. "Easy as pie."

Easton turns and starts walking toward me. "C'mere."

"What're you doin'?" I ask, backing up a step. I don't like the gleam in his eye.

Easton darts towards me then, and I don't have time to make a move before he grabs me around the middle just like that calf and drives me to the ground. I land on my back with an "Oof," and the two of us roll a ways downhill before coming to a stop.

"Shit," I groan out around a laugh, looking over at my friend. The laughter in my throat dies when I realize Easton's arm is hanging over me where we've landed, and his body is pressed against mine.

My heart starts racing at a breakaway pace, like a bunch of stallions are galloping inside my chest. I try to ignore Easton's close proximity, but it's hard to do. We're both breathing heavily after the short tumble, chests rising and falling as the sun attempts to bake us into the dirt, and the feel of his hard body against mine is causing my brain to short circuit.

"What was that?" I ask a little breathily.

Easton grunts, lifting up and looking me directly in the eye. For a brief moment, my heart simply stops. Because he's right there, inches in front of me with those deep blue eyes I so often get lost in. And, as absolutely unrealistic as it would be, it feels like he's about to kiss me. But then he grabs a clump of ground and smashes it against my cheek, breaking the daydream.

"Much better," he declares, grinning down at me.

My mouth drops open slowly in shock. "I can't believe you just did that."

He points at the cheek he dirtied and says, "You gotta little somethin' right there," before rolling over and landing on his back next to me.

I huff, hoping my flush can be explained away by our tumble and the sun overhead. "Y'know, some days I question why we're friends."

"Nah, you don't."

"No, I don't," I admit, laughing as I wipe dirt and mud off my face.

I'm still laughing when Easton and I finally pick ourselves up. And there's a smile on my face the entire time we trudge back up that hill.

We're both filthy, and the sun is doing its best to broil us alive as we finish our work, but up here on High Hill, it feels like we're on top of the world. Invincible. Just the two of us.

It's a good fucking day.

CHAPTER 6

Easton, age 19

"Wish me luck, Monty," I say, petting my horse before I let him loose to roam the portion of field Dad let me fence just for him. It gives him a consistent space to feel safe, now that he's mapped it out.

My dad's office isn't far as the crow flies, just over the hill from our house. I could walk there, but I decide to drive instead.

He had the office built long ago as a way to keep the business side of things separate from home life. I think his idea was to leave work behind when he came home, but he also has a home office he often works in, so I don't know what the difference is. But now that the ranch employs a whole bunch of ranchers and help, the building has several purposes, including an in-house exam room for the on-call vet.

While I make the short drive to see my dad, I go over the talking points I've rehearsed in my head dozens of times. I graduated a year and a half ago, I'm an adult now, I have a business plan, and I'm ready to strike out on my own. I hope he'll hear it.

I pull into the gravel parking area and find a space among the many employee trucks and other vehicles in the lot. Even on a Sunday, there're plenty of folks here. Animals don't take a day off.

A cool blast of air hits me as I head inside. There's no receptionist on the weekend, so the building feels empty, but I know my dad will be in his office. I checked with him earlier to make sure he'd have time to see me. I knock before I enter, and Dad's voice filters through the door.

"Come in."

When I step inside, my dad sets aside the papers in his hand, and I appreciate that he seems like he's going to give me his full focus.

I sit down across from him, working to keep my leg still. My dad always has a way of unsettling me. It's not that he makes me uncomfortable. He's just stern, and it feels like I'm always trying to earn his approval.

"What'd you wanna see me 'bout?"

"Well, I wanted to ask about the land you and Mama set aside for us."

My dad nods. My parents told us long ago that they separated out three parcels of property from this one. They're not hundreds of acres big like the ranch, but they're still sizable chunks of land, one for each of us boys should we decide we wanted them. Clive has already moved onto his, had a house built there and everything.

"You're thinkin' of buildin'?" he asks.

I tilt my head back and forth. "Yes, but it's a little more than that. I want to start my own business."

Dad leans back in his chair, crossing his arms. "You want outta ranchin'?"

"I want to train horses," I tell him, knowing better than to say anything bad about ranching. "I've saved up my money, but it's not enough to get a house and a business started. Now, I could keep on as I'm doin' and afford it in about five years, but I have it all planned out and was hopin' you could help me get that future started now."

My dad is silent for a while. Long enough that I start wondering if I should just keep talking, trying to sell him on my vision.

"What's your plan?" he finally, thankfully, asks.

So I explain it to him. The house, the large horse barn and adjacent pastures, the investment needed to get my business off the ground. I tell him in detail the costs, the turnaround to profit, and what I see myself doing. How I see my life playing out.

"I've trained a good many horses by now," I go on. "The Walkers had those horses they got at auction that I groomed to be good trail riders, and now they're doin' a steady business with 'em. Geraldine Allen's horse kept fallin' out of his turns durin' barrel racing, and I got him turnin' on a dime."

I open my mouth to keep going, but my dad holds up his hand.

"And you and Becca, you two are serious?"

I nod. Truth is I love Becca quite a lot, and I don't see there being another girl that could hold a candle. But with both of us still living at our parents', it'll be hard to move forward as a couple.

"Yessir, that's another thing I've considered. We'd need somewhere to settle down, should the time come."

My dad nods again, looking more pleased about that.

"All right," he says. "You get me those plans, and we'll get the financials settled."

"Really?" I push forward in my chair, surprised. I honestly thought there'd be a longer discussion, maybe a few drawn-out conversations over months or more.

My dad grunts, raising an eyebrow.

"Right," I say, standing up, not wanting him to change his mind. "Thank you, Dad. Truly."

"Mhm." He picks his papers back up, effectively dismissing me.

I scoot out of there with a wide grin on my face.

When I pull into Becca's driveway, her and Wyatt perk up from their location at the picnic table in the yard beside the house. I barely have the truck door closed before Wyatt is opening his arms wide, shouting, "Well?"

"I'm startin' my business," I yell back.

Wyatt jumps up with a big "Whoop!"

Becca runs over, meeting me halfway and jumping into my arms. I scoop her up easily, seeing as she weighs practically nothing, and she plants a smacking kiss on my cheek.

"So proud of you," she says, smiling wide before coming in for a longer, lingering kiss on my lips.

As I set her down, I notice Wyatt off to the side, looking away like he's giving us privacy. Becca holds my hand, tugging me back over to the table, and we sit side by side, feet hooked together. Wyatt plops down across from us, grinning.

"Told you he'd go for it."

"You did not," I say. "We both thought he'd hem and haw."

"Well, I told you he'd be a *fool* not to go for it," Wyatt amends, giving my arm a little shove.

"You're gonna do great," Becca says, face shining up at me, and it makes me proud that she really believes so.

"It's not gonna be the same at the ranch without you," Wyatt says, his eyes telling me how much he'll miss me. I get it; I'm going to miss spending my days with him, too.

"Yeah, but we'll still see each other plenty," I tell him.

Wyatt looks over at Becca then, a strange expression on his face, but it's over so fast I don't have time to try to decipher it.

"When will you start buildin'?" he asks.

"Not sure. It might take a bit, gettin' it all sorted. In the meantime, I'll get word out about business expandin', since I'll have a space to keep more horses with me."

"We'll help you," Becca says, ever my champion.

Wyatt nods. "'Course we will. Now," he says dramatically, pulling a bottle of whiskey out from under the table, "I propose we celebrate."

"That confident, were you?" I ask, chuckling.

He shrugs. "I figured, worst-case scenario, it'd be good for pissin' away our sorrows."

"Where'd you even get the booze?" I ask, considering we're not yet legal drinking age.

Becca waggles her eyebrows. "Bumped into your cousin Autumn when I was volunteerin' at the road cleanup the other week. She helped us out," she says with a grin.

Wyatt opens the bottle, holding it in the air. "To Autumn, and to Easton's big break."

We all cheer, and the bottle is passed around, each of us sipping and getting progressively more tipsy.

At some point, we end up on the ground. Becca and I are lying on our backs, side by side, with Wyatt sitting up next to me. Each time Wyatt hands the bottle back to Becca, he leans over my body, and I get a whiff of something earthy, like he was out chopping wood.

"When you gonna start datin' someone?" Becca asks Wyatt, handing the bottle to me.

I tense a little because even though Wyatt told me he suspects Becca knows he's gay, neither of us has asked her outright, and she hasn't volunteered the information. I agree that Becca is a good person, and she'd never say anything around town. But, I still worry every time the topic comes up.

Wyatt just shrugs, looking up at the darkening sky. "I dunno. Maybe when I'm thirty," he jokes.

Becca hums under her breath. "I know there aren't many options 'round here, but I bet you could find someone worthwhile somewhere close. You're a catch, Wyatt. Anybody would be lucky to be yours."

I notice she doesn't ever use feminine pronouns when she asks Wyatt about dating. I wonder if Wyatt has noticed that, too.

"I appreciate that, darlin'. But I think for now, I'll stick to bein' on my own."

I pass the bottle to Wyatt, and he takes a drink.

"Almost gone," he says, handing it back to Becca, sending another whiff of woodsy smell my way. "What about you, Bec? Not datin', 'cause I know you've got this one here hooked, but have you put any more thought into that summer session in San Antonio?"

"Maybe," she replies, referring to the short volunteer EMT training course she could take at the community college. "I just don't know what good it would do. The nearest hospital is almost an hour away. I don't know how often I'd be able to go volunteer."

"Hmm," Wyatt responds. "Well, look at it this way. It's only three months of your time, and then you can save my sorry ass the next time I take a horn to the thigh."

"Or just don't aggravate the steers," I tell him, chuckling.

"Or there's that," he agrees with a grin.

I take a sip from the emptying bottle and hand it over. Wyatt polishes it off, setting it next to him on the grass.

I don't say it out loud, but I have a feeling I know what Becca's holdup is. We haven't discussed it yet, but with all this talk about getting the land from my dad and building a house and future, I'm sure Becca can sense something in the air. We've been dating for a while now, and I'm serious about her. It's only a matter of time before I make her an honest woman, although she'd slap me in the chest if she heard me saying that. Probably say something about making me an honest man, instead. But in the meantime, Becca doesn't want to make any big commitments.

I know she wants a family and to raise children. And I want that, too.

We fall silent as the sky turns navy, highlighting the stars above. Wyatt lies down next to me, sandwiching me between him and Becca. Becca takes my hand, squeezing it with her own, and I hold on tight, smiling as my world turns a little hazy around the edges due to all the whiskey. Becca giggles at nothing in particular, and Wyatt and I follow suit, all of us laughing up into the night sky.

I reach over with my other hand until my pinkie hits Wyatt's. I loop it around his, feeling like we should be connected, too. Wyatt doesn't move his hand, just looks over at me and smiles.

CHAPTER 7

Wyatt, age 20

Like usual, I stomp my feet on the Moores' doormat before heading inside. I don't see Easton's dad or anyone else around. Not that Clive would be here. Easton's older brother moved out of the house a while ago. But it's not unusual to run into Hawthorne, since he's still in school.

Hawthorne reminds me a lot of Easton, at least in regards to looks. They have the same dark hair, same blue eyes and bone structure. Hawthorne isn't as reserved as his brother, though.

I don't see him, however, or Miller, as I make my way through the house. And it's not until I'm one foot inside Easton's doorway that I spot my friend, and when I do, I stop still.

Easton is standing in front of his full-length mirror, an antique piece that used to belong to his mama, adding cufflinks to his baby-blue button-down. He's wearing a dark gray suit over the top, the entire thing pressed and sharp-looking. I've never seen him in a suit, apart from the cheap rental at prom a couple years back, and it's having a strong effect on me.

He looks so handsome I'm dizzy with it.

His short hair is styled ever so slightly, and he's not wearing his nearly ever-present hat. He even shaved his face smooth.

Now, don't get me wrong, I love Easton dirty and a tad raggedy, but this is something altogether new. It's surprising to me that there are still new things to discover about the man.

His lips are pursed in concentration as he fiddles with his cufflinks, and I want nothing more in this moment than to simply kiss him. To walk over, take his face in my hands, and show him all the things I've never been able to say.

But then I realize he must be dressed like this for a reason, and just like that, my fanciful little bubble bursts.

I shore myself up tight before walking over. Easton's head lifts in surprise, and a smile spreads across his face.

"Hey, what're you doin' here?" he asks.

I reach for the cufflink on his left wrist, and Easton holds out his arm for me. I secure it, shrug, and then reach for the other.

"Just stoppin' by," I tell him. "Got a date with Becca tonight?"

"Yeah." He nods, shifting to adjust his tie in the mirror. His eyes lift to mine in the glass, a dopey smile on his face. "It's our second anniversary, so we're drivin' over to San Antonio to some fancy place that has ceviche on the menu, whatever that is."

I nod, not trusting my voice to hide the fact that it feels like my insides are being scooped out. But I find myself having to ask.

"You're getting serious, then?"

"Yeah," Easton sighs, a content sort of sound. "Aunt Perla's takin' me to look at rings next week."

Now, I've heard the expression "lower than a snake's belly in a wagon rut" before, but I never really understood it. Plenty of things are lower than that. Worms in the ground, the roots of trees. But standing in front of the man I love, hearing him tell me he's fixing to propose to the woman *he* loves, I suddenly understand.

I feel like that snake. Hot all over, breaking out in a sweat like the summer sun will do to you. Yet icy cold deep in my stomach, just how that snake's belly would feel with the cool muddy ground underneath it.

I feel lower than low, shocked and turned upside down, inside out.

"You'll have to tell me if it's any good," I hear myself saying, although, to my own ears, it sounds like I'm inside a tin can. "The restaurant, I mean. And, uh, wow. Congratulations, buddy. I know she's gonna say yes."

Easton smiles again, eyes crinkling in the corners, that damn mouth and those white teeth of his tempting me cruelly.

"Listen," I say as I clear my throat, "I gotta hoof it. But have a good time tonight, all right?"

I slap Easton's shoulder and hightail it out of there, leaving his confused expression in my rearview. I don't stop walking until I've reached the center of town. I don't even know why I decided to come here, what drove me, but all of a sudden, I'm standing in front of the one pub-slash-restaurant in all of Plum Valley.

Pushing my way inside the saloon-style doors, I shake the moisture that's accumulated on my hat and arms from the walk over. I was too inside my own head to even notice the drizzle.

My legs are sore from the lengthy walk, and my arms won't stop shaking, but I hitch myself up on an open stool and hang my hat on a hook. It's busy tonight, and the loud din of conversation fills the space. It all just sounds like white noise to me.

Easton is going to get married. Soon. To Becca.

I don't know if my heart can take it.

How am I supposed to watch that? Could I? They'll build a house together, probably have a few kids. And what about me?

I'll be the perennial bachelor around town. People will talk about me. *I wonder why that Montgomery boy ain't settlin' down.*

I should have been expecting this. I should have prepared better. They *have* been dating for a long time. And that's been hard enough to watch, like acquiring new, tiny little bruises every day that cover my body slowly until I'm hurt all over. But somehow, I couldn't, *wouldn't*, let myself think he would marry.

I was clearly in denial.

Nash, the bartender and restaurant owner, comes over, and I order two shots and a beer. He wings up an eyebrow, but he doesn't question me. Nash knows I'm still just shy of twenty-one, but he's been serving me since I turned twenty. One upside to small towns, I suppose.

I finish the shots quickly, relishing the accompanying sting, and am taking my first sip of beer when there's a lull in conversation. It only takes one look around the room to realize why. Newcomers.

The talking starts up again, only now, people are surely speculating on who those three men are. We don't get a whole lot of visitors here in Plum Valley, Texas. We're too isolated, nothing but cattle and a hot breeze.

Out of the corner of my eye, I see one of the men gesturing to his friends. Curious, I take a longer look and find deep-set, whiskey-colored eyes staring right back at me.

Ah, shit.

Dread slithers in my gut. I recognize him. I fucked him behind a bar several towns over, just the other week.

There's a reason I drive far away when I want to hook up. I don't need word of that getting back here. And now this man, who just happens to be visiting for who knows what reason, is smiling and making his way over.

His two friends veer off to grab a booth as the guy whose name I never got sidles up in the stool next to mine. I curse internally, a good five or six times, as his hand drifts along my shoulder and arm in an overly familiar way. I can sense eyes on me, wondering who this man is, wondering what I have to do with it.

"Hey there, cowboy," he says, flirty smile in place. It's the same smile that got me last time, the same cheesy line that started off our conversation, if you could even call it that. We didn't do much talking. The man himself doesn't look like he's lived in these parts long, and he definitely doesn't talk like it.

"Didn't expect to see you again," I say, hoping my tone is hint enough.

Apparently, it isn't. He angles his body toward me, leaning forward into my space.

"Neither did I. Must be my lucky day."

His hand brushes my arm once more, and I lean away surreptitiously. As politely as I can, I brush it off, deciding I need to be direct and shut this down before he gives me away.

"Listen," I say, but he plows right on.

"I have a room down the road. Want to join me? Have a repeat of last time?"

There's a loud gasp from right behind me—because, of course, this night just had to get worse—followed by Lou-Anna Smith-Travers's distinctive booming voice. "You're *gay*, Wyatt Montgomery?"

I close my eyes, squeezing them shut tight like I'll be able to black everything out. This, and what happened before. But it's no use. The entire restaurant is hushed now, and when I look over at my nameless companion, his face has fallen in regret. I can tell he realizes that he walked into my complicated closet and dragged me out behind him.

I could deny it. Could talk my way out of it. But, for whatever reason, I don't do that. Maybe I'm just tired of it all. Or maybe I know something has to change. So, like a bear swatting at the hive without much thought as to how it'll feel to be stung, I turn on my stool and look Lou-Anna Smith-Travers in her overly-mascaraed eyes, knowing I'll really be speaking to the entire room.

Am I gay?

"As Ms. Martin's peach punch."

She blinks rapidly, and with one last glance at the man who unwittingly toppled the domino that set my life to change course in this town, I grab my hat and walk out.

It's pouring now, but it doesn't matter. I have no choice but to walk, so that's what I do. I walk all the way to the Moores' ranch, hopping fences until I make it to my favorite one overlooking the valley. The entire time I walk, and for who knows how long as I sit there on that fence, soaked to the bone, I think about my life here. What I have and what I don't, and I make up my mind.

I have to leave.

It's not even because news will travel so fast that by tomorrow, everyone will know my sexual orientation. Sure, I'll get looks and be talked about even more than before and likely even take some hostility from more than a few folk who'll disagree with me as a person because of something I have no control over. At this point in my life, I can handle that. I've even been preparing for it.

What I can't deal with, day in and day out, is watching Easton love somebody else and make a life with them.

I don't *want* to leave. *God*, I don't want to. These hills, these cattle, even some of these people, they're part of me, as imperfect as they are. But if I stay here while my heart withers, then this place and all my memories here, all the *good*, will turn to ash. And I don't think I could handle having my heart broken twice.

What I feel for my best friend, it's puppy love. It's got to be. And getting away will let me see that. It'll let me move on and find someone of my own, someone who's capable of loving me back.

Mind made up, I feel myself settle. It's like a numbness washes over me, my very own sedative to dull the pain. I'll say goodbye to Plum Valley and fall out of love.

I'm halfway back across the pastures when Easton appears through the veil of rain, running toward me in his fancy suit that's likely ruined by water damage and dirt.

"Are you all right?" he shouts once he's a couple dozen feet from me.

"What're you doin' here?" I yell back.

He reaches me quickly, grabbing my biceps in his firm grip. His eyes ping back and forth between mine, like he's trying to read me from the inside out.

"Why aren't you on your date?" I prompt again.

"We just got back." He squeezes my arms hard enough I can feel his fingertips digging into my flesh. "Came as soon as I heard. Are you all right?" he asks again, each word slow and intentional.

I don't know what to tell him. Am I all right? No, I'm not, although not for the reason he thinks. But I could let him believe that; it would make all this easier. I could let him think I was outed, and that's why I have to go.

"I'm leavin'," I tell him.

The confusion, shock, and sadness on his face breaks my heart all over again. This is going to be so much harder than I expected.

Easton doesn't say anything, like he knew this day was coming. He simply pulls me into his arms, knocking my hat to the ground in the process. I don't mind. I just hug him right back, thankful for the rain washing away my tears.

CHAPTER 8

Easton

When Wyatt and I were thirteen, he fell out of a tree on my family's ranch. I remember the moment vividly. First, there was the sound of Wyatt's flannel snagging against the rough bark, followed by his shocked gasp. Next, a flash of color in my peripheral vision and the *whoosh* of his body in the air. Lastly, the sickening thud as he hit ground and the way my heart sank straight down into my Stetson boots.

I remember looking over the edge of the branch as time seemed to slow, giving me an extended moment to register the dread of what I'd find. And then there was Wyatt, far below, lying crumpled on the ground. For a split second, I'd feared the worst. But then Wyatt's chest heaved as his lungs reinflated.

His wide eyes met mine, and even though I could tell his arm was broken—no arm should bend that way—he still managed to give me a flash of a smile. Relief, that's what it was, that it wasn't worse.

But it wasn't good. And by the time I climbed back down to the ground, Wyatt was sitting with his arm held close to his chest, looking green and grimacing.

It had started out as such a good day, too. Wyatt and I, in one of our favorite spots, talking about the future and our plans together. How he could take over the ranch when Dad got too old, if neither of my brothers wanted to. How we'd build space for the horses I wanted to keep. How we'd have houses, side by side, so we could be together forever.

Because, of course, we thought it was that easy. We thought there would always be an us.

We didn't know any better back then.

When we made it back to my house, my older brother, Clive, was the only one around. He drove us right to the hospital, calling Wyatt's parents once we arrived. His ma consented to treatment over the phone, knowing it would take them near an hour to show up.

I sat in the room with Wyatt, holding the hand of his good arm tight, as the doctor set his bone. It was one of the most horrific things I'd ever seen or heard. The snap. The way his arm went from crooked to straight. The sound he made the moment the pain flooded his system.

I'll never forget it.

I could feel it, that pain. Deep in my gut, like it was happening to me.

It's the same pain I'm feeling now, watching Wyatt pack up his meager belongings.

I don't know what to say. I want to convince him to stay, to beg, but I know I don't have that right. Being outed makes everything that much more complicated, so I understand why he has to go. I always knew Plum Valley wouldn't be enough for Wyatt, anyway. It doesn't have anything to offer him, especially not in terms of a partner. And that's something Wyatt wants one day. He's a romantic at heart; I could always tell.

I can't ask him to stay for me. Of course I can't. It would be the most selfish decision I could make.

<u>And yet I don't know how to *exist* without Wyatt in my life.</u> What does that look like? It's not something I ever had to imagine before, and I don't want to now. But I knew—I always knew—it was only a matter of time before I'd find out.

Wyatt is leaving.

That's his choice, and I have to respect it.

I feel guilty, too, that I'm so broken up over Wyatt when I still have Becca. It shouldn't feel this bad, should it? Wyatt and I are just friends, after all. He's only moving to another state. He can still visit. Or I can visit him.

This isn't an end, and yet it sure feels like one.

"Are you ever gonna say anythin'?" Wyatt asks.

When I look over, he's finished packing his bags and is sitting next to them on the bed. I haven't moved from my spot on the dingy beige carpet right inside the door.

"Hadn't planned on it," I try to joke, but I'm pretty sure it falls flat.

"C'mon," he says, plopping down next to me and letting our knees brush together. "You've gotta talk to me before I go."

Before I go.

I scrub my eyes, stomach swooping dangerously, the same way it did when Wyatt fell out of that tree.

"This is harder than I expected it to be," I finally admit.

Wyatt bumps his shoulder into mine and leaves it there, so we're connected from shoulder to knee. I appreciate the warmth of his touch, knowing it'll be the last time we're connected like this for a while.

"I know," he speaks softly.

I don't want to make this harder for Wyatt. Don't want my mood to sour our final moments. So, as best as I can, I push it down.

"I'm gonna miss you, bud."

"Yeah," he says, those deep brown eyes crinkling at the corners, "I'll miss you, too."

There's a whole lot more we both could say, but neither of us do.

I help Wyatt load his bags into his beat-up truck, which he promises he'll replace as soon as he gets the funds, and then we're left standing there awkwardly. Wyatt's parents aren't even here to send him off. Truth is I think they're relieved he's going. Now that the whole town knows Wyatt is gay, his parents don't want a thing to do with him, their own son.

I just don't understand people sometimes.

"It's not goodbye, all right?" Wyatt says.

I nod, swallowing a few times as I stare at the stones beside my boot.

"Hey," he prods, squeezing my arm gently until I look up at his face. I hold back the tears threatening to fall, my insides curling every which way in a jumble I can't make sense of. "You and Becca are gonna have a good life, you hear? And so will I. It's a brand-new world out there, and I'm gonna explore it, all right? And we'll see each other again before you know it. This isn't goodbye," he repeats.

But fuck, it sure feels like it.

"C'mere," he says, pulling me against his body.

My arms go around him willingly, desperately. I cling to him, allowing myself one more minute to catalogue the smell and feel of him, like I can imprint it into my brain as sense memory. Available to recall at will.

"I love you," I tell him. It's not the first time I've said it, but I have to say it again now. It feels necessary.

Wyatt is quiet for a moment before he replies, "I love you, too," his voice choking over the words.

When we break apart, Wyatt turns his face quickly, getting into his truck without another glance back. I'm grateful for it, if only because it hides the tear rolling down my cheek.

The truck turns over with a big clunk, and then he's driving away.

And here I am, standing in his parents' driveway, watching him go, feeling like a part of myself is leaving, too.

Why is this so hard?

I let myself cry. Couldn't stop it if I tried, to be honest, but I let it happen fully. Let myself stand there and feel it. I can't remember too many times I've cried in my life. When my favorite barn cat, Bubba, disappeared. When Mama passed.

And now, as Wyatt moves on.

I can't say exactly how long I stay standing in the same spot, watching the empty space Wyatt left behind. Long enough that the sky has started to turn dark. Long enough that my tears have dried up. I feel empty. Hollow.

Becca is waiting for me when I get to her parents' house. She doesn't ask any questions; she just holds me, shedding a few tears herself. And she continues to hold me, over the coming days and weeks, when it feels too hard. She never judges, and for that, I'm grateful. I couldn't have asked for a better woman by my side.

★

"Buddy, are you there?" I ask the crackling sound in my ear.

"Hold on," Wyatt's tinny voice responds, sounding a world away. Sure feels like he is, at least. Half a minute later, the call sounds clear again. "Sorry 'bout that, had to go up to the roof."

Wyatt's living in a cheap apartment in Illinois, nearby to his college. He plans on moving into something nicer his second year, once he has some more money saved, but right now, it's the best he can afford. And the place, from what I've heard, is a dump. Our calls often drop inside the building because it's all concrete and the cell tower is far away, so he ends up climbing up the escape ladder to the top of the building so we can talk.

I have a hard time picturing him there, amidst a sea of concrete and metal, instead of green grass and wide open blue skies.

"What's new?" Wyatt asks, voice sounding a little clearer, more like my friend.

"Well, Dad officially signed over the land, and we're startin' construction next month. Two-story house, nice big barn, and we'll clear up the pasture land a bit before layin' fence."

"That's fantastic news," he says.

"And there's another thing," I say, smiling a bit, even though he can't see it. "Becca said yes."

There's a brief pause, and I wonder if I lost him, but then Wyatt is exhaling. "Congratulations, man. I'm so happy for you. Knew she'd say yes."

"Yeah, well, when have you ever been wrong, huh?"

Wyatt lets out a bark of laughter, and I can practically see him shaking his head.

"And you?" I ask.

It's been a good three weeks since we last spoke, a whole six months since he moved up to Illinois. It feels like our whole lives are changing, like I'm missing so much of his personal evolution. And he's missing mine.

I hate that we don't talk more often, but Wyatt is so busy with his classes—learning more about agriculture than he ever could've here—as well as working as much as possible so he can afford it all. I don't know how he does it, the constant hustle.

"You'll never believe it, but I got a new truck."

"You don't say?" I ask, surprised, even though I knew it was only a matter of time.

"Didn't have a choice. Trusty Rusty finally bit the dust." He chuckles. "I had to buy a new one to replace him. And by new, I mean used, of course. You'd like him, though. He's a pretty, blue thing."

Wyatt always calls vehicles "he," whether it's a truck, bike, or even my dad's tractor that he used to ride around. I used to find it funny because most folks call 'em "she." Wyatt told me that was just plain dumb, and he'd much rather ride a Dick than a Sally. Made me blush when he said that.

"Can't wait to meet him. How's Sadie doin'?" I ask.

Wyatt met Sadie in Illinois, and she's become a good friend. I'm thankful for that because the idea of him moving all that way alone made me worry. At least with Sadie there, I know he has support and someone to have fun with. And that's good because Wyatt needs that levity in his life. It's such a part of him, that ability to live big and a little wildly.

"Crazy as ever. She had to drop a class, long story, but she asked the teacher out right after. Claimed she dropped the class so she could, which wasn't true, but it completely freaked the guy out. Sometimes I think she just likes makin' folks blush," he says around a laugh.

"I'm glad you have her," I say, not for the first time.

"Yeah. She's great."

"Still workin' at the sub shop?" I ask.

"Still there," he replies. "Still hate it, but it's a job. Oh, I did talk to this lady 'bout thirty minutes away who needs some help with muckin' horse stalls. I'll be doin' that in the mornin's I don't have class now, too."

"Runnin' yourself ragged," I note.

"Yeah, well, not much choice. When I'm cleanin' up horse shit, I'll think of you. How's that?"

I laugh. "Sounds about right."

"How's Monty?" he asks, and I can hear the tenderness in his voice.

"Missin' his best human's best friend. Doin' real well, though. Healthy, happy."

"That's good," Wyatt says softly.

"And you?" I ask. "Are you happy?"

There's a long pause, and I start to worry maybe he *isn't*.

"Yeah, Easton," he says at last, sounding almost tired. "I'm learnin' a lot, and things here...they're different. It's easier to find folks like me, y'know?"

I swallow. "That's good," I tell him, not sure why it feels so hard to get the words out.

We talk a little bit longer, but pretty soon, Wyatt has to go study. It never gets easier saying goodbye, but Wyatt says he's happy, and I suppose that's all we can ever wish for the ones we love.

CHAPTER 9

Wyatt, age 22

"Tomorrow's the day?" Sadie asks, knowing very well it is.

"Mhm."

She flops down next to me on my cheap secondhand couch, curling around me like an octopus.

"What're you doin'?" I ask her, trying to blow her textured, black curls out of my face.

"Comforting you," she says, like it's obvious.

"By squeezin' out my insides?"

Sadie laughs, but she disentangles herself, linking just her arm with mine instead and laying her head on my shoulder. Her hair still tickles my face.

"You really are gay, huh?" she says, sounding wistful.

"Told you that the first time I met you," I remind her, patting her head.

Sadie and I met in one of my first classes, Intro to Biology. She complimented my boots, and when I opened my mouth to thank her, she asked me out on the spot. Not many Southern accents like mine here in Illinois, I guess. Sadie isn't the only one obsessed with it, either, much to my amusement.

We didn't go out, obviously, but she sat next to me that day and every one after, and we became fast friends. Now, we live in apartments next to one another. Much better apartments than where I lived last.

I'm thankful for Sadie. She's made life here not only bearable, but way more enjoyable than it might've been otherwise. Even when we just occupy the same space, it's easy and fun and comforting.

Like now, sitting on the couch together, waiting for this commercial about toothpaste to be over.

"Are you ready?" she finally asks, quietly.

"Don't think I'll ever be ready to watch my best friend walk down the aisle," I tell her, my insides clenching at the thought of it. Tomorrow, Easton will be married. And I'm the fool who's not over him, not even close.

"You still love him, don't you?"

"'Course."

"So why are you going to his wedding?" she asks.

I look at Sadie like she's crazy. "'Cause he asked me to. Truth be told, I would've gone even if he hadn't. I'm still his best friend."

"That you haven't seen since you left two years ago," she points out.

I nod.

"See, I don't get it," she says, shaking me slightly. "Why choose to go back to him now, to someone who's going to hurt you without even trying?"

I sigh, having gone over the same thing in my head many times. Maybe I'm simply a masochist, but it doesn't matter. Any way I look at it, I see myself going to that wedding. Exactly like, no matter what, I answer his calls.

He's just my Easton.

"I would always choose him. Over and over again, no matter how it ends. In any world where there's a Wyatt and an Easton, that Wyatt would find his Easton and fall in love. And maybe that's just my story, to be the brokenhearted. Maybe I'm okay with that."

Sadie blinks at me through sad eyes. "You deserve better," she says, voice soft.

I shake my head. "There's no better man for me."

"God, Wy," she says, sounding exasperated. "You're like a tragedy."

I laugh. "I'm well aware, darlin'."

"You deserve to be *happy*. To find your own happiness somehow. After this, I hope you can."

"Any advice on how to do that?" I ask, truly wanting to know.

"Look at me," she says, gesturing to herself. "The only person I have hanging off my arm is a gay cowboy. Do I look like I know what I'm doing?"

We both laugh, and yet again, I'm grateful to have Sadie in my life, to help me find humor, even in the hardest of times.

"I have an idea," she says, popping off the couch.

"What's that?" I ask, looking over at her.

"We're going to Blockbuster. We're going to rent *My Best Friend's Wedding*, and then we're going to get greasy Chinese food, cheap wine, and hang out together all night," she says, clapping her hands together.

"And that's supposed to help?" I ask, confused.

"Yes," she declares. "You're going to get life lessons directly from the great Julia Roberts herself. Plus, there's eye candy for both of us. And then," she goes on, "in the morning, after you're ten pounds heavier and much wiser, I'll drive you to the airport."

"All right," I say, hefting myself up to follow Sadie out the door. "Bring on the egg rolls and the eye candy."

I'm in a daze from the moment Sadie drops me off at the airport. Part of it may be the lack of sleep and the slight hangover, but I think mostly it's just this day. I barely remember the plane ride back to Texas or Easton's brother, Hawthorne, picking me up and driving us to Plum Valley. I don't remember the folks I talk to once I'm back in town, either, nor getting ready at Miller Moore's ranch house.

It's all a hazy gray. Until, suddenly, there's Easton. Standing in front of me like a dream come true.

Dressed in a black tuxedo with a white-and-yellow daisy in his coat pocket, he looks like a true gentleman and the most beautiful person I've ever laid eyes on.

It physically hurts, seeing him again for the first time in years. But it's also...good. Amazing, really. A shock of fresh air to aching lungs. I didn't know it was possible to feel so much pain and happiness, all muddled into one.

His face, when he sees me, breaks open into the widest grin, and I can feel my own responding like an inevitability. For a moment, all the rest just falls away, and it's me and Easton again. Simple and true.

"Wyatt." He rushes over, smashing me in his embrace. I breathe him in, relishing the feel of his smooth face against my lightly bearded one and the scent of hay ever present on his body. He feels good. Strong and right.

When he pulls back, he looks me over.

"This is new," he says, dragging his fingers over the short hairs on my jaw in a way that makes me want to purr.

It is new. I don't know why I grew it, the beard, and I'm not even sure I like it. Maybe I just knew I'd need a little armor for this.

When Easton's hand falls away, I look him over, too, noticing the now-rumpled flower in his pocket.

I cringe. "We crushed your daisy."

"That's all right," he says, not even looking down at it. "I'll get a new one."

I have so many things I want to say to my friend, but my lips stay glued shut. With Easton's blue eyes boring into me, I'm afraid if I open my mouth, the floodgates will rise, and I'll spew out things that need to stay firmly within my own mind.

Luckily—or not so luckily; I'm not sure which—Easton's Aunt Perla chooses that moment to interrupt, popping her head into the room.

"It's time to go to the church," she says. "Oh, hey there, Wyatt dear," she adds, smiling at me softly. I give her a nod in return.

"All right, just a minute. Thanks, Aunt Perla," Easton replies. When she leaves, he tugs me over to the decanter of whiskey sitting atop the bureau. He pours a finger each into two glasses, handing one to me. "I'm glad you're here, Wyatt. I wouldn't want to do this without you by my side."

So close and yet a million miles away.

"Cheers," I say, clinking my glass with his.

The whiskey goes down smooth, paving the way for what is sure to be one of the worst days of my life.

★

I stand off to the side of the dance floor, my fifth whiskey of the night in my hand, as some country love song rings throughout the barn. I can't get the image of Easton, standing at the front of the church with a fresh daisy in his pocket, saying "I do," out of my head. It's stuck there on repeat. Each time, the words are expected and yet shocking. Each time, there's the distinct feeling that I'm dissociating up into the ceiling, watching it all from above.

"Hey, you," Becca says, startling me, her smile a mile wide. She looks radiant in her white gown. It's simple, but beautiful. She, too, has daisies, lined like a crown through her hair. "Dance with me."

I nod, following her onto the dance floor.

"You know," she says a minute later, swaying gently in my arms to whatever country song is playing now, "I wasn't sure if Easton would ever end up givin' me the time of day back then."

It takes a second to get my brain in gear. I feel like I've been wading through molasses all day.

"In high school?" I ask, pretty sure I understand what she meant. They were friends long before anything else. We all were.

She nods. "Kept tryin', though."

I don't ask her why. I know. Easton is worth it.

"He's different than most," she goes on.

This time, it's me nodding. He's different than just about everybody.

"When I asked what took him so long, know what he said? He said he needed to see my heart before he saw my body. I damn near swooned when he told me that. Wasn't until years later that I thought about it some more."

I swallow, not exactly sure where Becca is going with this.

"He always said he only saw *me* like that. No one else."

Suddenly, I can't swallow at all. My throat is too tight.

"When I prodded about it, 'cause I couldn't quite believe that, he said he was probably just Becca-sexual. Now, the man sure knew how to make me feel good, I'll admit, but I didn't for one instant think I was the only person he'd ever be able to find attractive."

The song changes, but Becca doesn't let up her grip.

"Truth is Easton never was very good at seein' the forest for the trees."

I feel like my vision is spinning. What is she saying?

"Why are you tellin' me this?" I ask, trying to keep my voice even.

"Because Easton only saw me after I made it abundantly clear I was available. And I didn't... Christ, this is difficult. I didn't realize that at the time. And I needed to say I'm sorry."

I jerk my head back, meeting her gaze head on. "What could you possibly be sorry for?"

"For takin' him away from you," she says so quietly I'm not sure I even heard her right. She rushes on. "I could tell you had feelings for him, and I'll always wonder what would've happened if I hadn't pushed my way in. Don't get me wrong—I know Easton loves me, but I think he could've loved you, too. I just didn't see it until it was too late."

I reel back, shaking my head rapidly. There's no way. She's wrong.

I can't listen to this. I excuse myself, blood rushing in my ears as I make my way outside into the balmy night air. I don't even realize Becca is right behind me until she's turning me around and wiping the tears off my cheeks.

"I'm sorry," she says again, eyes imploring me, but I just shake my head.

"Easton never saw me like that," I say, voice hoarse. "Besides, it doesn't change anythin'."

"Maybe not, but he does love you. He misses you," she says.

And for a moment, I hate her, even though I don't hate her at all. I don't want more guilt over leaving my best friend. I don't want hope that he could ever see me as more. What good would any of it do? This right here is our reality. Easton is married to Becca. I don't figure into that.

And even though it feels cruel that Becca is saying something now, I know she doesn't have bad intentions. She's just honest, always has been. She loves Easton, and she wants what's best for him. And I truly believe she still loves me as a friend, too.

So I get it. That she wants to clear the air. That she feels bad.

But none of it *matters*. It doesn't change anything, and in fact, it just fucking hurts. If Easton ever could have seen me as anything more than his best friend, he would have. There was plenty of time before Becca came along. So she's wrong.

She has to be.

I don't say anything else, and Becca doesn't stop me this time as I walk away. I follow the fence line, listening to the sound of crickets and the occasional cattle call. The soundtrack of Plum Valley. It kills me that it still feels like home.

When I double around and see the first cars leaving, I walk back to the barn. Easton spots me as soon as I'm through the doors, and that kills me, too, that he still has the uncanny ability to know when I'm near.

"Where'd you get off to?" he asks, looking flushed and happy.

"Just needed a bit of fresh air. Listen, I should be gettin' on my way. I've got a red-eye to catch."

"who leaves a wedding early?"

Easton nods, even though his eyes look sad. "I wish you could've stayed longer."

"I know. Me, too," I lie. There's a reason I booked the first flight back to Illinois. I knew I'd need a hasty exit.

Easton hugs me, just like we've done a million times before. But this one feels different for me. It feels very much like I'm saying goodbye.

PART II: COMING HOME

CHAPTER 10

Easton, age 24

"Ohh," Becca coos, looking over the white, spindled crib. "That's just *perfect*. You thank your mama for me, Riley."

The teenager blushes, nodding his head quickly at Becca. I know the feeling. Even eight months pregnant, she looks radiant. Maybe even more so *because* she's eight months pregnant. And when she turns that megawatt smile your way, it's easy to feel like a million bucks.

"Will do, Mrs. Moore. She was glad to get it outta the house, though."

Riley and I pull the crib down from the bed of my truck, and he helps me carry it inside the house. We get it set up in the nursery, and after the teen leaves, I step back to admire the aesthetic.

It really does look perfect. The white paint goes well with the daisy theme Becca decided on.

When I asked her what would happen if the baby was a boy, she gave me a stern look and asked, "*And what's wrong with boys likin' daisies?*" She had a good point, and I felt rightfully ashamed. It made me wonder what Wyatt would've thought if he heard me saying something like that. He was always going on about gender norms.

Thinking about Wyatt puts a smile on my face, even though, nowadays, it's a bit of a sad smile. I miss my friend. It's been two years since I last saw him at the wedding.

"Looks good, doesn't it?" Becca asks, coming up next to me and squeezing my arm.

"Sure does. You did good."

"We both did," she corrects. "Come take a walk with me?"

"All right," I agree with a nod.

I follow Becca out to the deck and down into the yard. I keep the grass cut short here, behind the house. Otherwise, it would grow spindly and wild like it does on the unmaintained portions of our property. The yard itself is a good-sized rectangle that's boxed in on two sides by pasture fences. We have three large pastures in total for the horses that stay here, as well as a paddock I use for training and the big, red barn where the horses bed down. And then there's our house.

The house is Becca's pride and joy. She gave a lot of input into the design when it was being built, deciding on the floor plan, the paint colors—not surprisingly, she chose yellow with white shutters and windows—and she decorated most of the interior herself, picking things out at estate sales and putting them together in a way that feels both hodgepodge and cozy.

As we walk leisurely around the perimeter of the yard, Becca picks the black-eyed susans and thistles that are growing along the fence, collecting them into a little bundle that she'll put on the kitchen table later. Neither of us says much; we just enjoy the quiet and the occasional sounds of cattle that drift over from my dad's ranch.

We'll just do one loop of the yard this afternoon, not only because it's the hottest hour of the day, but because, being eight months pregnant, Becca gets tired easily. Even so, she determinedly takes a few short walks every day. At this point, walking for her is more of a waddle, but I would never tell her that.

When we reach the south pasture, Monty comes over to the fence and sniffs my hand. Usually, he'd be in his own personal field up by the paddock, but I have fewer horses staying here right now in preparation for the baby coming. Which means Monty is getting his own little vacation. He walks with us slowly, kicking up his mane on occasion, as we make our way along the fence line. Being near Monty always reminds me of my friend. Best horse. Best friend. It makes me wonder if Monty misses Wyatt, too.

Pretty soon, though, there will be a new little human to introduce Monty to. I wonder what he'll think of that.

"You're happy here, right?" Becca asks. My gaze shoots to her in surprise.

"'Course," I tell her. "Where's this comin' from?"

Becca stops walking, and I turn to her. A few tendrils of her light brown hair have blown into her face, so I reach over and brush them back behind her ear.

"Sometimes, you get this look in your eye. When you're missin' him," she says. "Been seein' a lot of it today."

I know who she's talking about. I just didn't realize I made a face when I thought of him.

"I do miss him. Does that bother you?"

She shakes her head. "No, of course not. He's your best friend. I just..." She sighs. "I just want to make sure you're happy."

"I am," I tell her, tugging her forward into my arms. She comes willingly, holding me close and looking up into my face. "Very happy. Here, and with you."

"You should go visit him," she says. I open my mouth to object, but she keeps on. "I know. It wasn't a good time when we were buildin' the house, and plannin' the wedding, and then gettin' your trainin' established, and now that we're expectin' a baby. But there's always gonna be an excuse. You could go now. We still have a month before he or she will be here."

I shake my head. "It's too risky."

She gives me her Becca look, that stubborn one, but it's no use. We've had this discussion before, and there's no way I feel comfortable leaving her while she's pregnant.

"What about after?" she prods. "When the baby is a few months, you could go then."

Realistically, I can't see myself going anytime soon. It's not that I don't want to visit Wyatt—I do. It's like an ache. But I can't leave Becca with a newborn.

She seems to read my mind. "We have plenty of family who could help out."

"He said he should be able to visit soon, maybe after the baby is here," I say.

"Have you spoken recently?" she asks, unwinding from my arms and pulling me along beside her.

We continue walking, and I nod. "'Bout a week ago."

"What's new?" she asks.

I like that Becca cares, that she's always asking me how he's doing. It feels like it keeps him here, at least a little bit.

"Said he got a full-time job. Farmin' vegetables, can you believe that?"

She laughs. "The cowboy has jumped ship."

I chuckle, nodding. "Mhm. Said he likes it there well enough. Not sure where he's goin' next, though."

"Is he datin' anyone?" she asks.

I shake my head. "Nah. I don't think he does that."

"Ever?"

"Not that I'm aware of," I tell her. "Just does casual."

"Hmm," she says. "That's too bad. He's got a lot to offer."

I agree with her, and I'd hoped Wyatt would find a boyfriend, even though the concept was too abstract to fully picture. I could never visualize him with anybody but me. Not like *that*, of course, but because we were always together. And even though I *want* him to be happy, it always felt weird to imagine somebody in my place.

But if Wyatt is dating, he's keeping it close to the chest. I don't know which would be worse: him dating and not telling me about it or him being lonely all the way out there.

"Did you ever get back to Nash about fishin'?" Becca asks.

"Nah," I reply. I thought about it. He's invited me a few times to join him out on the dock behind his house, and even though Nash is a bit older, it's not by much. We get along just fine, but he's not Wyatt.

"I know it's not easy for you to make friends," she says.

I simply hum. When Becca and I get back to the deck, having completed our circle around the yard, she pulls me close.

"C'mere," she says, rising up on tiptoes to give me a kiss. It's a little awkward around her belly these days, but I don't mind. I kiss her back, tasting the cherry of her Chapstick.

"Now," she says, pulling back with a mischievous grin on her face, "I know I'm as big as this house, but I'm also real horny. So, as soon as I can make it up these stairs, I need you to take me to bed."

"Yes, ma'am," I tell her, a huge smile forming on my face.

I kiss her one more time before letting go.

"Will I ever get enough of you?" I ponder.

"Sure hope not," Becca says, smiling.

Neither of us could've known what lay ahead.

★

"Hawthorne?" I say, one hand on the wheel, the other on my phone.

"Yeah?" my brother asks.

"It's time. We're headin' to the hospital."

Holy cow, it's really time.

"Good luck!" he says, adding a little cheer away from the phone, which makes me chuckle. "The horses will be in good hands, and I'll alert the family."

"Thanks, brother."

He hums his assent, and I hang up, swiveling my head briefly to Becca, who's in the passenger seat holding her belly and breathing deeply.

"Doin' all right?"

She nods, not speaking. I set down my phone, gripping the steering wheel with both hands as we travel to the hospital. Becca's contractions aren't very close together yet, but the hospital is far enough away that they told us to come early, rather than risk not making it at all. Becca seems to be doing okay, but I can tell she's at a point where it hurts, instead of just feeling like a nuisance.

"We'll be there soon, all right? And then we'll get to meet our baby."

She nods, a smile on her lips before she grimaces and closes her eyes.

The drive seems to take forever, and after an eternity, we pull up to the hospital, which thankfully has a valet service. I hand over the keys, and Becca and I make our way inside. They check us in, and after a waiting room, a private room to check

Becca's progress, and then *another* room for delivery, Becca is pushing. I can hardly believe it, but I just hold on tight, letting Becca squeeze my hand to death as she pants and groans and works to bring our child into the world.

There's a head, another grunt, and then, all at once, our baby.

The nurse gives the tiny, squirming thing a quick wipe down, swaddles it in a blanket, and then hands it up to Becca.

"Ready to meet your beautiful baby boy?"

A *boy*.

Becca's smile is a mile wide, even as she's covered in sweat and looking worse for wear. She holds the baby boy against her chest, looking up at me, and I'm sure my face is mirroring the same thing hers is. Joy. Because holy crap, that right there is our baby.

My chest is light, this feeling I've never had before rushing through me. I think it's the love reserved for our children. Must be because I know I would do anything for that little boy.

As I'm watching, one hand on the bundle and the other hand on my wife's shoulder, Becca's eyes shudder, and then the monitors start beeping wildly.

A nurse grabs our baby as chaos breaks out, my heart sinking in confusion and fear. I back up out of the way, and there's nothing I can do apart from watch as everything comes tumbling down.

CHAPTER 11

Wyatt

I wake to a warm, wet mouth wrapped around my morning erection. With a groan, I roll onto my back, blinking my eyes open.

"That's a helluva way to wake up, darlin'," I tell Adam, the guy I met at the bar last night. He's shorter than me. Slim, too. Not my usual type, but the guy is cute and feisty, and I found myself liking that.

"Oh god," he moans in an exaggerated manner. "That accent. Just keep talking. I won't even need anything else to get me there, I swear."

I can't help but chuckle, which was Adam's goal, I can tell.

"C'mere, anyways," I say, dragging him up my body until he's seated over my lap.

I spit in my hand, using the moisture to jack Adam off. He rocks back onto me, using one hand to trap my cock so it's sliding between his ass cheeks. I bite the inside of my cheek against the pleasure.

"Say something else," Adam says.

"At this rate, I'm gonna finish faster than a hot knife through butter."

He groans, and I burst out laughing, the sound a little sleep-roughened. He smiles down at me wickedly, clearly enjoying this.

"More," he says, adding pressure against my cock with one hand while grabbing my hair with the other.

"Honey, you're hotter than two rabbits screwin' in a wool sock."

"*Fuck*," Adam hisses out, pace faltering as he spills over my fist.

Before I can follow him over the edge, he scoots back down over my erection, taking me to the back of his throat. I cry out as I come, and my arms flop over my head while I catch my breath. Adam lands next to me, chest rising and falling like my own.

"I could listen to you reading the dictionary," he tells me.

"Maybe next time," I say.

Adam grins. "Oh, I like that."

The guy doesn't take any prompting to start getting dressed when I roll out of bed, which I appreciate. As I get ready for work, starting the coffee pot and then putting some toast into the oven, Adam picks up his things. He stops to write his number down on the pad of paper I keep on the countertop, sending me a wink when he's finished.

"I look forward to next time," he says, heading out the door.

Not five seconds later, Sadie bursts into my apartment.

"Oh, he was cute. I wish I'd been a few minutes earlier. I bet I could've caught the show."

I don't say anything, just raise an eyebrow.

"I knew it!" Sadie chirps.

"Coffee?" I ask, chuckling.

"Please."

Sadie sits down at the table as the pot finishes brewing.

"How's the new job going?" she asks.

I shrug. I started at an ag farm after I graduated. It's not cattle ranching by any means, but I still have yet to figure out where I want to settle now that I have my degree. Of course, my heart has an opinion on that, but my head knows better.

The nearby farm, which specializes in vegetables for local restaurants and stores, had an immediate opening. It's as good a place as any to work while I figure out the rest.

"It's fine," I say. "Keeps me busy."

"Good people?" Sadie asks, and I can hear the underlying question in her tone. Do they know or care that I'm gay?

"I've been keepin' to myself," I tell her.

She smiles a little sadly, and I know she understands. Sadie herself is open to just about anybody, so she knows what it's like to struggle with how the world views you. It's better here in Illinois than it was in Plum Valley, that's for sure, but it's still hard. You can never predict who will react badly or with outright hostility. Most of the time, it's easier to just keep that part of yourself hidden, unless you're in a safe place.

I bring two mugs and the entire pot of coffee over to the table, and Sadie and I sit side by side as we drink our caffeine, talking about nothing and everything. I always like this time of day, waking up with a friend.

"Any leads?" I ask Sadie.

Sadie has been looking for a job. She'd love to do yoga, but the studios around here aren't hiring, so she's been applying just about anywhere relevant to her kinesiology degree.

"Not yet," she sighs in disappointment. "I might have to start looking further out."

"Well, if you wanna pull vegetables in the meantime, let me know. I can put in a good word."

Sadie chuckles before checking the time, standing, and bringing her mug to the sink to wash.

"Later, apartment husband," she says, shooting me a finger gun, of all things, on her way to the door.

"Later, darlin'."

Potatoes might be my least favorite. Not to eat, because who doesn't love a good loaded potato, but to harvest. It's back-breaking work, digging them from the soil, row after row after row.

At least the sun here in Illinois doesn't bake me in quite the same way as it did back in Texas. One good thing, I suppose. I always seem to be trying to find good things to make up for how much I miss my home.

I miss connection, too. I have Sadie, of course. And, when the mood strikes, I can find a man for the night, like Adam. But it's not the same. It's not Easton.

I know I should make more of an effort to put myself out there, try dating for once in my life, but it always comes back to the fact that I did *not*, in fact, fall out of love with my best friend. Even after I left. Even after he got married. It's still there, that feeling, stuck like a bad tick.

Except maybe something a little less gross.

I don't know how to get over him, and until I can figure that out, I don't think I can give dating a try.

"Hey, can I ask you a question?" Mark asks from a couple rows over.

I look up. "Are you talkin' to me?" I check. Having been in my own head, I might've missed something.

Mark makes a point of looking left and right before raising an eyebrow. There's no one else around. "I'm not talking to the potatoes."

I chuckle, swiping some hair out of my eye. It's at my shoulders these days, so it tends to get in my face if I don't tie it back. "Sorry, I was a little distracted. Go ahead," I tell him.

"Were you, like, an actual cowboy?"

Ah, this question. "Sure was."

"Of actual cows?"

"Yep."

"What's that like?" he asks, pushing his potato-collecting bin further down the row to keep up with him.

"Mmm, peaceful," I say, my mind immediately placing me in the past, Easton by my side and a whole field of cattle and bluebonnets spread out in front of us. "Assumin' you like the mooing, that is, and I always did. It's nice. You're just out there, carin' for 'em, watchin' 'em grow, helpin' 'em live their best cow life."

"Before we eat them," Mark says, pulling a laugh from me.

"Well, sure. Doesn't mean we can't give them a good life, too. And I always liked that. From calvin' onward, the cycle never really ends. It's just life. And a nice, open field," I say, realizing I'm talking like I'm *still* a rancher, when that's not really the case.

"Sounds a little like playing God," he jokes.

I shrug. "Never really thought of it like that. The cattle sure are more entertainin' than these here potatoes, though."

"I like vegetables," Mark says. "No talking back. They just go where I tell them to."

"I guess you have a point there."

My phone rings from within my pocket, interrupting our conversation, and I fish it out, startled to see a familiar name there. I answer right away as my body breaks out in goose-bumps. Easton's brother wouldn't be calling unless something was wrong. I walk off, away from Mark, for a bit of privacy.

"Wyatt? It's Hawthorne," he says as soon as the call connects.

"What is it? What happened? Is Easton all right?"

The questions come out rapid fire, and I can barely hear Hawthorne's response over the deafening sound of my own heart.

"Uh, no, everythin' isn't all right. Easton isn't hurt, and the good news is that he has a son now. Born just yesterday mornin'," he says, a little catch in his voice. "His name's Will. But, well, it didn't go right, and Becca..." He peters off, and it feels like my heart stops, suspended in time as I wait for him to finish his sentence. "Becca died, Wyatt."

Oh, God.

She died? I clutch my chest, feeling like I've run out of air. Aching for what Easton must be going through this very minute. What he's been going through since yesterday. While I was at a bar, picking up a guy, laughing and joking and having a good time, Easton was dealing with the unimaginable.

Becca's gone. Easton lost her. And now he's alone, with a newborn baby to take care of.

There's no question. I'm off like a shot, racing to my truck.

"Wyatt?" Hawthorne asks in my ear.

"Yeah," I croak, "I'm here."

"Just thought you should know."

"I'm comin'," I tell him.

"You are?" he asks, sounding relieved.

"Yeah, I'll be there soon as I can."

I hang up as I reach my truck. I call my employer on the road, letting them know what happened and apologizing profusely.

And as quickly as possible, I drive to my apartment and pack some essentials. With no more than a single parting glance at my temporary home, I'm on my way back to Plum Valley.

CHAPTER 12

Easton

I just get Will down for the night when I hear a soft knock at the front door.

I rub my eyes and let out a sigh, my very bones feeling weary. Who is it now? My cousin Autumn is already here, helping out with the laundry. My family wouldn't hear it when I said I wanted time alone tonight after we got back from the hospital. I was just so tired of the looks and whispered comments and the goddamn pity in the crinkled corners of their eyes. I wanted a moment to breathe. But they insisted someone stay, just in case. I didn't have it in me to ask "In case what?" or argue the point.

Having them here only reminds me of the person who's missing. And the truth is I don't want to think about it. Any of it. I've cried more in the last forty-eight hours than, heck, probably ever. Maybe it makes me selfish, but I just want to push it all away. I don't want to think about the fact that my wife is dead. I don't want to worry about what comes next. I don't want to have to field concerns from my family, however well-meaning their intentions.

I just want to *be*. At least for a little while, between bottle feeds and rocking Will back to sleep, I want to ignore the fact that everything is different now. But I can't do that.

The knock sounds again.

Grudgingly, I tear my eyes off my sleeping newborn and walk down the hall. Autumn appears at the bottom of the stairs before I have a chance to descend.

"I'll get it," she says, walking away when I nod.

I head back to the nursery, leaning against the doorframe and peeking into the dark room. I listen to Will's quiet breaths, mentally bracing myself for whichever member of my family is on their way in, feeling guilty that I wish they'd all just go away. But I don't have any fight left in me, and as such, I resign myself to conversations about the future and the past and how *it will be all right*. Nothing is all right at the moment.

But when soft steps ascend the stairs and a head appears, followed by a body, it isn't my aunt or my dad or anyone I expected to see.

It's Wyatt.

My best friend, who drops his bag lightly at the top of the stairs and steps towards me. My friend, the one person I couldn't admit to needing the most, who's here instead of miles and miles away. My friend, whose face is mirroring all the things I'm feeling inside, but who musters up the tiniest smile to send my way.

He's just a foot in front of me, and when he says the simple yet heavy words, "I'm home," I crumble.

Wyatt follows me down to the floor in front of the nursery, scooping my body into his arms as best as he can, holding me tightly while I well and truly fall apart. I must cry for an hour, maybe more. Relief, sadness, fear; they all pour out, draining me dry. The whole time, Wyatt holds me, shushes me, rocks me, kisses the top of my head.

Stays with me.

When it's done, I feel wrung out, empty, as if I purged myself of some sort of sickness. And yet having Wyatt here makes me feel safe for the first time in days. He makes me feel a little less alone in that way only he's capable of doing. I wish I could keep him here forever because I don't know how I'm going to manage all of this on my own.

When a soft cry comes from inside the nursery, I inhale shakily.

"Uh," I say, voice sounding croaky as I speak to my friend for the first time tonight. "Want to meet my son?"

"Yeah, I really do," Wyatt says, a crooked grin on his face, even though there's moisture in his eyes.

I stand up, holding my hand out for Wyatt to grab a hold of. A quick look through the doorway assures me that Will is all right; he's waving one fist in the air and making soft little grunting sounds.

I clear my throat, canting my head down the hallway. "Let's grab a bottle first. He'll be hungry."

"You can show me how to feed him," Wyatt says softly.

And *Christ*, I don't know why those words get to me, but they do. Maybe because it feels like a life raft when, with the way everything else is tugging me down, I can barely keep myself afloat. I nod, inhaling a shaky breath through my nose.

Wyatt follows me into the kitchen and watches as I prepare a bottle, reading the instructions three times just to make sure I don't screw it up. My hands shake as I try to twist on the cap, until Wyatt squeezes my arm, his touch grounding me. When we get back to the nursery, I show Wyatt how to hold Baby Will while making sure his head is supported, and much to my relief, it doesn't take much persuading to get him to drink the whole bottle. Will falls back asleep immediately after burping, and I stand there, watching Wyatt hold the tiny baby in his arms, a goofy expression on his face as he gazes downward.

I know I need to change Will's diaper, log his feeding time, and wash the million bottles on the kitchen counter, but I can't take my eyes off the scene in front of me.

It doesn't feel like it's been years since Wyatt was here last. It doesn't feel like any time has passed at all. Having my friend back is the most natural thing in the world. And when he looks up at me, a sleeping Will in his arms, there's so much adoration in his gaze that it takes my breath away. I'm hit with the full force of it and the realization that Wyatt is looking at my child with true happiness. Not pity. Not sadness. *Happiness*. And that's exactly what I want for him. He *should* be celebrated. He *should* be shown a world of love and joy and support. And I haven't been giving him that, too caught up in my own grief.

Seeing it in front of me, seeing my best friend show me what *should* be, uncorks some of the pressure in my chest, and for the first time in days, I can feel a small smile tugging at my own lips.

I have a son. A beautiful, healthy son. And my best friend is here, at least for now. It's not going to be easy, but maybe I can do this after all.

It's the tiniest sliver of hope, but I latch onto it.

In the morning, everything feels a little grayed. Will slept well for his first night home, waking up every few hours to eat, but I never felt comfortable leaving him for any stretch of time, even while he was resting peacefully. Wyatt insisted on staying, too, and even though I tried to convince him to get some rest, he wouldn't budge. He set up a bunch of blankets and pillows on the floor of the nursery, and that's where we spent the night, watching over Will. Truthfully, I was glad for the company.

I didn't notice Autumn leaving, but at some point after Wyatt got here, she must have, only not before finishing the laundry and cleaning all the dirty bottles. I know she deserves my thanks for that, but right now, I'm preoccupied with the bundle in my arms. Will is still sleeping, but since Wyatt finally conked out an hour ago, I decided to bring the baby boy with me so my friend could get some rest.

I'm making coffee one-handed when he reappears, the sound of his footsteps alerting me to his presence. I turn my head just in time to see a sleep-rumpled—or sleepless-rumpled—Wyatt turning the corner into the kitchen, rubbing at his eyes.

"Caffeine?" I ask quietly, knowing the answer will be yes. I already have two mugs set next to the machine.

Wyatt scoffs lightly. "'Course."

I bring a mug over to the table, setting it down in front of Wyatt, who accepts it gratefully. Then I grab the other and take a seat, slowly so as to not disturb Will. I watch a few dust motes puff up into the air in the early morning light, circling around Will's head like a tiny halo. I can feel Wyatt's eyes on me from across the table, but I shake my head.

"Not yet," I say.

Wyatt nods, content to sip his coffee. I do the same.

I'm not quite ready to talk about any of it. I know I have to, and soon, but I just want a few more minutes to sit here and drink coffee and pretend like my world wasn't upended in the blink of an eye.

Of course, the real world doesn't listen to wishful thinking.

Will stirs, letting out a little cry, and I push away from the table, setting myself to make a bottle of formula before the wailing begins. Wyatt grabs the supplies before I have a chance, however, measuring carefully and making the bottle just the way I showed him.

"Thank you," I say. Wyatt just nods.

When the bottle is ready, I take a seat in the family room, cooing at Will as he eats slowly, his little hands clenching repeatedly into fists. For a few minutes, I'm consumed by this tiny baby. My son. And it hits me all over again that Becca will never get this. She won't get to feed her child or watch him grow. She won't get to celebrate birthdays and graduation and all the things that should have been her right as a parent.

It doesn't make any sense, and I don't know that it ever will.

I wipe my sore eyes dry as Will finishes his bottle, thankful I have him to focus on. He's my priority, the push I need to move forward instead of getting too lost inside my own head, no matter how strong the pull. After burping him, I change his diaper—checking the stool chart twice to make sure that *yes*, it really is supposed to be that color—and with a content, full, clean baby in my arms, I return to the kitchen.

"What's this?" I ask in surprise, finding Wyatt flipping bacon on the griddle.

"Cookin' breakfast," Wyatt replies before turning around. Golden-brown eyes hold mine a moment before dropping to Will. Wyatt's face breaks into the goofiest smile again, nose all scrunched up, as he steps closer and leans down to give Will a hello. Under different circumstances, I would've laughed at this side of my best friend. As it is, I choke up again, over-whelmed by the gratitude I feel for him.

For all of it. For coming home and being here, and for looking at Will like he's the most important person in the world.

Before I start crying again, I divert my attention to breakfast. "You didn't have to do that."

"I know. I wanted to," Wyatt says, pulling himself up to his normal height and heading back over to the stove. "Fixin' bacon and eggs and toast. I can go to the market later and pick up more food. You're gettin' a bit low."

"You don't have to do that, either," I inform him.

"I know," Wyatt repeats, fixing me with a stern look that seems off on his face but is effective nonetheless. "I want to."

"Thanks," I mumble, watching Will's sleepy eyes take in the room.

A minute later, Wyatt drops a plate onto the table and holds out his arms. I look at him, dumbfounded.

"The baby," he prompts, laughing. "I'll hold him so you can eat."

I pass off Will and watch as Wyatt coos at him, walking around the kitchen and swinging him gently. When he sees me staring, he gives another pointed look toward my plate. I take my cue, sit down, and dig in, feeling the briefest glimmer of warmth infuse my chest, despite the events of the past few days.

Although thinking about that immediately puts me back in a dour mood.

I finish my plate on principle, but it ends up feeling a little like lead in my stomach. "I can take 'im, now," I tell Wyatt.

He simply shakes his head. "He's already asleep. Should I put him back in the crib?"

"Actually, I have a portable one we can set up out here. Hold on."

After some fussing, I get the foldaway crib set up in the archway to the family room, right next to the kitchen where we can keep an eye on him. Wyatt lowers Will down gently, and we both stand there for a moment, gazing at the sleeping baby.

"Shit," Wyatt says wistfully, making his way back into the kitchen and sitting down with his own plate of food. "I can't believe you have a son."

"I know." And it *is* pretty amazing. Except that Becca won't be here to see it, any of it. "How long are you stayin'?" I ask, throat tight.

Wyatt shrugs, like it isn't a big deal, when we both know it is. "However long you need."

I swallow heavily, asking the question I was always afraid to voice aloud. "And what if I always need you?"

"Then I'll stay," Wyatt says, gaze solid, and I know he's speaking the truth. He *would* stay, but I can't possibly ask that of him.

"What about Illinois? You have a life there now," I remind him.

Wyatt just laughs, finishing the last of his eggs before setting his fork down gently and leaning back in his light oak chair. It doesn't match the one I'm sitting in or the table itself. It's a mismatched set, all of it. Becca found each piece, one at a time, at garage sales, saying she didn't see the point in buying new furniture when there were plenty of good pieces out there waiting for a home. I clear the lump in my throat, the memory hitting me hard.

Wyatt sighs. "I left Plum Valley and got a degree in agricultural animal breeding and a minor in ranch management," he says wryly. "Maybe I always knew I'd be comin' back."

I don't know what to say to that. I didn't think Wyatt would ever be happy returning. But one thing I know about my best friend is that he's more stubborn than a mule at water. If he's made up his mind about this, nothing I say will change that.

"You're really home?"

"Yeah," he breathes out. "I really am."

And somehow, that's exactly what I need to hear.

CHAPTER 13

Wyatt

"It happened really fast," Easton says, voice low. His eyes shoot up to mine briefly before he looks back down at the table, tracing its rough surface with the tips of his fingers.

I know without asking that he's talking about Becca.

"The delivery seemed to go fine, and then, all of a sudden, she was closin' her eyes. There was so much...blood, and they just..." Easton drops his face into his hands, scrubbing up and down. "She was just *gone*. There one minute and then gone. I still don't understand how it could've gone so wrong. Rare complication, they said."

Easton's throat is working like he has more to say, so I stay quiet, letting him work through his thoughts. I can't believe Becca is gone, either. It doesn't feel real. Her presence is still here, in the house, everywhere I look. And I have a profound sense of guilt that the last time we spoke, I walked away from her.

But more than that, my heart is absolutely breaking for my friend. I never would've wished this on him, no matter my own feelings. I never wanted to see him hurt, and he's hurting badly. So badly it's palpable, a denseness in the air like thick fog.

"Her parents were...fuck." Easton shakes his head, like he can't stand to think about it. And if the man is swearing for real, it must've been bad. "I still have to make arrangements. There's so much to do. I don't even know..." He peters off again, and I can't stand it any longer.

I push out of my seat, dropping down onto the hardwood floor in front of Easton, gripping his knees. He looks so lost and scared and overwhelmed that I just want to hold him tight.

"I don't know how to do this," he says, barely a whisper. His eyes are bloodshot and glistening once more with tears. I wish I could grab his face and kiss those tears away. But, of course, I can't do that.

I don't know *what* to offer that he hasn't already heard. It all seems so pointless. The *I'm sorry's* or *it's all right*. So, instead, I just grip his knees harder and say what I know to be true.

"No one knows how to lose somebody they love. There's no goddamn manual for that sort of thing. But Becca brought a beautiful, healthy, baby boy into the world. She made a *life*: your son over there. So we'll honor that. We'll honor *her*."

Easton's hands close over mine, holding tight as tears spill freely down his face. He looks up at me through dew-damp lashes, his breaths shallow and harsh. I'd take his pain in a heartbeat if I could, but I know there's no shortcut when it comes to grief. The best I can do is make sure Easton knows he has somebody by his side for the journey.

"We'll make sure she knows all about him, you hear?" I free one of my hands, wiping the moisture from below his fluttering lashes. "And Will will hear all about Becca, too. He'll know his mama. And you," I go on, "you just *do* it. One day at a time. You just keep movin' forward until, one day, it feels like livin' again. And until then? You won't be doin' it alone, babe."

Easton inhales sharply, his arms coming around me in a crushing hold, pressing my head against his stomach. I wrap my arms around him and hold on tight as Easton's body shakes with his shuddered breaths, knowing with one hundred percent certainty I'm exactly where I'm supposed to be.

It's ten in the morning when the brigade arrives. Three cars, all in a row. We can hear them before they reach the house, tires crunching over gravel and dirt.

Easton and I are sitting on the couch, little Will in his arms. I was telling him about Illinois, things I hadn't updated him on yet. Things about Sadie and details of my new job, which I left mid-shift. I don't worry Easton with that particular detail. I'm sure he can figure out I lost my job, but there's no use bringing it up right now and adding to his guilt in any fashion. Knowing my friend, he's already feeling guilty about a million other things.

It was a peaceful morning after Easton's tears dried up. Just the three of us sitting around and ignoring the outside world for a little while longer.

But now, as we hear those cars rolling in, our little bubble crashes. I can see Easton's shoulders pull up, the tension ratcheting. I hop up before anyone can knock on the door and wake Will. Instead, I pop outside, close the door behind me, and wait as three cars' worth of Moores walk up, eyeing me with varying levels of surprise.

"Wyatt, dear, I'm so glad you're here," Easton's aunt says, reaching me first. She has a hamburger casserole in her hands because of course she does. It is Plum Valley, Texas, after all.

The land of polite, well-intended folk, who show their love through beef and cooking.

"Came as soon as I heard." I accept the side hug she offers, casserole held out of the way. "The baby is nappin'," I announce to all, hoping that's enough to get the hint across to keep their voices low.

Aunt Perla nods and pats my cheek before heading quietly inside. Easton's brothers each shake my hand as they pass, and I make sure to thank Hawthorne again for keeping me in the loop. Then it's hugs from the cousins, Christabell and Autumn, the latter of whom gives me a smile. Easton's dad is last, and his reception is less hospitable than the rest of the family, which is no more than I expect. Miller Moore was never a man who cared for me, maybe even downright hated me, even before I was outed to the town. He believes in much more traditional family values, far as I can tell, and sees me as a bad influence on his son.

A nod is all I get before the man passes, and I follow him inside, cringing slightly when I see everyone huddled around Easton in the family room. Easton looks resigned to the fact that his entire family showed up unannounced and is now invading his space, because even though he's not happy about it, he's too polite to ask them to leave.

I keep my distance, but I make sure I'm never far away in case he needs me. Every once in a while, Easton's eyes seek me out, and each time, it validates that my being here—in this house, and in Plum Valley—is the right thing.

After a while, Will starts to stir. The family oohs and aahs over the little bundle, but I can tell Easton is getting antsy. He's keeping the baby firmly in his arms, but Will is squirming, hungry. And Easton is stuck in a conversation with his aunt, while his cousin, Christabell, plays with the baby's foot. Every time Easton opens his mouth to excuse himself so he can feed Will, he's cut off. Another question about baby supplies or what he'll do about the horses he's training.

So I make my way into the kitchen and prepare a bottle. Easton looks relieved, and without discussing it, he hands Will over the moment I approach. I sit in a chair across the room, feeding the baby boy, not realizing at first that most of the family has turned my way. Hawthorne is asking Easton something, but Aunt Perla has stopped talking altogether and is watching me with her hands clutched to her chest, looking pleased. Christabell and Autumn are exchanging whispers, and Miller is appraising me with his arms crossed, disapproval in his eyes.

I ignore them all in favor of watching Will. His scrunched face is peaceful as he nurses on the bottle. One tiny fist is clenched around my finger, and ten tiny toes rest against my bicep. He looks like a little, wrinkly old man, but he's perfect.

Eventually, around the time I'm burping Will, Aunt Perla starts dishing out the casserole, along with rolls and salad the cousins brought. Easton comes over to take the baby, mumbling a quiet but sincere "Thank you" before disappearing into the nursery.

When I join the rest of Easton's family in the kitchen, there's a lull in conversation.

"I'm so glad he's acceptin' help," Autumn says, breaking the silence. "It's gonna be hard for him as a single dad, and we just wanna be there for him, but he's always so determined to do everythin' himself."

"What d'you mean?" I ask. "Y'all were with him the past few days, weren't you?"

"Yeah, but he wouldn't let any of us help with Will," Christabell says, chomping down on a bell pepper she snuck from the salad bowl.

I don't quite know what to make of that. I'm not exactly surprised. Autumn is right. Easton *has* always felt like he needs to be strong and do everything on his own. Yet, he's letting me help, trusting me to do so, and knowing that makes me feel warm and a little bit breathless.

"Well, I'm glad to be here."

"How long you stayin' for?" Miller asks, tone clipped.

"I'm back for good, sir," I reply, keeping my tongue civil and a smile on my face.

"Why? My son don't need you. He's got his family."

"Dad," Clive gasps at his father's outright rudeness.

"What?" the older man says. "'S'true."

"Leave it be," Clive hisses. "Easton could use a friend right now, after everythin' he's been through."

Miller huffs but doesn't say any more. Everyone looks downright uncomfortable at this point, so when my phone starts vibrating in my pocket, I gladly take it as reason enough to excuse myself.

"Yeah?" I answer, walking out onto the back deck and closing the door behind me. Monty is in the south pasture, a lone figure standing in the shade, his tail whipping periodically.

"How's it going?" my friend asks, her voice laced with sympathy.

I let out a long sigh. How do I answer that? "Not good."

"I can't even imagine," Sadie replies. Her nails are tapping something in the background, and the sound fills the silence. "Well, let me know if you need anything. I'll check your mail and water your plants and stuff until you're back."

Another silence, longer this time. I swallow roughly, my throat clicking with the motion.

"Wyatt?"

"I'm not comin' back, Sades."

"*What?*"

She sounds shocked, and I can't blame her. I never would have expected to uproot my life and move back to Plum Valley in the blink of an eye, all for the man who was such a big part of my leaving. But everything is different now.

"I know, but Christ, I can't leave him like this. He needs me," I tell her.

This time, it's Sadie who sighs. "You're a good man, Wyatt, but why does it have to be you? It isn't your responsibility. I don't want to see you get hurt."

I don't know how to explain it to her. How the moment I stepped back inside this house and brushed past my friend, it felt like a piece of myself that had been untethered snapped back into place. Like my very atoms recognized Easton's and settled back into my skin and bones. It doesn't matter that it means something more to me. That's never changed. Trying to convince myself it wasn't love didn't work. Moving half a country away didn't work.

Easton is my soulmate.

He's part of me, and even if there's never *more* than what we have now—and let's face it, I've already accepted there never will be—it doesn't matter. It'll never matter.

When I look at it like that, I guess the answer is easy.

"Because my fool heart has, and always will, love that man. I would do anythin' for him, and right now, he's broken and alone. If I can help him feel that a little less, it's what I'm gonna do."

Sadie is quiet for a moment.

"Goddamn poet," she finally sighs. "Wy, love, how is this going to turn out for you? If you're there, taking care of your friend, the man you've loved your entire life, who's going to take care of you? What if *you* end up broken?"

"Doesn't matter."

"You've made up your mind about this?"

"Yep." That very first minute. Maybe the moment I dropped everything to rush back to Plum Valley.

Sadie sounds sad, but still very much like my hardass friend. "Dammit, I'm going to miss you."

I smile, just a little. "I know. Same here, darlin'. I'll be back at some point soon, though. I'll need to pack up, move my things."

"Egg rolls and chardonnay?" she asks.

"You got it."

When I click off the call, I hear a rustle over my shoulder. Panic sets in as I spin, afraid of who I'll find. Afraid it'll be Miller, as if he needs more of a reason to dislike me. I mentally comb over what I said, how much I gave away, wondering why the hell I didn't move somewhere more private when I was talking about Easton that way. So many things fly through my mind in that moment, but when I turn around, it's Easton's cousin in front of me, and relief hits.

Christabell holds up her hands. "I didn't mean to eavesdrop, I swear. But I didn't feel right duckin' away before you could realize, either. I swear I'm not gonna tell anyone."

"I appreciate it," I reply, rubbing the corners of my eyes.

Christabell looks like she's struggling to decide whether or not to say more. I don't know why—maybe I'm just not ready to face the rest of the family again—but I take a seat and gesture for her to do the same.

"Have you two ever?" she finally asks, fidgeting with the hem of her black-and-gold sunflower dress.

Christabell is close to our age, just two years younger. Out of all Easton's brothers and cousins, she would've seen us together the most at school or the bonfires. I can't say I'm surprised she asked—I'm sure I wasn't actually all that discreet about my longing—but I laugh nonetheless.

"No. Unfortunately for me, Easton is straight."

Christabell's eyebrows pull together, but she nods. "It sounds like maybe your friend asked the same thing, but why stay? I don't think I could. If I loved someone and they didn't even see it, I don't know if I could stick around."

I shrug. I've asked myself the same thing. Hell, I did move away for years. But that was when Easton had Becca. When it comes down to it, I can't deny Easton anything. I love him, plain and simple. If that means being a friend, that's what I'll be.

"It's worth it to me. He's worth it. That's enough."

Neither of us have a chance to say more, as Easton himself pops his head outside.

"There you two are. Hungry? Food's on."

With one more quick smile at Christabell, I get out of my seat. Easton cocks his head as I walk by, but I wave him off.

Lunch is a fairly quiet affair, the mood a little more somber without baby Will in the room to make everybody giddy the way babies do. Aunt Perla keeps shooting Easton quick glances, but he keeps his eyes down. Hawthorne and Clive keep the conversation alive, talking about the new batch of Longhorns at the farm and the pastures being turned over for reseeding.

I finish my food quickly, not all that hungry, and set to work cleaning bottles at the sink. I'm so in my own head, I don't even notice that Easton is standing at my side until he speaks.

"I feel like it's all I say lately, but thank you."

"No thanks necessary," I reply, bumping my hip against his.

He nods, a fleeting smile gracing his lips. The man looks tired, which, of course, is to be expected of a brand-new father. But it's more than that, too. Grief and weariness hold prominent positions behind the blue of Easton's eyes. I don't have any delusions that it won't be that way for a long time to come, but this right now, entertaining family, is not helping. They mean well; they want to help. I get it, but Easton needs quiet. He needs a damn nap.

I dry my hands, clapping them together as I turn around. The whole table looks up, falling silent.

"All right y'all. Thank you for comin', truly, but Easton needs some rest. Why don't we pack it up and set up another time this week that would work better for visitin', all right?"

I don't wait for a reply; I just grab Easton by the shoulders and lead him out of the room. His steps falter as we move past his bedroom door, but I just keep pushing.

"Where're we goin'?"

"My room. Yours is right next to the nursery, and I need you to sleep, all right?"

Easton chuckles, the sound tired and broken by a large yawn. He doesn't correct me about the room being *his* guest room, not *my* room, and I don't stop moving us until Easton crashes onto the bed.

"What about Will?" he asks, rolling onto his side and stuffing my pillow under his face, eyes already closing.

"I'll handle it, bud."

"Mmph."

I'm almost out the door when Easton speaks, barely a mumble.

"This pillow smells like you."

I stop, pivoting on my heels, and wait to see if there's going to be more, but it seems that was it. Easton is out cold.

I don't know what to make of the fact that Easton knows my smell, and I know I shouldn't read anything into it. But my heart speeds up nonetheless.

CHAPTER 14

Easton

As I wake up, there's a brief moment when I panic. I'm not in my room, the house is quiet, and the sun is almost set. How long was I asleep?

I shoot out of bed, tripping in the sheets and barely catching myself before eating a face full of hardwood. I hurry down the hall, finding the nursery open and empty. For a fleeting second, my gut sinks, but then I remember Wyatt.

Wyatt is here, and he wouldn't let anything happen to Will.

I find them out on the deck, Will's back against Wyatt's chest, as the bigger man watches the sun setting against the rolling hills. He looks over when the door snicks shut, a smile on his face.

It does funny things to me, seeing my best friend and my son together. It feels right, like the two most important people to me are important to each other, too.

Becca's not here, but I have this.

"Why'd you let me sleep so long?" I ask quietly, settling beside them.

"You needed it."

I shake my head. I slept the entire afternoon away. He could've woken me sooner.

"Did you really kick my family out?" I ask, remembering what happened before my head hit the pillow.

Wyatt just shrugs. "Well, yeah. Told 'em you'd set up some visits, but that you needed time to settle in. They seemed to understand."

"Thank you," I tell him. Wyatt has always been able to speak his mind easier than me. Mama raised us boys to be accommodating and polite, always. I've never had an easy time breaking out of those habits. "Maybe I should have someone come by tomorrow," I say, thinking out loud. "I need to get..." I clear my throat to get her name out, "Becca's affairs squared away."

"Already taken care of," Wyatt says softly. My eyes shoot to him, and at my confused, inquisitive gaze, he nods and goes on. "Talked to Autumn, who's gonna get with the Thompsons. They'll handle the service, pick everythin' out. I told her you'd insist on payin', so they'll get a bill for you."

"Wyatt," I say, at a loss for words.

"And Aunt Perla will take care of the reception. We'll have it here, o'course, but she volunteered to handle food. And you know, what with probably all of Plum Valley comin', there'll be plenty of casserole." Wyatt finally pauses, looking up at me. "If it's too much, just say the word. I can call everybody off."

"No," I answer quickly, shaking my head to clear the tears I can feel threatening to escape. "No, thank you."

"Mhm," Wyatt hums, and that's that, my best friend looking out for me, like he always has.

After we head inside and eat some supper, Will falls asleep in the portable crib, and Wyatt flops down onto the couch.

"You should get some sleep now," I tell him.

"In a little bit," he says, flipping through channels with the volume on low.

I sit down next to him, our legs bumping. It feels so normal I could cry. But, I've been doing plenty of that lately.

"The beard is gone," I comment. The longer growth he had at the wedding is shaved back to stubble.

"Yeah," he replies, rubbing at his jaw. "I never really liked that thing."

I hum. "I like bein' able to see your face," I tell him. He looks good either way, I suppose, but this is the face I'm used to looking at.

Wyatt blinks at me, quirking his mouth a little, and then he goes back to flipping channels.

"Requests?" he asks.

Truth be told, I don't really care what we watch. Just being here with Wyatt is enough. It makes me feel less like I'm falling apart at the seams.

"Whatever you want," I reply.

Wyatt stops on the opening credits to some action flick. It can't be more than fifteen minutes before his eyes close, head relaxing back against the couch. I smile, glad he's getting the rest. I figure I should do the same—they're always saying to sleep when the baby sleeps—but I can't seem to make myself move.

Instead, I stay on the couch until the movie is over, watching it and, occasionally, my two guys.

★

The next few days pass in a blur. Will keeps me busy, eating, sleeping, and pooping like it's his job and I'm his personal assistant. The Thompsons stop by after calling Wyatt to check that it's all right—a fact that doesn't bother me in the least—and they thank me for letting them have a part in the planning. They're grateful to be able to contribute to putting Becca to rest, and I could kiss Wyatt for setting all that up. I never would've thought of it. In fact, I would've thought it a guilty thing to do, putting the responsibility on them. But they don't see it like that. To them, it's an honor. A parent caring for their child one final time.

Becca's funeral is held at Plum Valley's oldest church, and nearly half the town shows up. I wish I could say I remember the words that are said in her honor, but the truth is, I'm too preoccupied with my own sadness, too wrapped up in myself, for them to register.

I think Wyatt anticipated that, too. He asked Billy Ruskin, who's studying to be a filmographer, to videotape the whole thing so I could watch it when I'm ready. When he told me that, I wasn't even able to thank him properly. At a loss for words, I simply grabbed him in my arms and squeezed the daylights out of him.

When it's my turn to speak at the service, I read a few words I prepared the other day. It's not much, but then again, I never was a man of many words. I talk to Becca, telling her how much I love her, how grateful I am that she gave me years of joy and a beautiful son. I tell her that we'll always remember her.

The service is open casket, but I can't bring myself to look. I don't want to remember her this way, waxy and devoid of life. I want to remember the way her hair would blow in the breeze and how she always wore my flannel shirts in the morning before the sun warmed the valley.

Wyatt says his goodbyes in person, and he tells me she looks beautiful. I nod, and when I look down at Will in my arms,

Wyatt seems to understand what I can't bring myself to ask. He scoops up the sleeping baby and goes back to the front of the church, reintroducing Will to his mother and Becca to her son.

I cry silently, watching them through bleary eyes.

Becca's casket is lowered in the afternoon. A beautiful white thing with floral inlay. It reminds me of her, and I thank the Thompsons for picking it out. It feels strange to thank them for such a thing, but what else do you say on the day someone you loved is buried?

I stay at the cemetery long after the last person has left, Wyatt with me, Will asleep in his stroller. A final goodbye, a promise to visit, to never forget.

It's hard to sort through my feelings, as overwhelming as they are. But there's one thing I know for certain. Having Wyatt here is like being wrapped in a comforting blanket, his warm presence keeping me sane, keeping me going. I think Becca would've been grateful for that, too. She always loved Wyatt.

After I drop a handful of dirt in the grave, I make myself turn away. There's no changing this. Tragedy happens all the time. We can't prepare for it, can't ever know how or when it will affect us. And even though I know I won't stop loving Becca just because she's gone, and there will be plenty of grieving ahead, I have to do what Wyatt said. One day at a time, move forward.

So that's what I do.

By the time Wyatt drives us home, Becca's reception is in full swing. It looks like the entire population of Plum Valley is in attendance, cars lining the driveway, driven onto the grass, and parked down the road. No one seems to mind that I show up late, or that I disappear with Will into the nursery without saying a word.

I don't want to do it again. The platitudes and pitying looks. The grabby hands that want to meet her son.

Luckily, Wyatt doesn't come to get me until everyone has left. I wake from my slumbering position flat on the rug to my friend's face hovering above me, telling me they're gone. Will is still napping in the crib, and I don't move, so Wyatt joins me on the ground. The pair of us lie side by side, hip to hip, as we look up at the little neon stars dotting the ceiling of Will's room. Becca put those there. Maybe, now, she's one of them.

CHAPTER 15

Wyatt

Will was two weeks old when the crying *really* started. At first, Easton and I were stumped. Finally, Easton admitted we needed help and called Aunt Perla, who assured us it was perfectly normal.

"He's wakin' up!" she said excitedly.

We weren't as enthused.

He cries all the time. He doesn't want to sleep unless he's in our arms, and sometimes he doesn't want to sleep period.

He's now two weeks and four days old, and for the fourth night in a row, Easton and I are taking turns pacing Will around the house while he wails. The little man's face is red, his tiny hands clenched into fists. I can tell Easton is beside himself, and he'd probably be pulling out his hair if it were long enough.

We already checked his temperature, his diaper, and everything else. He's keeping food down and gaining weight steadily. He isn't sick. He's just a baby.

Easton chews his fingernail as I bounce and hush Will to no avail. He's been crying for two hours straight at this point.

"He's gotta fall asleep at some point, right?" he asks.

"He will," I assure him.

"Is he hungry?"

I shake my head. "We just fed him, remember? He burped. Diaper is dry. He's fine. He's just bein' a li'l stubborn."

Easton scoffs at that, and Will lets out a particularly loud screech.

Easton scrubs his hand over his forehead, and I can tell he's retreating into himself, wondering if he's a horrible father, assuming he's doing something wrong. We're both exhausted, but Easton seems to hold these things closer, like he feels personally responsible. And he'll overthink and get anxious and feel like a failure.

He's not, of course, but it's especially hard to hear reason when you're so tired you can't even remember what day it is.

So, in an attempt to lighten the mood, I do the first thing that pops into my head. I sing. Loudly, and off key.

Easton's head pops up the moment I start off "I Say a Little Prayer," singing about waking up and putting on my makeup. He looks at me like I've lost my marbles, but little Will's hiccupping slows, so I power on, walking out onto the deck and into the balmy night as I do my best to lull the newborn in my arms.

Will's face is still blotchy and red, but he stays quiet, watching me with those big, blinking gray eyes of his. The breeze ruffles the handful of baby hairs on his head, and I can't help but smile. My heart feels full, and I know I'll love him forever and ever, just like the lyrics say.

When I glance up, my smile slips. Easton is leaning back against the house, arms crossed in front of him and one leg kicked up. He's watching us, or more appropriately, he's watching the little boy in my arms as I attempt to sing him to sleep. And even though his body language is casual, his face is anything but. There's so much *love* there, in Easton's gaze.

It's blinding. And for a moment, during that brief suspension in time, I feel encompassed by it. Pinned under the weight of that gaze.

And I want that. I want it *so* much. I always have.

And suddenly, those lyrics I'm singing? Those words about the person you love, how you think of them through every part of your day, how you pray they'll love you, too? It feels like they were made just for him, for how I feel about him.

Easton's eyes find me at last, and I quickly duck my gaze back to Will, afraid he'll be able to read the truth written all over my face. As I repeat those begging words, I turn away, walking Will to the railing. I keep singing to him until I'm sure he's asleep, and then I hum, rocking him slowly as I look out at the dark night sky and the stars above.

Easton comes up beside me after a moment, running his fingers gently along Will's forehead. "You're ridiculous, y'know that?" he says quietly.

"Sorry for subjectin' you to that," I joke because my feelings are too raw for anything else.

Easton grunts, his body so close to mine I can feel the vibration of it.

"You ain't that bad of a singer, cowboy," he says, a smile on his face as he watches a resting, and silent, Will.

His words cause my breath to stutter. They stoke a little fire inside my belly, filling me up from the inside out with a dangerous sort of heat that I do my best to ignore. Oblivious to the effect of his words, Easton just holds out his hands, silently asking for the baby. I pass Will over, letting out a soft breath of relief when he transfers without waking, only to be rocked to my core the very next moment when Easton opens his mouth again.

"Good job, Papa," he says, tucking his son more firmly against his body.

I swear my heart plain stops.

Papa.

I watch Easton, the man of my dreams, walk back inside with the little boy that's quickly stealing my heart.

I want to be Papa.

"How's being a dad?" Sadie asks.

I clench my eyes shut, heart tripping over itself at her words.

"Woah, I didn't mean to touch a nerve." She sits down next to me and rubs my thigh. "What's going on?"

It feels weird to be back here in Sadie's apartment. I finally made the cross-country trip to Illinois to collect my things, seeing as I only had a bag's worth of my possessions in Texas, and doing laundry every few days was getting to be a chore. A daily load of Will-related laundry is about all the folding I can handle.

It only took a day to pack up and load my things once I arrived, but I'm waiting until the morning to drive back. I can tell Sadie's a little bummed I won't be staying longer, but I didn't want to leave Easton alone for more than a few days. Sure, Hawthorne is helping with the horses as needed, and Easton's various family members all offered their assistance with Will, but Easton is still so wary of accepting outside help when it comes to his son. He's protective of that little boy.

I'm sure that will get better, once Will is a little older and it's not quite so scary, worrying about any little thing that could happen to him. But right now, Easton can barely hand him off without watching like a hawk the entire time. Except with me, of course.

So this is my last night in Illinois, and even though I've sat in this exact spot on Sadie's couch countless times before, it feels foreign to me now. It's not home, not anymore.

Home is back with Easton and Will, the little boy who's growing up much too fast.

"He's only two months old, and I'm already so attached," I tell my friend, trying to articulate why it is that the topic of dadhood is a sensitive one. I *am* attached. Hopelessly gone for that little baby in a way I never knew I could be.

Gone for the way he looks up at me with his light gray eyes that haven't started changing color yet. Gone for the way his little gummy mouth tips into a smile every once in a while. Gone for his fingers and toes and that tiny little belly button that's impossible not to poke.

I never thought much about having kids before. Couldn't really let myself. In my head, I always pictured a home with a cowboy, some acreage to call our own. And my mind always tried to cover up the image of Easton with somebody else, some faceless, unknown man. But my heart knew the truth. I just wanted him, and since I knew that was impossible, dreaming up kids was too dangerous a concept to entertain.

If I let myself go there, if I let myself fantasize about having kids with a man who would always turn out to be Easton in the end, I'd just be setting myself up for a world of heartbreak. Because reality would eventually crash in, and I'd remember I was dreaming about a man who could never love me back. And then those fictitious kids I allowed myself to want? They'd be ripped away, too.

It was an impossible fantasy I refused to entertain, and yet, somehow, in some cruel twist of fate, I ended up living it. And I love that little boy. I love Will.

But I'm not his dad, not really.

So I'm just waiting for the moment it all gets torn away.

"Oh, honey," Sadie coos, curling her arms around me when the dam breaks. She hugs me as I cry, seeming to understand exactly what's on my mind.

"I don't ever want to say goodbye," I manage to croak out.

"Maybe you won't have to," she says, rubbing my back soothingly.

After a few minutes of wallowing, Sadie hands me a napkin out of the to-go bag. I wipe my face as she unboxes the egg rolls and sticky rice. She shoves the containers in front of me, a wrapped pair of chopsticks on top, and I accept them gratefully. I've always appreciated Sadie's form of food therapy.

"I won't live there forever," I point out, opening up my chopsticks. Of course I won't. Eventually, I'll have to find my own place. Maybe not right away, but at some point. Easton won't want me there forever. Not once he starts dating again sometime down the road. And I want that for him, I do. I've always wanted him to be happy.

"Maybe not," Sadie agrees, pouring two glasses of cheap wine. "But that doesn't mean you'll lose that boy. You'll always be something to him. Maybe the cool Uncle Wyatt."

I can't tell her I don't *want* to be just Uncle. It sounds too petty. Too pathetic to admit I want a fake life with my best friend and his son.

"I suppose."

"God, I've missed your country ass," Sadie says, sighing.

"I've missed you, too, darlin'. I'm sorry for how this happened."

"Psht," she says, waving my apology away. "Don't be sorry. You couldn't help it. And it's not your fault I don't have any other friends here to occupy me."

"You could always move down to Texas," I say, enjoying the crinkle of Sadie's brow.

"Could you really see me down there?" she asks, shoving a piece of pork into her mouth.

I shrug. "Maybe someday."

"Hmph. What're we watching?"

Her question brings a smile to my face, because it reminds me of watching *My Best Friend's Wedding* in this very spot nearly three years ago, crying—because Christ, how could you watch that movie without crying—and singing along. What would Sadie think if she knew that night ended up being a god-send, since that song we sang over and over again until I had it memorized got Easton and I through Will's two-week-long crying stint? For whatever reason, that little boy loved my mediocre singing. Or, maybe, he simply fell asleep to avoid it.

I could tell Sadie about that night I sang to Will for the first time, but for some reason, I don't. It feels too personal, that memory, and I want to keep it close to my chest, keep it between just Will, Easton, and me.

Besides, tonight is about Sadie and me. I've already taken up enough time talking about Texas and everything going on there. Right now, I want to stop worrying about all that and just enjoy my friend. It might be some time before I see her again after this, unless she decides to visit us down south.

Sadie looks over at me, remote in hand, waiting for my movie pick.

"Lady's choice," I tell her.

She scrolls down, stopping on a channel that's playing *Three Men and a Baby.*

"Really?" I ask around a laugh. Leave it to Sadie to find the perfect comedic relief to my real-life drama.

She reaches over and squeezes my arm, giving me a wink. "It'll get easier," she says after a few minutes, her tone serious but gentle.

I nod. I know what she means. This complicated situation, over time, will sort itself out.

The thing is I never expected it to be easy. But that doesn't mean it won't be worth it.

CHAPTER 16

Easton

"Got 'im?" I ask.

Wyatt nods, detaching the infant seat from its base. "Little man is locked and loaded," he confirms, sliding his hat back on his head.

I chuckle. "Nine months, can you believe it?"

I hardly can. The past several months have gone by in a flash. Yet there have been days that felt like a lifetime. Funny how that works.

"Course I can," Wyatt says. "The man weighs a ton."

"Oh, please," I reply with a snort. "You haul calves on the regular. I doubt he's much more than twenty pounds."

I hold the door open for Wyatt and the baby carrier. He tips his hat, which makes me chuckle again. He's good at getting me to do that.

"We'll see," Wyatt says. "Bet he's a solid stone and three quarters."

"What, are we guessin' his weight like he's at the county fair?"

Wyatt snickers at that, but then he falls silent as we reach the check-in counter.

"Will Moore for his nine-month visit," I tell the woman.

She nods, eyes pinging from me to Wyatt before falling back to her computer screen. "Fill these out," she says, handing me a clipboard full of papers, "and have a seat over there."

I nod, and Wyatt and I head to the waiting area. [There are a few other couples there with their kids. Not that Wyatt and I are a couple.]

I fill out the paperwork, which seems like exactly the same thing I filled out three months ago, while Wyatt peeks inside the car seat cover. Will hasn't made a peep, so my guess is he's still asleep.

We get called back before long and are led into an exam room.

"All right," the nurse says. "Go ahead and undress him, and we'll get his measurements. Are you the dads?" She looks between Wyatt and me.

Wyatt points my way while he bends down to get Will out of the seat.

"I'm his father," I say, nodding.

She looks at Wyatt again, furrowing her brow, before asking me the same barrage of questions they do every appointment. Smoking in the home? Lead paint? Is he sleeping?

I don't know why folks act so confused any time Wyatt and I are together with Will. Is it really that strange? Doesn't make sense to me.

Will starts making some noise now that he's been woken up and promptly dressed down to his diaper, exposing him to the chilly room. But the nurse quickly finishes with her questions and leads us out to the scale. She gets his head circumference, height, and weight.

"Twenty-four pounds, two ounces," she declares. "He's a big boy."

Wyatt shoots me a shit-eating grin, and I roll my eyes. Guess he was pretty darn close to the mark.

After that, we're ushered back into the room to wait for the doctor. Will complains all the while, even as we walk him around, bouncing him and pointing out the pictures on the wall. I don't understand why there's always such a wait in between. Don't they realize kids don't like being cold? They're pediatricians, for gosh sake.

Will is downright wailing by the time the doctor comes in. I'm trying to soothe him, but he's not having it. Plus, it's almost his feeding time, so I'm sure he's getting hungry, too.

"All right," the doctor says, scooting onto his wheely stool. "This must be Will."

"Yep," I say, ready to get this part of the exam over with.

"Set him on down over here," he says, pointing to the table covered in that crinkly paper. As soon as Will is on top of it, he quiets, kicking at the paper in deep concentration. I wish I'd thought of that sooner.

Wyatt chuckles. "He sure does like making a ruckus."

The doctor smiles as he checks Will over. "Looks like he's already a strong sitter. Has four teeth pokin' through, that's good. Eyes, ears, heartbeat are all fine. How's he doin' with solids?"

"Good," I tell him. "He eats most things we give him. Except for peas, doesn't take kindly to those."

"He likes the soft carrots, though," Wyatt puts in.

The doctor looks between us, nodding. It's there again, I can tell. That curiosity. Is it because folks assume we're *together* together? That's gotta be it. I can't think of a single other reason. Not that I think it should matter one way or another. People can think whatever they want. It doesn't bother me.

We go through a few things with the doctor, like what to look out for once he starts moving and tips for baby-proofing. It's helpful, all things considered.

When Wyatt and I walk back out into the Texan heat, Will having been declared healthy with an appointment to be seen again in three months, my friend tips his hat up, looking over at me.

"Whatcha gonna give me for winnin' the bet?"

"Oh, Lord," I exhale, eyes Heavenward. "We've got a comedian here, folks."

Wyatt laughs loudly, a big ol' smile on his face.

"Wyatt, c'mon, he's doin' it," I call out.

Will and I are out back after his appointment, sitting in a nice shady spot on the grass, on top of a big, old blanket I've had since I was a child. I remember sitting on it with Mama. She would knit out in the backyard while I colored or played with my little cowboy figurines.

Now I'm the parent, making use of that same blanket out back with my child, weaving a new generation of memories into the fibers.

Will is up on his hands and knees on the soft, worn material, rocking back and forth a bit. He's been doing that a lot lately, and Wyatt and I are just waiting for him to crawl. It looks like he might be ready.

Wyatt himself is inside, getting our lunch together, but as soon as he hears me calling, he comes barreling out of the house. He stomps down the deck stairs now, taking two at a time in his haste, and rushes over with an expectant expression on his face.

Will's little body is still perched on all fours, swaying and wobbling a bit as he tries to kick out a knee. There are a handful of toys in front of him, and he has his eye on the prize.

"C'mon," Wyatt encourages, crouching down low on the other side of the toys.

Will's little face is scrunched in concentration, looking wiser than his young age would suggest. He rocks over and over until, finally, one little knee moves forward.

It feels like Wyatt and I collectively hold our breaths as Will balances there, but then his other knee shoots back and he drops down onto his stomach.

"So close," Wyatt says, ruffling Will's little fluffy hairs. He shoots me a smile before standing back up. "I'll finish up our sandwiches and be right back out."

"No mustard," I remind him.

"Please." He rolls his eyes. "Like I don't know you."

I suppose that's true.

Wyatt heads back inside and returns only a minute later, three plates in tow. There are sandwiches for us and an assortment of cut-up foods for Will. We all eat, Will making a mess of his meal, and enjoy the temperate day.

"Did I tell you I saw my parents in town the other day?" Wyatt asks out of the blue.

I shake my head. "No, tell me."

"I saw my parents in town the other day."

"Smartass," I say, chuckling.

Wyatt finishes chewing his food before he continues. "I was headin' out of the market while they were walkin' in. They saw me, and we locked eyes for a moment. But then they kept on, went right past me. Didn't say a word."

"Wyatt," I start, wanting to tell him how sorry I am, but he shakes his head.

"I walked right back in," he says.

"You did?" I ask in surprise.

He nods. "Told 'em I was back in town. That I was doin' well. That there was an amazing little boy here they could meet if they ever got their heads out of their asses."

"Did you really?" I ask, my heart clenching.

"Not quite those words," he admits.

"What'd they say?"

"Nothin' good," he replies, shaking his head. I reach over and squeeze his leg. "It's no more than I expected from them. We haven't had a relationship in a very long time. I don't even know why I tried, considerin' nothin' has changed with me comin' back. I'm still gay. They don't approve. Well, they made it clear, yet again, that they don't want any part in my life."

"It's not the way it should be."

"No," he agrees, "but I'm not gonna let it bother me. I have a good life. *We* have a good life goin' here."

"That we do," I put in.

"I don't need to hold onto a couple of folks who can barely call themselves parents."

I nod, and that's that. Wyatt doesn't say any more on the matter, and we finish our lunch in silence, albeit not an uncomfortable one.

After Will is cleaned up, Wyatt tries encouraging him to crawl again. He flips him gently onto all fours, Will easily holding the position now, and then gestures for him to move forward.

"C'mon, buddy," he says.

Will just smiles, wiggling back and forth.

"Like this," Wyatt says, showing Will how to pick up his arms and legs.

I hold in my laughter, but Will doesn't. The little boy starts giggling as Wyatt crawls around the grass, which quickly turns into a game of Wyatt trying to make Will laugh even harder. Wyatt looks like a total goofball as he rushes around on all fours, whipping his long hair out of his face each time the breeze blows it around.

"Woooah there," I call out, chuckling at last. "Easy."

Wyatt stops, shooting me a look. "Don't you use that tone on me, Easton William Moore. I am not one of your horses."

He sounds so indignant I can't help but laugh harder.

"All right, all right," I say, holding up my hands when Wyatt's stare promises swift retribution if I don't shut the hell up. "I won't say another word."

Wyatt flops down. "It's no use. The kid is gonna crawl when he's darn ready for it, and not a moment sooner."

"Sounds like somebody else I know," I say.

Wyatt pushes himself into a sitting position before handing a ball to Will, who immediately flings it away in an uncoordinated movement.

"Are you talkin' about me?" he asks.

"'Course. You're both stubborn."

Wyatt purses his lips, thinking about something. "Sure, but he doesn't get that from me," he says, grabbing the ball again and giving it back to Will.

This time, it's me pursing my lips. "What d'you mean?"

"I mean," he says slowly, not meeting my eyes, "I'm not his dad. If he's stubborn, it's not 'cause of me."

"Wyatt," I say, scooting close enough to grip my friend's knee. "Just 'cause you didn't contribute any biological parts, that doesn't make you less of a dad to Will. You're his papa, and you always will be. And, whether you like it or not, he's gonna take after you, too. So watch out, 'cause in twelve years, you may be drivin' him to the hospital when he falls out of a tree."

"You really mean that?" he asks, voice soft and a little raspy.

"'Course," I tell him. "Maybe not the tree part, but the rest of it I'm sure of."

Wyatt nods, a small smile on his lips as he plays ball with Will.

It's true—Wyatt *is* Will's parent. It's not a turn of events I would've predicted, but having Wyatt here has been a life-saver. He stepped in without being asked to, just showed up of his own volition and has been caring for Will and myself ever since. He moved into the house officially, making the guest bedroom his own. He started working the ranch again with my dad and has even been putting his degree to good use, offering up tips that I've heard my dad begrudgingly talk about as useful. He changes diapers, feeds Will, puts him to sleep, holds him and loves him and parents him.

He's my partner in the truest sense of the word when it comes to Will, and I wouldn't have it any other way.

Even though losing Becca has been like losing a part of myself, having Wyatt back has replaced a different void. A Wyatt-shaped hole that never quite healed during all the time he was in Illinois. Now that he's back, here with me, that part of me feels whole again. Complete and right.

Wyatt hasn't replaced Becca because no one could do that. But he's here, as himself, and Will will know him as his papa, just like he'll know me as his dad, and he'll know Becca was his mother.

Plus, having Wyatt here simply makes me, and Will, happy. He's my best friend, and he's always had the ability to make my day bright. Like now, as I watch him boop Will on the nose, making the little boy giggle, it puts a smile on my face.

I don't know exactly when it happened, but Wyatt was right. At some point, it did start to feel like living again. And I can finally see the future ahead of me. I've been making plans and looking forward to what lays ahead, and it looks a whole lot like a good life. A happy one.

PART III: THE ROAD IS WINDING

CHAPTER 17

TEN YEARS LATER

Wyatt, age 34

"Will Mr. Moore be joinin' us today?"

I struggle to keep my patience in check. It's been a long day already. Things were hectic at the ranch with new calves being born and a few downed branches from last night's storm that we had to clear out. I'm sore. I'm caked in mud. And now I have to have another go-around with Will's principal.

"Easton is outta town on business."

"Right," Mrs. Tomlinson says, face dripping with disapproval. "Well, you have to understand how unusual this is—"

Will's huff brings her sentence to a halt. "What's the big deal? Wyatt's my dad, too."

"Not officially," Mrs. Tomlinson replies.

"Who cares? You're just as bad as those Merchant brothers, sayin' what they did. I don't understand why I'm the one in here!" Will shouts.

I shoot Will a look to cool it, even though, on the inside, I'm grinning like a fool. No normal ten-year-old is this righteous.

I try to appease the woman. "Mrs. Tomlinson, I will make sure to relay all necessary information to Easton...Mr. Moore...as soon as he's home."

Will crosses his arms, as does his principal, but she continues on, ever unhappily about it.

"Will is bein' suspended for instigating a fight. We don't tolerate violence at this school," she says.

"And yet you tolerate a whole buncha stuff you shouldn't," Will grumbles under his breath.

"How long for?" I sigh.

"A week."

"A *week*?" Will and I both ask. "That's longer than last time," I inform the woman, as if she doesn't remember.

"Yes, well, harsher punishment for harsher crimes."

Christ, the woman sounds like she's talking about a hardened criminal, not a pure-hearted ten-year-old boy who has the displeasure of growing up in a town that's stuck in the Stone Age.

I ruffle Will's hair as I nod.

"All right. Well, if that's all?"

Mrs. Tomlinson nods, and Will pushes out of his chair, causing it to screech backwards. He grabs his backpack, flings it over his shoulder, and leaves the room.

"Mr. Montgomery..." the principal starts.

"Wyatt, please."

"All right. Wyatt, then," she says. "He's a smart kid. Good grades. But this behavior is inappropriate."

I give the woman a clipped nod, knowing anything I say would only fall on deaf ears. This is far from the first time Will's gotten in trouble while the other kids don't even get a slap on the wrist. Will's not wrong. The school may be strict about physical violence, but they don't do a thing to discourage the hurtful words being thrown around.

I find Will outside the front door of the school building, kicking at a dandelion weed that's growing up through the pavement.

"It's not fair," he says before I even have a chance to speak.

"No, it's not. But that doesn't mean you should hit everyone who says somethin' that's not right."

Will peeks up at me, his russet-colored hair falling over his forehead. It's wavy, like Becca's. Same color, too. He has Easton's eyes, though.

"I only hit Diesel. Bobby, I kicked."

I snort before I can stop myself, shaking my head quickly after.

"What'd they say this time?" I ask, leading Will down the steps towards the truck. He waits until he's buckled in before speaking.

"That you and Daddy ain't right. That you'd rot for bein' faggots."

My chest constricts tightly, and I have to breathe through the familiar ache. It's no different than the stuff I've heard since I was Will's age, but it doesn't make it any easier. And, if anything, it's harder. Knowing I'm dragging Easton into it. And knowing Will has to deal with that, too, because of me.

No one wants that for the people they love.

"I'm sorry, kiddo. I never wanted this for you. Or for your daddy. The things they say that aren't true—"

"Nuh-uh," Will says, turning to look at me with that fire back in his eyes. "It's not your fault. It's theirs. It shouldn't ever matter who we love or how we do it. You, Daddy, and me, we love each other. That's family, and there ain't ever anythin' wrong with that."

Fuck, this kid.

As surreptitiously as possible, I wipe the moisture from my eyes.

"What say we stop for ice cream? I think you've earned it."

Country Cones has a short line when we arrive, not that I'm surprised, considering school just let out. Will and I step up behind Rick Inman, an older gentleman that's worked at the post office ever since I was a boy and is notorious for having a sweet tooth. I heave an internal sigh, hoping the man ignores my presence. It's always fifty-fifty with him, whether he'll ignore me outright or glare at me until I'm out of his sight. He used to be nice to me, but that was before he learned I like dick.

When he looks over his shoulder, I discover it's a *glare* sort of day. I give him a wan smile and then focus my attention on Will.

"What flavor are you gettin' today?"

Will's face is buried in his new phone, but he purses his lips like he's deep in thought before declaring, "Mint chocolate."

I nod. "Good choice."

When I look forward, Rick is still glaring. I lift my eyebrows in question, and the man finally turns back around, just in time to place his order at the counter. Before moving aside, he mutters, "Wouldn't serve him, if I were you," to the kid behind the register.

I blink my eyes heavily. *Christ.*

The kid, who's Cindy Davenport's eldest son Jeffrey, looks confused as he asks, "Why?"

Rick leans closer, and even though I can't hear what he says, based on the way the kid's eyes widen, I know it's not pleasant. Jeffrey stammers something before giving the man his ice cream. Rick leaves slowly, his eyes burning a hole through the back of my head all the while.

Will, who certainly would've had an opinion or two for the man if he wasn't too distracted with his phone to notice the interaction, places his order, and Jeffrey scoops it out. As I'm paying, he leans close, his cheeks a little red.

"I'm real sorry," he says.

"What for?" I ask. "If anythin', I should be apologizin' for whatever you just had to hear."

"I can't believe..." He shakes his head and hands me my cash. "My mom always said you're a good person and that treatin' folks different for any reason wasn't nice."

I smile, my heart giving a little squeeze at knowing the Cindy of today is still the good-hearted person I remember from school.

"You tell your mom I said 'hi' and that those lemon meringue bars she dropped off for the school bake sale were darn good. I bought two."

"I'll do that," Jeffrey says with a little smile. "Have a good day, Mr. Montgomery."

I shove a ten-dollar tip in the jar before Will and I walk out into the balmy late afternoon air.

It happens a lot, days like this. The bad with the good. In a town our size, it's hard not to know one another's business. And the sad fact is my business is common knowledge. It has been since that day in the bar before I left, when Lou-Anna Smith-Travers called me out. Lou-Anna, much to my surprise, apologized profusely for that when I came back, but more than a handful of folks around here wish I'd never returned.

But the good outweighs the bad, every single day. And those folks like Rick? I do my best to ignore them. It's not worth getting my hackles up when I know any trouble I cause will come back at me and the ones I love.

And yet, despite my best efforts, trouble keeps finding us. And that boy of ours, God love him, doesn't know the meaning of keeping his hackles down.

"Are you gonna tell Daddy?" Will asks as we walk back to the truck. As if I could even keep his being home for a week a secret.

"Yeah, kiddo," I say with a small sigh, ruffling his hair. "I'm gonna tell your daddy."

★

"Again?" Easton asks, rubbing his eyes in a way that tells me he has a headache coming on.

"You know that kid's just stickin' up for what's right. He's defendin' our honor. *Your* honor, 'cause what they're sayin' about you isn't even true. And I'm not sayin' he should have to do that. Of course he shouldn't—he's just a kid. But I can't be mad at him for it," I hiss out quietly.

Easton places his hands on my shoulders, and immediately, my pulse starts to come down. He squeezes lightly, his touch warm and familiar.

"First of all," he says, "it doesn't matter whether or not it's true. There's nothin' wrong with bein' gay, and I don't care if that's what people think about me. Second, I'm not mad at him, either. But I am worried."

I nod, feeling myself deflate, before a chuckle finds its way past my lips.

"You two are so similar, y'know. I see so much of Becca and you in him."

Easton looks at me earnestly. "And you," he says, causing my heart to trip over itself.

Sometimes it's easy to forget the truth. That Easton is only my friend. That we're not more. When he says stuff like that, I want to kiss him. I want to tug him into my arms and show him how much I love him.

But I can't.

"Well, of course. He had to get that fool-headedness from somebody," I joke.

Easton shakes his head but chuckles. When he looks into the kitchen, I follow his gaze. Will is at the table, doing his homework.

"Maybe it's time I move out," I ponder.

Easton's gaze whips in my direction. "What?" He shakes his head. "No. Listen, I don't give a damn what folks in town say. And I like havin' you here. I don't see that ever changin'. So, if you're movin' on, it's gotta be because *you* want to. Not for them, and not in some misguided attempt to protect us. Only if it's right for you, you hear?"

I nod once, throat tight.

"What about if you start datin' again?" I ask, even though I don't want to.

"Well, then, we'll tackle that when it happens. *If* it happens. Although, out of the two of us, I'm pretty sure you findin' somebody is more likely."

I don't tell him that my somebody is standing right in front of me.

"Was my dad cross that you had to skip out early?" Easton asks.

I shrug. "You know Miller. He didn't say one way or the other. But, if his grunt was anythin' to go by, he wasn't happy 'bout it."

"I can swing by there tomorrow, talk with him."

"Easton," I laugh, and this time, I'm the one placing my hands on his shoulders. "I have worked with your dad for a decade. Longer if we're countin' the years before I left. I can handle the man."

"Right," Easton nods, rubbing the back of his neck. "I just don't like how he treats you sometimes."

"I appreciate it, but I'll be fine. Hawthorne always has my back. Clive, too, y'know."

"Good, good," Easton says, looking miles away all of a sudden.

I realize how tired he must be. He's been on the road for three days straight, lugging that horse back from Tennessee. I'm so proud of Easton for building his business from the ground up. Starting with horses in town, training them for all sorts of purposes—herding, competitive sports, trail riding—and growing through word of mouth. He's been getting clients from further and further out these days, and he always has a steady rotation of horses in the barn that he's working with.

Plus Monty, who's always here. Easton's best horse.

"Why don't you wash up and head to bed?" I suggest, squeezing the back of his neck. "Nothin' else needs to get done tonight."

"You sure?" he asks.

"Yup, get on," I say, giving him a gentle shove.

When I look back at Will, I find him watching me.

Later that night, once Will's homework is done and he's fallen into bed, I peek into Easton's room. Through the sliver in the doorway, I can see him spread on top of his mattress, over his covers and all.

Not for the first time, I wonder if maybe, just maybe, it's time I find someone I can share a bed with.

CHAPTER 18

Easton

"Hey, you got a minute?"

My dad looks up from the mound of paperwork on his desk. I can't help but notice how much older he looks these days. The wrinkles are more prominent on his face, and his hair is fully silver, barely a fleck of brown left. He moves a little slower, too, and I'm glad to see him taking more steps back from the manual work.

He grunts, leaning back in his chair, which squeaks under the shifting of his weight. I sit down in the old, gray leather chair across from him, setting my elbows along my knees.

"How's the ranch?"

"Good, as always. Good rain this year."

"Glad to hear it," I say, brushing some dirt off my pant leg, second guessing my being here. Wyatt won't be happy if he hears.

I'm two seconds away from aborting my plan when my dad pipes up and stokes my ire.

"Spit it out," he says. "You didn't come here for idle chitchat."

I huff a breath.

"Why are you so hard on Wyatt?"

My dad doesn't even look taken aback by my question, which tells me he *knows* he's doing it.

"I'm hard on everyone."

"No, you're worse with him," I shoot back, sitting upright. "Is it 'cause he's gay?"

I've never confronted my dad directly before, but it's always been my suspicion that his behavior has to do with Wyatt's sexuality. What else could he have to complain about in regards to Wyatt? Not that being gay should be a reason to dislike a person, but this *is* Plum Valley, where progressive thinking moves at the speed of molasses.

"He's not a good influence on you," my dad says in reply.

"In what way?" I ask, truly baffled.

"Him livin' there with you. Folks talk, Easton. They worry 'bout you. About Will."

"What folk?" I practically explode. "You? Who else even matters? I don't give a good Goddamn about what people think. And what's more, there's nothin' at all wrong with bein' gay!"

"Everythin' all right in here?" Hawthorne asks, peeking his head around the corner of the office door.

"Nope. Dad's spoutin' off some homophobic bullshit, and I've about had enough."

"Now, c'mon," my dad sputters as Hawthorne comes into the room. "It ain't like that."

"No? Then explain why you have a problem with Wyatt livin' with Will and me. Why you have a problem with him in general and always have."

I've never yelled at my dad before, but I've reached my limit. He's been treating Wyatt like trash for long enough, and it's time to stop.

"I just..." He rubs his hand over his mouth.

"You just what?" I prompt.

"I just want what's best for you," he finally says, looking sad and suddenly tired. "When you were young, I worried about you and that boy. You've always been too close."

Suddenly, it's making a little more sense.

"And you worried, what, I would turn out gay, too?"

He doesn't say anything, just looks out the window at the steady drizzle outside. Sad and tired, too, I push up out of my seat.

"Newsflash, Dad. Wyatt *is* what's best for me. He's the best friend I ever could've asked for. He stepped up when Becca died, and he helped raise your grandson. The things you say and the way you treat him? That not only hurts Wyatt, but it hurts me, and it hurts the little boy who looks up to him as a father. If you can't be civil with him...if you have a problem with him bein' gay, then you have a problem with me."

"And me," Hawthorne speaks up, reminding me of his presence. He grips the back of the chair in front of him, leaning forward as he looks directly at our dad. "'Cause this son of yours *is* gay, and he's had enough of your passive-aggressive bullshit, too."

Hawthorne turns on his heel and is out the door before the meaning of his words can fully saturate my brain. I barely spare my shocked dad a glance before I hoof it after him.

"Hey," I call out, catching up to my brother at the parking lot fence.

Hawthorne turns, looking like a cat with its hackles up. I don't stop; I just walk right up and pull him into my arms. He deflates with a deep sigh, hugging me back.

"I love you, brother," I say, squeezing him tightly before letting go. "I hope it goes without sayin', but your sexual orientation doesn't change that fact one bit. I didn't know, and

I can't say I saw it comin', but I'm glad I know now. And I'm proud of you for standin' up for yourself back there."

"Yeah. Well, thanks," he replies on a sigh, looking older than his thirty years. "I never expected for a second you'd have a problem with it, Easton. You're a good person." He lifts his hat, brushing his hair back before replacing it. "It was just time, y'know? I've been puttin' off sayin' somethin', and I finally realized—what's the point? I've got to live for me, not Dad or anybody else."

"I'm sorry you had to hide," I tell him truthfully, wishing our world were a little less harsh and a lot more accepting.

"I wasn't always," he answers, shrugging. "Just figured it out this past year."

"Really?" I say, surprised. I want to ask a million questions. What about the girls he dated? How didn't he know? How'd he figure it out?

"I can see your gears turnin'." He chuckles.

"I just figured it would be somethin' you *know*. That's how it was for Wyatt."

Hawthorne shrugs again before leaning his weight against the fence. "For some, I'm sure that's true. For me, I just didn't put it together. Maybe if things 'round here had been different, I would've pieced it together sooner. Don't think I'll ever know one way or the other for sure. But, it is what it is."

"How *did* you figure it out, if you don't mind me askin'?"

Hawthorne chuckles, looking down at the ground and shaking his head.

"Porn," he admits. At my confused expression, he snorts. "I clicked on gay porn by accident. Only when I realized I was pretty darn excited 'bout it, more excited than when there were chicks involved, I did some investigatin'. Figured it out from there."

"Oh," I say, mind whirring.

"Yeah, *oh*. Listen, I gotta run to the feed store, but we can pick this back up later if you want. You look like you have more on your mind," he says, clapping my shoulder.

"Yeah, all right."

Hawthorne turns to walk away, but I snag him before he can get too far.

"Hey, thanks. For bein' there for me and for Wyatt. I hope I can do the same for you."

"You already do, brother," Hawthorne says with a smile. "Don't let Dad get to you."

He turns away with a nod, and I watch him go. But my mind is stuck on some of what he said.

Hawthorne didn't figure out his sexuality until nearly his thirties.

Becca's the only person I've ever been attracted to, and I figured that was just me being a late bloomer or something. Except, ever since she's been gone, I haven't felt the need to look for anyone else. Is that normal after ten years?

I've never been interested in having casual sex. I know lots of folks do it, but that's not my thing. I've gotten by just fine without. Maybe I simply don't have a strong sex drive. That's a thing, isn't it?

It's probably time I do a little digging of my own. If nothing else, I'm finding out there's a lot about sexuality I don't know. And that's my own fault for not educating myself.

I bet I could ask Wyatt. He wouldn't judge my naivety on the matter.

Mind made up, and knowing there's no further I'll get with my dad today, I drive home and do my daily chores and training. When Wyatt walks through the door in the evening,

I'm in the kitchen, checking the stew that's been cooking in the crock all day.

"Smells good," he says, carefully placing his boots on the rubber mat to the right of the door. That's something he's always meticulous about, making sure his boots are off the minute he's inside the house. He always scrubs the excess dirt off outside, too.

I'm not so orderly with my own footwear, but Wyatt doesn't seem to mind.

He pads into the kitchen and peers over my shoulder, the smell of cattle and oil reaching my nose. It's a strangely comforting mix that reminds me of my childhood.

"Mm," he hums. "I'm gonna take a shower. Then I'll set the table."

That's another peculiar habit of his. If I make the food, he wants to set the table. And yet, on his nights to cook, he insists I do it. I reckon it's his way of keeping things balanced, and I find I don't mind that.

Fifteen minutes later, the three of us, Will included, are seated at the table, enjoying our supper.

"Did y'know that some frogs, when they're still tadpoles, can change their sex?" Will asks out of the blue.

My head pops up in time to see Wyatt coughing to hide his laugh.

"Really? No, I didn't know that," Wyatt says.

Will nods, like he's satisfied, and continues to chew his food.

"Female kangaroos have three vaginas."

I nearly choke on my carrot. "Where's this comin' from?" I ask.

"It's interestin'," Will says with a shrug. "We had a class about human parts, but it wasn't very detailed."

Wyatt shoots me a look, eyes wide and dancing with humor.

Will goes on. "And the teachers didn't want to answer my questions, so I found a book that did a better job. And it got me thinkin' 'bout other animals, so I found a book on that, too. There's a lot more diversity out there than they want us learnin' about."

Wyatt grins, biting his bottom lip. "School doesn't always teach us everythin' worth knowin'," he agrees.

"So how are we supposed to figure it out?" Will asks, and I love his inquisitive mind, even though I know it'll get him into trouble from time to time.

"Seems like you're doin' a mighty fine job of figurin' it out yourself," I tell him. "They had those books in the school library?"

"No." He shakes his head, stabbing a potato and chomping it down. He doesn't stop chewing as he speaks. "I called the library over in San Antonio. They found what I was lookin' for and pulled some books for me. Gramps picked 'em up," he says, referring to Becca's dad.

I make a mental note to thank Brady Thompson next time I see him.

"That was a good thing he did," I tell Will. "And that's how you do it, I reckon. If you have questions, ask me or Wyatt or Gran and Gramps, and we'll help you figure it out. Pretty soon, you'll know more than all of us."

Wyatt smiles at me, and I can practically tell what he's thinking. That we're in trouble where it concerns Will Emory Moore.

"So, why *do* kangaroos have three vaginas?" Wyatt asks.

Will throws up his hands. "I don't *know*. It seems like two would be plenty," he says in exasperation.

"Still two more than I need," Wyatt mutters under his breath, making me laugh.

Will continues to entertain us with strange animal facts all throughout supper, and then after, while he does the dishes, Wyatt helps me make my nightly rounds. As I scoop feed and Wyatt portions hay, my mind goes back to my conversation with my brother and the thoughts I've had ever since.

I don't think I should mention to Wyatt that Hawthorne is gay. It doesn't seem like my place. So, I think carefully about how I can word my questions.

"You always knew you were gay, right? You told me when we were, what, eleven?"

"Uh-huh," Wyatt says, brows scrunched together.

"And, you're, uh, attracted to plenty of guys?"

"Yeah, sure," Wyatt says slowly, spearing his pitchfork into the ground and leaning against its handle.

I stop, too, holding the scoop loosely at my side.

"How does that work for you? You just see somebody and think, 'I wanna have sex with 'em?'"

"Easton, buddy, can you speak clearly? 'Cause I get the feelin' you're beatin' around somethin', and I'd rather just cut to the chase."

I sigh, rubbing my forehead. "I don't get like that," I finally say. "And it makes me wonder if somethin' is wrong with me."

"And when you say 'get like that,' you mean you don't want to have sex with folks you see?"

"Well, yeah."

Wyatt is quiet for a moment, wringing his hands against the pitchfork. It reminds me of the rhythmic way in which he kneads dough.

"You had sex with Becca, though."

"Yeah, she was different, I suppose."

Wyatt nods and keeps on wringing.

"Is it somethin' you feel like you're missin'?" he finally asks.

I think about that some more. In a way, I miss the connection of it. The intensity. But, for whatever reason, I *was* attracted to Becca. Anytime I think about having sex with someone random, it doesn't appeal. I can't even picture it. What's the point if I don't care about the person?

I like sex—I do. But I need that connection.

"Not really, no. I loved it with Becca," I feel like I have to explain, "but I don't miss it without her. I just miss her."

Wyatt nods, mouth tugging into a small, sad smile that seems reserved for talk of Becca.

"I think, maybe, you're just not into casual sex. And there's nothin' wrong with that. Maybe, one day, you'll find someone like Becca again."

"You think?" I ask, not sure if I hope that's true or not.

"I do. Now, c'mon, these horses aren't gonna feed themselves."

CHAPTER 19

Wyatt

I can't stop thinking about my conversation with Easton last night. The man hasn't had sex in over *ten years*.

Part of me assumed as much, but I never wanted to look too closely into it, in case I was wrong. And yet, what right would I have to be jealous, even if Easton was out there having sex?

Lord knows I am. Random men in towns adjacent to ours, or even further in San Antonio. Heck, they even have apps for that sorta thing nowadays.

But that isn't Easton's thing. The more I think about it, the more I wonder if he's demisexual. It's not a term I even heard of until recently, and I want to do a little more research before mentioning it to Easton.

It would explain a lot, though. Why he's not attracted to women frequently. Why he wasn't even attracted to Becca until after they became friends. Maybe he needs that emotional bond.

Which means, considering Easton and I have had an emotional bond most of our lives, the probability of him ever finding me attractive is likely damn near zero. It's a depressing thought, even though it's something I've known for a long time.

Maybe Easton just needs to get out there, form some friendships so he has a chance of finding love again.

Another depressing thought.

It's not that I don't want him to be happy. I do. But I also worry about what it would mean for us and my role in our little family.

I'm still thinking about it as I move a herd of seasoned Longhorn down from the northeast pasture, when I see Clive riding up on a four-wheeler.

"Yeah?" I call out.

Clive works the ranch like the rest of us, but these days, he focuses more on administrative duties, since he's being groomed to take over the business one day. I remember, when I was younger, having dreams of that being me. Of course, Miller has never seen me as a son like I'd hoped. I've come to terms with that, but the Moores are still family to me. Just like this land is still home. I'm content simply being here on the ranch, any way she'll have me.

But with Clive stepping into the role as soon-to-be-boss, we see less of him out in the field, so I'm curious as to why he came out all this way.

"Easton called," he says, swinging off the vehicle.

I immediately pull my phone from my pocket, groaning when I realize it's dead.

"You really need to keep that thing charged in case one of these steers decides to put a hole through you."

"Gee, thanks for the vote of confidence," I joke.

Clive grins before his face falls serious again. "That new horse you have back at home got into some trouble. Wrapped her foot up in wire. Easton's got the vet on the way, but he could use some help."

"Shit," I mutter. "I'll finish movin' this group and then head over."

"Nah." Clive waves me off. "I've got this. You go on. Take the four-wheeler. I'll ride Junior and put him back in the stables when we're done."

"Thanks," I tell him appreciatively.

He just nods as he hands me the keys, taking Junior's reins and swinging up onto the horse. I climb onto the four-wheeler and make my way back across the ranch.

When I arrive home, I can see Easton out in the paddock he uses for training, attempting to keep the new horse, Dixie, calm. She's clearly agitated, swinging her tail around, huffing and hopping around on three legs. The fourth is held up in the air, cable wire and a broken piece of wood hanging from the limb.

"Shit," I say again, debating whether I should hop the fence and rush over or keep my distance, lest I make it worse for Dixie.

Luckily, Easton looks over and notices me. I can see the relief painted across his features.

"How can I help?" I ask, letting my voice carry across the space without being louder than necessary.

Easton keeps a hold on Dixie's lead, keeping her in his peripheral vision as he calls out, "She got stuck in the gate between east and south, took half of it down. Tempest was still in the east pasture last I checked, but Sun Over Mason"—another horse he's currently training—"is in south. And if those two get together, all hell will break loose."

"Got it," I tell him, stopping by the barn to grab a few extra leads, just in case, before I run over to the east pasture.

Tempest is still in it, but barely. He and Sun Over Mason—these names, I swear—are facing off, tails twitching, ears back. Half a gate stands between them, and I have a feeling each horse is just waiting for the other to make a move.

I approach slowly, clicking under my teeth quietly so that Tempest isn't surprised by my arrival. His one ear flicks over, listening, but he doesn't stop his staring contest as I walk up. Tempest lets me clip the lead onto his bridle, and I'm thankful he's not in a combative mood, at least not with me.

After a couple gentle tugs, I lead him away from the broken gate and secure him to a nearby post. Sun Over Mason watches the entire time, and as soon as I turn to make my way over to him, he takes off.

I sigh, resigning myself to a chase. But first, I use one of my extra leads to reinforce the gate, so at least it'll hold if Sun Over Mason decides to try his luck at getting to Tempest after all.

Once it's secured, I follow the horse into the south pasture. Twenty minutes later, both horse and human sweatier, I lead Sun Over Mason back towards the barn. I give him a quick brush down and a small pile of hay, lock his door, and set back out to grab Tempest.

Before I can get that far, however, I hear vehicles pulling up. Easton does, too. His head turns toward the driveway from where he's still standing with Dixie, who looks a little less agitated but not quite calm.

"Tempest is still out," I call, heading that way.

Easton nods, acknowledging he heard me. I make my way back to where I left the horse tied up in the shade and find him munching on some grass.

"Good boy," I tell him, patting his withers.

I lead Tempest back to the barn, giving him the same treatment as the other horse. When I get back outside to the paddock, two men have joined Easton and Dixie. I hop the fence, approaching quietly. I can see the man I recognize as Doctor Jake Hanson unwinding the wire from around Dixie's leg as Easton holds onto her lead, stroking her shoulder and shushing her. The other man feeds her pitted dates, keeping her attention on him, instead of what the vet is doing.

It seems to work. Within a few minutes, the debris has been freed from Dixie's leg.

"Let's get her back to the barn if she'll walk," Doc Hanson says, scooping up the small pile of wire and wood. "I'll take a look at her there where it's cooler."

Easton nods, and the three men turn my way, horse in tow. It takes me a second of staring into surprised eyes to realize I recognize the third man, and he clearly remembers me, as well. I met him just a few weeks ago in a bar in San Antonio. We hit it off. Enough to enjoy mutual blowjobs in the back of his car before the night was out.

Harrison, I recall, is his name.

His lips tip into a grin as he passes, head swinging around to watch me a moment longer.

"Oh, hey there, Wyatt," Doc Hanson says, pulling my attention.

I return the vet's smile and shake the free hand he offers.

"Jake. I can't say I'm glad to see you under these circumstances."

The man chuckles, and we follow the others, Dixie walking slowly and not putting much weight down on her injured leg.

"You make me sound like the harbinger of death."

"Let's hope that's not poor Dixie's fate."

"Oh, please." The man scoffs good-naturedly. "She's not a runt calf. One bum leg won't put her out."

"I'd appreciate it if y'all could stop talkin' 'bout euthanizin' Dixie," Easton calls from up front, his tone deadpan.

Doc Hanson mimes zipping his lips, and Harrison shoots me another look over his shoulder, eyes sweeping up and down in a rather appraising manner.

Dixie lets Easton lead her into the stall, where she immediately begins lapping up water.

"Y'all stay out here," Doc Hanson says to me and Harrison as he passes by. "Don't need anybody gettin' kicked."

"And what am I, chopped liver?" Easton mutters under his breath from inside the stall.

Doc inspects Dixie's leg as Easton runs interference. Harrison and I watch through the bars, but every once in a while, I can feel his gaze on me.

"You live here?" he finally asks, voice pitched low enough so only I can hear.

"Mhm."

"With…" He tips his chin toward Easton, asking an unspoken question.

"No," I tell him. "Not like that." Unfortunately.

"Hmm," is all I get in return.

Doc finishes his exam, determining Dixie needs an X-ray to make sure her leg isn't broken. Easton is suitably upset about it. Her condition, not Doc's recommendation.

After brushing her down, Easton, with Doc's help, leads Dixie up front to the vet's trailer. Harrison stays behind to clean up Doc's tools that are still inside the stall.

"What're you doin' here?" I ask, my curiosity getting the better of me as I rake some loose pieces of straw back into Dixie's stall.

Harrison looks up from his position on the ground. "An apprenticeship. I'm finishing up my schooling under Doctor Hanson."

"Hmm," I grunt. "So, you're gonna be 'round here for a while."

Harrison looks up again, fire lighting his eyes. He sweeps his gaze over my face and body, looking at me like I'm something he wants to eat, not the sweaty, dirty guy I am who spent the entire day chasing ungulates.

"Yeah," he says. "I'll be around."

I nod but keep cleaning, making sure the hall stays clear like Easton likes it, raking the excess straw into the end stall. Harrison follows me, setting the vet's bag down next to him. I still have the rake in my hands when he descends upon me, pulling me in by the back of my neck. I let out a surprised grunt as his mouth clashes with mine, but when Harrison goes to pull back, I chase him forward, walking us until he hits the wall.

It's his turn to grunt in surprise, but he grips me harder, wasting no time before cupping the front of my tented jeans.

It's not a good place for this; I know that. Easton is right outside, and he could come back at any minute. The only saving grace is that I know Will will be at his grandparents' today after school. Otherwise, I wouldn't consider engaging Harrison like this. As it is, I'm hard, I'm horny, and letting off some steam sounds like a fine idea.

I shove Harrison again, knocking him back against the wall before I drop down, taking his pants with me.

"*Fuck, yes,*" he mutters, canting his hips forward like an offering.

As soon as his taste is in my mouth, my brain quiets. Yes, this is what I need. Everything is a little softer around the edges when I stop thinking and just let myself feel pleasure for a little while.

CHAPTER 20

Easton

I finish loading Dixie into the vet's trailer, and minutes later, Doc Hanson is pulling away. I watch them go, dust kicking up behind the truck and trailer as they roll down the long dirt road away from the house. I send a little prayer up for the new horse that her leg is just a bit bruised and not broken.

I still need to bring the rest of the horses in, and daylight is quickly fading, but the sight of the apprentice's car taking up space on the grass gives me pause. I would've expected him to leave with Doc Hanson, so I'm not sure why he's still here. Assuming he lost his way or maybe just needs a little help packing up, I change course for the stables.

As I step inside the shadowed interior of the big barn, I don't catch sight of the man, leaving me perplexed. Dixie's stall is closed up, and the doc's tools aren't inside anymore, so where's the apprentice? I reach into my back pocket with the intent to call Wyatt, since maybe he'll know where the other man is, but then I remember Wyatt's phone is dead, so I abandon that plan.

With no better ideas, I turn around to check outside. One or the other of them has to be around here somewhere. I've only taken one step in the other direction when I stop still, a noise giving me pause.

Feeling a bit like a horse myself, I cant my head to listen. There it is again. Almost like a huff. But Tempest and Sun Over Mason, the only two horses in the barn, are both staring right at me, not making a sound.

I walk closer to the source of the noise, keeping my feet light as I move. I don't know why for sure. Only a feeling, I suppose. Something telling me to be quiet and keep out of sight. As I approach the stall at the end, the one currently used for storage, the sounds get louder. Someone breathing. A muttered curse. Gagging.

That last noise is what propels my feet the final step towards the stall, my body tensing instinctually. I don't know what I expect to find—someone in distress?—but the sight of my best friend on his knees in the straw is not it.

I freeze. Absolutely turn to granite, as unfamiliar tingles race down my body, landing heavily in my hands and feet, making it feel like tiny fire ants are crawling under my skin.

The vet apprentice is there, too. Harrison. His head is thrown back against the stall wall, his jeans hanging loosely around his thighs as he shuttles his cock in and out of Wyatt's mouth. His fingers are threaded through my friend's long hair, grip tight, and the sight of it has my hands balling into fists. Anger rises up in me, sudden and profound, because Wyatt is *mine*. And how dare he handle him like that.

Except *Christ*, Wyatt isn't mine. Not like that. And he doesn't seem to have a problem with Harrison's rough treatment. He's sitting there on his haunches, one hand gripping Harrison's thigh, the other down his own pants, stroking furiously as Harrison stands above him, using his willing mouth.

Fuck. *Fuck.*

I have to get out of here. I shouldn't be watching this.

Move!

"Wait," Harrison breathes out, his hips slowing.

Wyatt drops back, releasing Harrison's cock with a soft plop sound that goes straight to my own dick, making me realize, rather shockingly, that I'm hard.

"What?" Wyatt asks, brushing his hair back from his face. "You seemed close. I know I was."

"Fuck me instead?" the man replies, one hand on his own dick.

"Oh, well, why didn't you say so?" Wyatt drawls, his grin widening as he pushes off the ground. "We have to be quick, though."

"Yeah, that's not going to be a problem," Harrison answers, reaching into his pocket for his wallet. He pulls out a condom and packet of lube and hands them to Wyatt before turning around and pushing his jeans down to his ankles. He leans forward, bracing his arms against the rough barn wall, but I barely notice him. My eyes are locked onto Wyatt.

Wyatt, my friend, who drops his own pants. Wyatt, my friend, whose dick is long and rock hard and just feet in front of me. Wyatt, my friend, who suits himself and spreads lube along his erection before pressing his fingers roughly against the other man.

I can't peel myself away. Can't stop watching. It's like time slows as I catalogue every familiar detail of the man I thought I knew better than anything. His long coppery hair, falling loose in front of his face as he stretches the other man with his fingers. The line of his neck and those broad, strong shoulders. His tanned, lightly haired forearms and the meat of his thighs, which are unveiled now that he's kicked his pants out of the way.

His cock, which I've never seen erect, that stands proudly before him. The swell of his ass, whiter than the rest of him, but firm and tensed slightly as he steps closer to Harrison.

It's like I'm seeing him for the first time. Seeing him as something other than my best friend. Seeing him as a man, stripped of all the veneer I've built around him our entire lives. The layers of friendship and familiarity and comfort that, when pulled back, let me see Wyatt as something altogether different.

A guy who is gay—and even though I knew that, it's somehow different seeing it in person—and virile. A guy who, based on what I'm watching, doesn't mind getting rough and dirty.

A guy who must be lonely, living with my sorry ass for all these years. Lonely enough for a quickie with the vet apprentice in a barn stall.

A guy who I can't take my eyes off of.

And I don't know what to do with any of that.

Wyatt presses forward, seating himself inside Harrison, and both men groan. He doesn't wait long before retreating and snapping his hips, slamming into the other man over and over. The sound of it, the sight, it makes me nearly lightheaded.

"Touch yourself," Wyatt tells Harrison, who complies.

The two rut because there's honestly no other word for it. It's dirty and hard and animalistic. And I know I need to turn away. That I can't keep watching this.

But as I take a step back, Wyatt's head swings my way. His eyes widen in surprise, his tempo faltering for only a moment, but he doesn't stop. He just keeps fucking Harrison as his gaze remains snagged on me.

His brows furrow, eyes pinging all over my face, probably reading the shock I must be showing. But neither of us looks away. Neither says a word.

When Harrison grunts out, "Close," Wyatt tightens his grip on the man. I can see it in the flexing of his muscles and the way his fingers indent further into Harrison's hips.

"Come on, darlin'," he says, looking me in the eye as the other man comes against the barn wall. My mouth drops open, and a gasp escapes my lips as Wyatt's lidded gaze drops forward, his hips stuttering and his whole body shivering as he comes inside the other man not a moment later. His hair is draped in front of his face, and that veil is what finally breaks the spell.

I turn around and get out of there as fast as I can.

I don't stop until I'm inside the house, slamming the bathroom door shut behind me. I have my dick out in two seconds flat and am coming into my fist before I can even feel guilty for jerking off over my friend. It goes on forever, or feels like it. Pulse after pulse, pulling from my whole body, leaving me slumped and dazed against the bathroom door.

I blink over and over again, my pulse hammering, my breaths coming out in short spurts. After what feels like an eternity, I tuck myself back in and wash my hands. Knowing I can't hide here forever, I head into the kitchen for a glass of water. A quick check out the window shows Harrison and his car are already gone.

As for Wyatt, I see him leaving the barn. I tense, unsure what to say to him after that, but he doesn't come up to the house. Instead, he turns on his heel and goes off in the other direction.

The rest of the horses, of course.

I don't know what to do. Don't know what to think. But I've never been one to avoid my problems, so I pull on my metaphorical big-boy pants and trudge out of the house in the direction Wyatt went.

I need to finish my work. And then I'll apologize and clear the air.

Plan in place, I stride through the grass and breathe in the evening air to clear my head. It's still hot, of course it is, but there's a breeze that indicates a cooler night coming in. The sun is getting low in the sky, and it casts a warm yellow hue over everything that makes it feel cozy. And it would be—I've always liked this time of night—if it weren't for all the thoughts inside my head making me decidedly uncomfortable, regardless of the night's beauty.

I see Wyatt already in the north pasture, so I head in the other direction to Monty's private field. My horse pivots his ears as I get close, and as soon as I give him a call, he trots over, slowing as his feet hit the dirt that surrounds the field in a three-foot wide perimeter. I keep it tilled along the fence so it stays grass-free, giving Monty a clear delineation of where the field ends. That way, he's able to avoid the fence easily, giving him the confidence to move around the space a little faster than he does in some of the other areas.

Once he's in reach, I grasp his bridle gently, and the two of us walk in. Although Monty would never bolt unless under duress, it's easier for him with a solid lead. His steps are surer, seeing as he trusts us not to lead him astray. He can still navigate the world just fine on his own, but I like being the tiller that gives him a little extra confidence, that makes things just a touch easier.

But that also means Monty is so tuned into my emotions and body language, he seems to sense something is wrong right off the bat. He presses his nose against the side of my head, and his hot breath fans across my face.

"'S'all right," I tell him softly, even though I'm not sure that's true.

Wyatt and I end up back at the barn at the same time, and Monty huffs softly as my body goes rigid, seeming to say *is that so?* I lead him quickly to his stall, keeping my eyes down as I pass by Wyatt, afraid that as soon as I see my friend, the image of him half-naked will resurface in my mind. Of course, I can't avoid him forever, don't even want to really. So, as soon as Monty is settled, I step back into the hall and wait.

My eyes ping up the moment I hear the sound of Wyatt's boots clomping toward me. He shifts his gaze toward the ground, his hat obscuring his face as he does so, and that surprises me maybe more than anything else I witnessed tonight. It's a rare sight for my best friend to be nervous.

Unsurprisingly, Wyatt tries to play the whole thing off. "Well, can't say that one should go in the scrapbook under friendship bondin' activities."

"I'm sorry," I tell him seriously, ignoring his attempt at a joke. Wyatt shakes his head, but I plow on.

"I should've walked right away. I don't know what I was thinkin'. I just..." Christ, how do I finish that sentence?

Wyatt saves the day. "You were surprised and froze. I get it," he says, waving his hand in the air. "No need to apologize. Honestly, it's me who should be sayin' sorry. We shouldn't have done that there. It was irresponsible."

He's likely right, and yet I hadn't even thought of that. If anything, the idea of doing that in the barn is, frankly, hot.

I clear my thoughts. Not helpful.

"Probably best if you just forget you ever saw that," Wyatt says. "We don't ever have to bring it up again if you don't want to."

Can I forget it? Can I get the sight of my best friend in a compromising position out of my head? Can I forget the way he looked, let go of the sound of his voice rolling around the word *darlin*? I don't know.

Right now, it seems like an impossible ask.

But I don't say that. Of course I don't. It would only make Wyatt uncomfortable.

So I nod, say, "We'll forget it, then," and go on pretending like everything is the same when it's most definitely not.

CHAPTER 21

Wyatt

"Hey, stranger."

I look up from the beer I'm nursing. I don't know what I'm expecting to find at the bottom of my glass tonight, but I guess I'm not in any hurry to figure it out, seeing as I've been here for an hour already.

"Hey, Harrison."

The man takes up the open stool next to me. Nash comes over, and Harrison orders a Guinness.

"Haven't heard back from you," Harrison says, not unkindly.

He's not wrong. It's not that I've been avoiding answering his question—all right, maybe I have been a little bit—I just don't know what to say. And I've had a certain best friend on my mind, as well as his shocked expression when he found me fucking Harrison in the barn.

Christ.

I haven't come that hard in forever, and I know it was because Easton's eyes were on me. It makes me feel like a shitty friend. At least things have mostly continued on as normal between us. No harm done.

I divert my attention back to the man next to me.

"Haven't figured out if it's a yes or a no," I answer honestly.

Harrison shrugs. "That's all right. I can wait."

I look over at him. Harrison is good-looking, and I have a feeling he knows it. His dark blonde hair is just long enough to be set in a stylish way that makes him look too sophisticated for these parts, but not so long it looks rakish. His lips are puffy and distracting. And he's bigger, like I like 'em. Versatile, too.

He's about the same height as me, just a little less roughened. That probably has to do with him being a bit younger, although I'm not sure by how much. He doesn't have years of sun and dirt baked into his skin. Or muscles honed by decades of manual labor. *Like a certain horse trainer*, my mind speaks up, but I swat the thought away.

Not to say Harrison isn't fit. He is, and I can tell he's a hard worker in his own way, what with all the large animals he deals with.

There's a reason I approached him at the bar all those weeks ago. I'm attracted to him, plain and simple.

"Why bother?" I ask in a self-deprecating manner. "Is it 'cause I'm the only gay man in a thirty-mile radius?"

"Well, that's not true. I've met a couple others." That's news to me. "But no, I like you, Wyatt," he says, shrugging as he takes a sip of his dark beer.

"Really? How can you tell? We've only had a conversation and a half."

"I don't know, just a feeling."

"Huh," I say.

"You could always give it a try," he says, bumping his shoulder into mine.

"Give what a try?"

"Saying yes. Going on a date with me. Worst-case scenario, it's not for you, we have one last goodbye fuck—cause, let's face it, we know we're good at that, at least—and that's that."

Nash's eyes widen behind the counter of the bar, but he doesn't say a word. Just keeps on wiping the counter dry. I sigh internally, but what's the point in even being polite anymore? Everybody in this town knows I'm gay. Who cares if they get a little more information than they bargained for? Lord knows Plum Valley loves its gossip.

Plus, I respect that Harrison is just *out there*. No shame. No hiding. Screw anyone who looks at him sideways.

I drink the last sip of my beer, not having gained any wisdom in uncovering its bottom.

Harrison is right—what is the harm?

It's giving up, that little voice in my head says. And that's the hard truth. Giving it a real shot with someone, *anyone*, means finally giving up on Easton for good. I didn't realize until just now that I was still hanging on.

Easton has known me for decades. He knows my good and my bad. And now, he's seen me naked. If he still doesn't want me, he never will.

Fuck, I'm so tired of this.

This constant go-around in my mind. These feelings.

I stick a ten on the counter and return my hat atop my head.

"Give me one more day to think about it," I tell Harrison.

He nods, and I head home.

As I walk in the door, I find Easton awake, even though it's late by our standards. Country folk start their day before the roosters, after all. He's squatting on the ground, my friend, back bent over the ottoman, arms high above his head. His shirt has ridden squarely up his stomach, far enough to see every muscle in his abdomen working with the stretch he's attempting to pull off. I have to shake my head before I start either laughing or crying.

Clearing my throat, I get his attention.

"Back botherin' you again?" I ask.

Easton lifts his head, looking like he's performing the world's worst yoga pose. The man is not exactly pliable. He sighs, coming out of the awkward position and plopping his butt onto the floor, legs pulled up and spread wide in front of him. Another distracting view.

I avert my gaze from his crotch as he rubs the back of his neck.

"Yeah, Glory Bird was givin' me trouble again."

"I swear that horse is a witch," I joke. She has the uncanny ability to make things disappear. Her bridle, a brush, the water bucket. We always find them some time later, tossed over a fence or hidden in the corner of a stall.

"Yeah, you might be right," he concedes, stretching his arms out wide.

"C'mon, then," I say, motioning towards the stairs. "Let's get you sorted."

"You sure?" Easton asks, looking guilty. "You don't have to."

"How many times do I have to tell you? I know I don't have to—"

"*I want to*," we finish at the same time.

I chuckle but point at the stairs again. At my insistent stare, Easton rises and walks ahead of me toward his bedroom.

Years ago, I had the physician next town over show me some tips for setting Easton's back. The man did an extended residency with a physical therapist before he went into general medicine instead, and he was gracious enough to teach me a few basics, since Easton showed up several times with his shoulder stuck in place.

The problem is Easton keeps straining the same muscle groups. And since he doesn't take the time to loosen them regularly, they just keep ratcheting tighter until he's thrown his whole back out of whack.

Of course, he never complains about it. He just tries lying over the furniture to stretch out, like that'll actually do any good. *The damn fool,* I think with a smile on my face.

I follow my friend into his room, and he strips off his shirt without me having to tell him to. My tongue promptly gets glued to the roof of my mouth as the broad expanse of his back comes into view, a sight I'll never get sick of.

Easton crawls onto his bed, and I detour into the master en suite to grab the lotion he prefers. I refuse to think about whether or not he uses that lotion for other activities, too.

When I get back to the bed, I set it aside and climb up over his back. Per usual, I remind my dick that this is *not* the time to get excited, but per usual, he doesn't listen.

I start by checking the alignment of Easton's spine. As I expected, he's got a couple vertebrae spun out a bit, so I place my palms on either side of his spine, nice and flat, and press down in short, hard bursts. They pop back into place, and Easton breathes a sigh of relief.

After that, I grab the lotion. For the next several minutes, I work the knots in Easton's upper back and shoulders. It's like he has tiny boulders in there, and each time I feel one release, I get such a strong sense of satisfaction. I did that. I helped him feel better.

And yet, at the same time, it's a tortuous process. Running my hands over his naked skin and feeling the dips and swells of his muscles. Listening to his soft, happy little moans. It reminds me that this is all I will ever get. And I have to be okay with that.

For the most part, I am. I've made my peace with it. Doesn't stop me constantly fantasizing about more, though.

For whatever reason, as I knead Easton's pain away tonight, it hits me a little harder. I have the best friend in the world, and I love him. I love living with him and raising that not-so-little-anymore boy who's sleeping down the hall. I love laughing with him and watching the sun set out beyond the back porch. I love family suppers when we all make it home in time and the fact that I'm *Pop*. I love it all, and yet I'm still a little lonely.

When I finish up, Easton's back is looser and red from the constant attention. I slide off the bed and give him a little slap on the side of his arm.

"Make sure to drink a glass of water before you go to sleep," I remind him.

Easton turns his head, looking over at me. There's something in his eyes I can't quite read, so I stop on my way to the door.

"Everythin' all right?" I ask.

He clears his throat. "Yeah, o'course. Thank you."

"No thanks needed," I tell him.

"Wyatt."

"Yeah?" I stop again, hanging in the doorway.

"Y'know I love you, right?"

Fuck.

The things he says sometimes.

I force a smile. "You tell me often enough."

"Do I?" Easton asks, peering at me from across the room.

I swallow around the discomfort in my throat, not quite sure why this conversation has taken such a strange turn. The way Easton's talking, the tone of his voice, it makes me feel like something is wrong. Although I have no clue what.

It just feels like there are some words hanging in the air, being left unsaid.

Maybe it's just in my own head. I have had a lot on my mind.

"Sure do," I aim for joking. "I think you'd be lost without me."

"That's the truth," Easton replies, sounding enough like his usual self that I feel like I can breathe normally again.

"Night," I say, closing his door behind me, hearing his answering "*Night*" through the wood.

I make it down the hall and into my room, closing my door just in time for the tears to come.

"*Shit*," I mutter, wiping at my face. "Get it together."

Maybe I won't ever find a person better than Easton, but don't I deserve *someone* for myself?

Before I can overthink it, I pick up my phone.

"Unless this is a booty call, phone calls can wait until daylight," the teasing voice on the end of the line says.

"Yes, I'll go on a date with you," I tell Harrison, hearing the resolution in my voice loud and clear. I'm doing this.

CHAPTER 22

Easton

It's official. I'm lusting after Wyatt.

I don't even know how it happened. It makes no sense. I've known the man my entire life. Thirty-four years. Twenty-two if we're talking about the time since puberty hit.

And I never, *never*, got a boner over him before. Yet now, it's happening all the time.

Seeing him in the barn with Harrison.

Standing next to him in the kitchen after he showered and was smelling like something orange and woodsy.

Catching a glimpse of him hauling a hay bale over his shoulder, his muscles tensing, his body covered in sweat. I've seen him do that a thousand times or more. So why, now, is it like some sort of erotic show?

I can't stop thinking about it, about *him*.

Or about the fact that, for the first time since Becca, I want someone. Badly.

But that someone is my best friend. There's probably some code against that, right? Don't hit on your best friend just because he's gay?

I feel like I'm in over my head, and I don't know what to do about it. If I tell Wyatt, there's only one way it could go right and about a million ways it could go wrong. Is that a risk I'm willing to take?

I don't know.

One thing I know for certain is I'm jerking off more these days than ever before.

Including now. As soon as I hear Wyatt shut the door into his bedroom, I roll over and free my cock, which has been rock hard ever since Wyatt started massaging my back.

I could barely stand it and was almost certain I could come from the feel of his hands on my skin and nothing else. But just when it was almost too much, he stopped. I wasn't sure how I felt about that—disappointed, almost—but it was surely for the best. Coming in my pants like a teenager would've been a dead giveaway. As it was, I did worry that a few of the noises I let slip were going to alert Wyatt to my predicament. Luckily, they were easy enough to chalk up to the massage itself.

I decide to hold off on trying to solve the new mystery of me and my friend and instead focus on the straining erection in my hand.

I stroke myself with some of the lotion Wyatt left behind, the smell reminding me of him now that I have a firmly established link in my mind between its scent and the feel of Wyatt's hands on me. I think of his work-hardened fingers and the firm pressure he applies when he runs them over my body. I think of the stubble along his jaw and wonder what it would feel like against my own. If his lips would be sweet.

I imagine myself mapping his body with *my* hands for a change. I wonder what that would feel like, the hard planes of him versus the softness of a female.

I wonder what it would feel like to have his mouth around me, instead of my own hand, or have his fingers digging into my hips like they did that time with Harrison. Would I like getting fucked?

The visuals flash through my mind too fast to keep up with. Wyatt. Me. Our bodies tangled.

I bite my fist when I come, worried my shout will break free otherwise. It takes a couple minutes before my body stops shaking, and I'm close to drifting off when I remember Wyatt's warning to drink some water.

With a good bit of effort, I force myself out of bed. I clean up in the bathroom, and, per Wyatt's instruction, drink down a good eight ounces before falling back atop my mattress.

What would it feel like to curl around him in sleep?

It's the last thought I have before my eyes drift shut.

Questions of Wyatt follow me for over a month. Over a month of wondering *why now*, wondering why him, questioning what it all means. Weeks and weeks of jerking off and thinking of his hands on me. I can't get him out of my head. Can't stop fantasizing about him.

And yet, I'm no closer to understanding any of it.

But it's a nice, peaceful morning, so I try to clear my head and focus on work. On the here and now. Will is helping today, mucking horse stalls for chore money, and the sound of his rake scraping the ground helps center me. I've almost accomplished my goal of putting Wyatt out of my mind when Will asks a question I'm not expecting, even though I've been waiting years for it.

"Do you ever think about datin' again?"

I look over at my son. He's really sprouted up over the last year. I can't believe he's almost eleven.

"Not sure. Can't say I've been inclined."

"Do you have sex?"

I cough, sputtering over nothing but air. I swear kids these days are much more advanced. Pretty sure at eleven, Wyatt and I were more interested in my brother's comics or chasing tumbleweeds than sex and body parts of the animal kingdom.

I stop what I'm doing, setting down the rake so I can give him my full attention.

"Why do you ask?"

He kicks at some straw with the toe of his boot and rubs the back of his neck, a gesture I now recognize as familiar. Wyatt is always telling me I do that when I'm nervous.

"Well, I hear Pop talkin' 'bout sex sometimes—"

"'S'cuse me?" I interrupt.

"Chill," he says, rolling his eyes and sounding exactly like the almost-teenager he is. "Not to me. On the phone once, and when Harrison was over here the other day."

Right, *Harrison*. The man he's been dating for the past month, much to my disappointment. I don't want to dwell too long on that.

I take a deep breath. It's not that I think Wyatt is being irresponsible, but I don't know how I feel about Will inadvertently hearing about sex at such a young age. We've had a few variations of body-positivity conversations and the "sex talk," but this is different.

"You shouldn't be hearin' that."

"Well, I can't turn off my *ears*, Dad."

I have to hold in my laugh. "Then he shouldn't be sayin' it."

"Dad, stop," Will says, all serious with his hands on his hips. "I won't have you shamin' Pop for talkin' 'bout somethin' as natural as sex."

Christ, this kid. I shake my head, fighting the smile that wants to break free. I can tell Will wants to have a real talk about this, and I don't want him thinking I'm not taking him seriously.

"You're right," I concede. "I apologize."

Will nods his head once and goes back to toeing the straw.

"Anyways, it got me thinkin'. Pop has sex."

I don't need the reminder, but I nod. "Sure."

"But I don't ever hear you talkin' about sex. And I wondered if that's 'cause you don't have a man or woman to date."

I stand there, completely gobsmacked by the simple and direct honesty of my son. It's not the first time he's taken me by surprise, not by far. Like that time he told me I had *three* gray hairs on my head, which means I'm old now, *duh*. Or when he gave me a ten-minute lecture about how I was killing the planet because I wasn't recycling our milk cartons.

And now, here he is, asking me plainly about sex and dating, with zero judgement. Just curiosity, maybe with a dash of caring about my happiness thrown in, too.

"Would it bother you if I dated?"

"Nah," he says. "I wish you could date Pop, though, so he wouldn't have to go."

Again, I find myself choking on air before my brain catches up with his words.

"Wait, why would Wyatt have to go?"

"*Dad*," Will scolds. "If he falls in love with Harrison, he'll move in with him."

It's like a sucker punch to my sternum. It's too soon for that, isn't it? So far, I've been doing a pretty good job of avoiding thoughts of Wyatt with his new boyfriend. It seems cruel that it would happen now, only after I realized my feelings for him. Except I know the world doesn't work like that, with malicious intent.

It just is what it is. I'm trying to be happy for him. After all, I haven't figured out what I would even do if Wyatt were single. Would I, *could* I, do anything about my new revelation? I don't know, and I wish I had someone to talk to about it.

Will accepts my silence, going back to his task. We don't talk anymore about Wyatt moving out, thankfully, only more benign topics. When we're done with chores, he saddles up Monty and takes him for a nice, long stroll.

As for me, I head around to the side of the house, where a single, old plum tree still stands. The thing is more dead than alive at this point, and I don't think it'll hold up much longer. When Becca and I built our home here, she had grand plans of putting a whole new orchard in this spot. She always thought the idea of revitalizing plums in Plum Valley was romantic.

I can't say I blamed her. It's a nice thought. She passed before she could make that dream come true, and I never did get around to clearing out this old tree and planting fresh.

I like coming here to talk to Becca. It feels like our spot. I prefer it over visiting her at the cemetery. It feels too stagnant there. A place for mourning. And I like to remember Becca alive and vibrant.

Sitting here, under this old tree, it's easy to see her in my mind's eye. To imagine her sitting cross-legged next to me, the breeze in her hair.

"Hey, Becca," I say, realizing maybe I do have someone to talk to after all. "I know—I haven't planted the orchard yet. I promise to get to it soon, all right? I have some news, and it might be a surprise to you. It sure was to me."

I rub the back of my neck, feeling a little nervous because it's the first time I'm going to say it out loud.

"I'm attracted to Wyatt."

I puff out a breath. There. I pause, waiting to feel something monumental, but all I feel is relief at putting it out there.

"I didn't see that comin', and it's new. It wasn't like that back when you were still here. I don't understand it, Bec. How did this happen? How does somethin' like that just...change? After so many years. The problem is he's in a relationship now. I want to *be* with him, I think, which, Christ, sounds crazy to say, but I can't even talk to him about it."

That wouldn't be fair of me to do.

"What do you think, Becca? Could Wyatt ever feel the same? I worry...that if I *did* ask him out... Wait, do folks still do that these days?" I shake my head. "If I do, it could wreck us. I mean, this is *Wyatt* we're talkin' about. My best friend. We've known each other our whole lives. What right do I have to potentially implode all that?"

Although a big part of me wants to believe we would be all right. If he didn't feel the same, I think we could get through that and come out strong on the other side.

"It would be worth it, if he could feel the same, don't you think? Can you picture it? The sort of life we could have together? I hope you don't mind me sayin' that, Becca. I don't think you would. You said you wanted me to be happy, and I believe that."

I exhale, drinking in several lungfuls of air.

"It's a right mess, Becca, and I'm in the middle of it."

CHAPTER 23

Wyatt, age 35

"Hey, stranger," Harrison says, his standard greeting for me.

"Howdy," I reply, toeing off my boots and melting onto the couch next to my boyfriend, laying my head in his lap.

Harrison runs his fingers through my hair, sifting and tugging gently. I hum my approval.

"That feels so good, thank you."

"Happy to," he says back.

"Sorry I'm late. Will needed some help with his homework."

"You know I don't mind," Harrison says, tone kind. He really doesn't. He's so understanding about my relationship with Will and Easton, and he knows there are certain responsibilities I'm not ready to give up.

"How was your day?" I ask.

I feel, more than hear, Harrison's chuckle. "Pretty typical. Had my arm up a cow's vagina."

"Oh, wow. Another one. I've never had anythin' of mine up a vagina."

Harrison laughs, and I chuckle in response.

"I have," he says.

"Well, 'course. You just told me you have."

"No," Harrison says, "I mean a woman."

"Wait, really?" I ask, rolling around so I can see his face. "You've slept with women? How come I didn't know this?"

"Well," he shrugs, "we never really compared past lovers. And it was just the one. First time sort of thing. Pretty easy to figure out it wasn't *my* sort of thing."

"Huh," I reply. "Was it weird?"

"You really want to know?" He chuckles.

I shrug. "Sure, why not?"

"It was likely awkward for both of us. We were fifteen, probably way too young, didn't know what we were doing. I couldn't stop staring at her boobs, and not because I liked them. They just kept moving, and it was like I was hypnotized."

I burst out laughing, and Harrison grins down at me.

"Not a boob sort of gay man, huh."

"Nope," he replies.

"More of an ass man?" I ask, waggling my eyebrows playfully.

"I do love yours," he says, sliding his hand under my waistband.

I spring right to life, blood rushing south instantly. "Hmm, show me?" I nuzzle my face closer to his crotch.

"Happy to," Harrison says again, squeezing my ass cheek. "But first, I wanted to ask you something."

"Is it whether I'm a boob or an ass man?"

"No, the answer to that is an obvious one." He laughs before slipping his hand back up to my head, brushing my hair lightly off my forehead. "No, I was thinking about the fact that we've been dating for over a year now."

I sit up, displacing Harrison's hand. "Yeah?" I prompt, not sure why I'm frowning, even as I can feel myself doing it.

"Relax, Wyatt, you look like you're expecting me to propose. That's not it."

His words don't exactly relax me. It still feels like something is going on, and it's making me uneasy.

"All right then," I say. "Go on."

"Well, I wanted to give you something."

He reaches into the side table, pulling out a key and handing it over to me.

"A key? I already have one of those."

"I know you do. This one is more symbolic. I was hoping you'd move in with me."

Harrison watches my face as I process his request. My first thoughts are of Will and Easton. I don't want to leave them. I'm not ready. I'm not sure I'll ever be ready. Harrison seems to guess that much as he goes on.

"I'm not asking you to give them up," he says, scooting closer and running his hand over my leg. "You could start with staying here on weekends, maybe? We could get Will a key, too, so he knows he's always welcome. We could even set up the guest room as his so he could stay here at night if he wanted to. I just want more of your time, Wyatt. Maybe that makes me selfish, and I won't pretend otherwise, but I think we have a shot at something real here. I'd like to give that a chance."

Well, shit. What do I say to that? He has a good point, all of it.

Do I want to take that step? Am I ready to give us a fighting chance?

------------------★------------------

"What's goin' on?" Easton asks. "You've been pretty quiet lately. Not like yourself."

I look over at my friend, who's chopping vegetables for supper. I've been sitting at the table for a while, thinking about Harrison's proposal. Haven't stopped thinking about it for two solid weeks, in fact.

With a sigh, I bring it up. "Harrison asked me to move in."

The sound of the knife stops abruptly, and when I look up, Easton is looking down at the cutting board.

"Didn't cut yourself, did you?" I ask, standing up and going over to where he's standing.

"No." He shakes his head. "Was surprised, is all."

So was I.

He resumes chopping, occasionally dumping handfuls of ingredients into the soup pot.

"What'd you say?"

"Haven't given him an answer yet. I'm afraid to," I answer honestly.

"Why's that?" he asks, setting down the knife and facing me. He grabs a dish cloth and wipes his hands.

How do I explain it without telling Easton the truth? That I'm afraid to say yes, afraid that I will actually fall deeply in love with Harrison and forget about him? And even though I would've jumped at that chance when I was younger and living in Illinois, now I'm terrified to stop loving Easton. It doesn't make any sense. It just feels like Easton is this integral part of me, and if I stop loving him, who does that make me? Wouldn't I be a different man?

Harrison loves me; I know he does. I love him, too, in a way. Just not the same way I love Easton. But could I? Maybe, with time.

Yet I'm terrified of it.

And then there's the fact that moving in with Harrison would mean moving out of my home. Well, Easton's house, but it *is* my home, too, after all these years. I have memories here, Easton is here, and Will is here. How could I turn my back on them, Will especially?

"He'd understand, y'know," Easton says, like he can read my mind.

"You think?"

He nods, setting the dish cloth down. "He wants you to be happy, and he'll realize it's not about leavin' him. It's about goin' towards love. He'll be all right. He's resilient, just like his papa."

Shit, don't cry.

"And you?" I voice. "Would you understand?"

"'Course," he says, a sort of resignation and sadness in his gaze. "I didn't expect you to stay forever, Wyatt. In fact, I never expected you'd even stay this long. These last eleven years, livin' here with you, have been a gift. I wouldn't trade 'em for all the Angus in Texas."

"Well, 'course not," I joke. "Everybody knows Hereford are superior."

Easton just shakes his head. "My point is we got longer than I expected, and I don't begrudge you wantin' to live your life. You helped me when I was at my lowest, and I'll be forever grateful for that. But now it's time for you to follow your own dreams."

I can't tell him *he* is my dream, always has been. I've been living my dream here with him and Will for the past decade. With the exception of one tiny, little detail—the lack of a romantic partnership—I'm exactly where I want to be.

"Besides," he goes on, "it's not like you'll actually be gone. We'll see you all the time still. I'm sure of it."

"He has to be all right with it," I say, talking about Will. "If he's not, I won't do it, not yet."

"Fair enough."

"And I *will* still be here all the time, so don't get any ideas into your head that you'll be able to get rid of me."

"Wouldn't dream of it."

"And if you have any problems with the horses, or Will is upset and needs his pop, or—"

"Wyatt." He cuts me off. "It'll be just fine. And if it's not, I'll call you. Always, all right?"

"All right," I say. "*Shit*, am I really gonna do this?"

"I think so," Easton says, reaching over and squeezing my hand tightly.

It seems like the right step, so why does it feel like there's a thousand-pound weight strapped to my heart?

CHAPTER 24

Easton, age 36

It's been about six months since Wyatt moved out, and I've been missing him something fierce. Sure, I still see him plenty, but not like before. He doesn't live with us anymore. There aren't a million small ways in which he fills my day.

Apart from in my thoughts, that is. There, he occupies a large portion of the available retail.

That wide smile and his laugh. The way he moves, so sure and strong. And the sight of his nearly naked body, glistening with sweat.

Those are the visuals that haunt me, in a way, and have for the past two years.

I regret it, I realized long ago. I regret not making a move the moment I registered my reaction. Not while he was fucking Harrison in the barn, of course, but after. When I knew my feelings had changed from purely platonic into something more. I should've told him. I should've taken the chance, and not a day goes by that I don't regret that.

It's a frustrating feeling, that regret. If I could go back in time, I'd do things differently. If only.

I won't ever pass up that chance again, should I be able to take it.

I'm helping my dad out at his house today, clearing out the attic. It hasn't been done since before Mama passed, and Dad wants to get things in order. My guess is he's thinking about his own time coming, even though I personally don't want to linger too long on that thought.

We have our issues, my dad and I, but I don't want him dead.

Will is helping, too. Supposedly. But he stopped dragging piles down the ladder an hour ago and is now flipping through an old stack of newspapers.

"Woah," Will says, pulling my attention.

"What'cha got?"

"Grandpa was in the newspaper," he says, turning the page toward me.

I dust myself off and go over to Will, looking at the article. I heard the story of how Dad hung a sign saying, "Willa, will you marry me?" below the Plum Valley steer on the outskirts of town. Mama was on her way back from visiting family when Dad surprised her with the proposal.

I didn't realize they ran a story on it, including a picture of Dad standing next to the sign, hands crossed in front of him, looking serious and happy all at once.

"He had a soft spot for her, huh?" Will says.

"Sure did," I reply, squeezing his shoulder.

"How come Grandma wasn't in the picture?"

"Story goes they got delayed and didn't make it back to town 'til two in the mornin'. Your grandpa stayed out there the whole time, but I'm guessin' whoever took this picture didn't want to wait around."

"What was she like?" Will asks, a question he's asked before.

"Kind," I tell him. "Big heart. Always doin' somethin' for somebody else. She was patient, too. And opinionated. She wouldn't hit you over the head with it, but she was pretty fierce about what she felt was right. You're a lot like her in that way. Your mama named you well."

It blew me away all those years ago when Becca told me she wanted to name our child after their grandma. Willa, for a girl. Or Will, for a boy.

"I miss them both," Will says, and even though he never knew either, I understand.

I ruffle Will's hair, which is getting pretty shaggy, and go back to the box I was sorting through. The next piece of paper I lift gives me pause.

Wyatt

I open the envelope addressed to my friend, feeling my heart rate pick up when I unfold the contents inside and reveal a familiar piece of stationary. Daisies.

"Dad?" I call out, already on my way down the ladder.

"What is it?" he asks, sticking his head around the corner from his study.

"What's this?" I ask, hand shaking slightly as I hold out the letter.

My dad's face pales. He blinks several times and then, seeming to steel himself, comes fully out into the hall.

"That was from Becca's affairs."

My breathing becomes shallower. "And why do you have it, when it's addressed to Wyatt?"

He doesn't answer right away, and I can feel myself getting hot, waiting to hear what I know will make me angry.

"Dad," I snap.

"I didn't think it was right for him to see it. What with him bein'...what he is. And what Becca was sayin' in that letter. I didn't want him gettin' ideas."

"*What* ideas?" I say, starting to read the letter, even though I feel a little wrong doing so. It's not my letter to read, after all.

I can hear my dad saying something as I turn around, but it's muted in my mind. I scan through Becca's letter to Wyatt, and it feels like my heart is going a mile a minute.

> *"I know I upset you at the wedding."*
>
> *"If you're still in love with him."*
>
> *"He loves you more than he understands."*

What is this? What was Becca saying?

I read it over and over, and when I finally stop, it feels like I'm breaking through fog, like everything around me suddenly reappears.

"You had no right to keep this," I tell my dad, turning around. "No right."

My dad just clenches his jaw tight.

"How'd you even get this?" I want to know.

"It was delivered to your house, same as your letter, the day the will was read."

"The day after we buried Becca. When you and Hawthorne and Clive were there as support. And you, what, grabbed it before anybody else could see?"

He doesn't need to answer; it's there in his eyes.

"Unbelievable." I shake my head.

I storm outside, needing a little space, and I don't stop storming until I'm at the tree Wyatt fell from all those years ago. The branch is still there, about twenty feet up, and before I can think too hard about what I'm doing, I climb up. I don't go too far out. I just sit on that branch with my back against the solid trunk, and I scream.

I scream until my voice is hoarse.

I don't even know why I'm screaming. It's not something I've ever done before, as far as I can remember. I just feel so angry. Angry at my dad. Angry at time, for passing on by, with me none the wiser. Angry at Becca, even, for knowing back then something I didn't figure out until recently.

I'm just so *angry*.

And sad. Did Wyatt really love me then?

The thought of my friend feeling all that and never saying a word... Christ. If it's true, he must have been so hurt. I never would've wished that on him.

Then again, if he loved me once, maybe he could love me again. Except he's dating Harrison now.

And once more, I'm reminded of the chance I so narrowly missed.

I think about that letter all that day and on through the next.

While dragging boxes from the attic, because I promised I would, Becca's words are on my mind. While bedding down the horses at night, I stop at Dixie's former stall, and I wonder if I should deliver the letter to Wyatt. In the morning, as I tromp through the dew-thick grass of the north pasture with Monty in tow, I contemplate if it would only hurt Wyatt to receive it at this point and whether or not it's fair of me to factor that into my decision.

It feels like a heavy burden, this choice. And, all over again, I'm angry at my father for putting me in this position to begin with.

Would it be right to deliver the letter, knowing it might bring Wyatt pain? Would it be a selfish decision, hoping it would somehow bring him back to me?

It's a terrible thing to hope for because it wouldn't be fair to Harrison, and guilt rips through me at the thought.

Does it make me just as bad as my dad if I hold onto it? What would Becca think?

It doesn't feel like there's a right answer to any of it. And after mulling it over for the past twenty-four hours, I haven't come to any sort of conclusion about what to do with the daisy-embellished stationary burning a hole through my dresser drawer.

CHAPTER 25

Wyatt

As soon as I step through the door, I can tell something is off.

Harrison is sitting in the kitchen, elbows resting on the table. The lights in the apartment are low, and he doesn't even turn my way when I close the door.

"Everythin' all right?" I ask, leaving my dirty boots on the mat to take care of later and walking over to the slumped form of my boyfriend.

Harrison looks up then, although he doesn't rise from his bowed position. He looks...sad, tired, and maybe a little angry.

"Not so much," he says.

I take a seat next to him, reaching over to clasp his arm, but he merely looks at my hand and then back up at my face.

"Have you loved him this entire time?"

My whole body tenses and then deflates in the matter of a second. I pull my hand back, rubbing it over my eyes. I'm not going to pretend I don't know what he's talking about, and there's no use in lying. That's one thing I'll never do to Harrison.

"Yes."

He tucks his arms closer to his body. It reminds me so much of a wounded animal, and I want to comfort him, but his body language is screaming *stay the fuck away*.

"Our anniversary was last week, you know," he says, and my gut sinks even further.

Shit, I've fucked this all up.

"Two years," he goes on. "I told myself I wouldn't be *that* person. The partner who gets upset if his boyfriend misses a date on the calendar. Not everyone is hardwired like that, to put stock into those moments."

He glances at me, and I know there's worse coming.

"But then, just yesterday, you were talking about how it was the anniversary of when Easton got Monty, his horse. And I knew you *did* remember dates, just not ours."

I puff out a breath. "I'm sorry," I tell him, although I'm not sure what I'm most sorry for. Missing our anniversary or being in love with someone else.

Harrison just shakes his head. "Why are you even dating me?"

"I tried," I tell him. "I did try to love you."

A couple tears fall down his cheeks, and I feel terrible that I'm the cause.

"It doesn't work like that, Wyatt. You can't just will love into existence. You should've told me. I had a right to know I was your second choice."

"And that would've made a difference?" I ask, baffled.

"Yes, it would've made a difference!" he huffs, slapping his palms against the table. "Then it would have been *my* choice whether or not I was okay with that. If you had been up front, hadn't lied by omission, I would've known what I was getting myself into. I thought... I thought you were *in* this. But you never were. I was just your distraction."

I don't know what to say. No words are going to fix this, and he's right. I've had one foot out the door this entire time, never fully committing, never handing over my heart, knowing it belonged elsewhere. Even if I could fix this, would I want to?

"You deserved better," I tell him.

"Damn right, I did."

"What now?" I ask, giving Harrison that choice, at least. He can kick me out right this minute if he wants. He has that right. He can yell at me for another five days. I'd deserve that, too.

"Now," he says, turning to face me more fully, "I'm going to kiss you one last time, and then you're going to pack your bags."

⁎

I don't knock before entering Easton's house. I never have before, and I'm not about to start now.

His head pops out of the kitchen, and he looks at me in confusion. "What're you doin' back already?" he asks.

His eyes drop down to the suitcases in my hands, and I can see the moment it dawns on him. His face drops, sympathetic, as he comes toward me.

"Shit, what happened?"

"We're through," I tell him.

"Wyatt, I'm..." He doesn't finish his thought, just shakes his head.

I shrug, bags heavy in my grip. "Was a long time comin', to be honest."

"And you're sure?" Easton asks, rubbing both hands behind his neck. "It's definitely over?"

"Yeah, I'm sure," I say with an exhausted sigh, wondering why he seems so agitated.

"All right," he mumbles, pacing around a couple steps. "*Shit*, all right. Hold on."

Easton turns on his heel and disappears up the stairs, leaving me thoroughly confused. I finally set down the bags in my hands and make my way into the family room, slumping down onto the comfortable brown couch I've missed so much.

When Easton breezes back into the room, he has an envelope in his hands. He's looking down at it with as serious of an expression as I've ever seen on my friend's face. When his eyes lift to me, there's something in his gaze that I can't quite decipher. An intensity of sorts. Some sort of steely determination as he holds out the slightly wrinkled paper toward me.

"This is yours," he says.

"What?" I ask, looking down at the swooping letters, indeed spelling out my name.

Easton takes a seat in the chair kitty-corner to the couch, elbows on his knees as he watches me. I don't have time to dwell on the disappointment I feel at his distance, sitting in the chair instead of on the couch at my side.

"It's from Becca. I got one, too, when she passed. And this one was supposed to be for you, *is* for you. My dad," he says, exasperation lacing his tone as he shakes his head, "held onto it."

"Why?" I ask, not even sure which question I'm asking. Why did Becca write me a letter? Why did Miller keep it from me?

Easton doesn't answer my question as I sit fully upright and gently open the flap. It isn't sealed, and I look up at Easton.

"You read this?"

He nods slowly, eyes on the envelope in my hands. I pull out the contents, and when I unfold the paper from inside, the first thing I notice is my name, again, at the top. *Wyatt*. Along the left side are little daisies, and filling up the rest of the page is big, scrolling penmanship.

I force my throat to swallow before I start reading, somehow just *knowing* this is big. Important.

> *Wyatt,*

> *I'm sorry. I know I upset you at the wedding. And if—Christ, I hope this doesn't happen—but, in case we never get a chance to clear the air, here is me doing my best.*

> *I didn't want you to give up hope. That's why I said the things I said. Nothing is certain in this life, and maybe there will come a time when I'm not with Easton anymore. And, if that happens, and if you're still in love with him, I think you should tell him. He was brokenhearted when you left. He didn't realize that's what it was, but I could see it. He loves you more than he understands, but he didn't ever know what to do with it.*

> *Don't give up hope, Wyatt. I pray you lived your life, found love where you could. But I truly believe we're capable of loving more than one per-*

son in our lifetime. And, if you have the chance to show Easton that love, do it. Don't regret a thing, Wyatt. Go to him. Make him see.

No regrets this time.

With love,

Becca

I feel like I can't take in a full breath. I'm afraid to look up, to see the pity in my friend's eyes, now that he knows the truth. That I'm the fool who's been in love with him this whole time, who stayed close for so long like some stray looking for scraps.

I just keep staring at that piece of paper, wondering how, after all these years, things could've blown up so spectacularly. I can't move back here. I'll have to find my own place. Easton probably won't want me around anymore, either.

"She was right," Easton says, voice barely above a whisper, and it's so far from what I expect to hear that I finally look up.

When I do, it's not pity on my friend's face. It's something softer.

"About which part?" I ask, unwilling to let myself believe he's talking about what Becca said about *him*. I can't believe it. It's been too long, and there have been too many chances for Easton to see me as something more, and he never has.

Easton comes over to me, dropping down and gripping my knee. It reminds me so much of that day nearly twelve years ago when I came back home and was comforting my newly widowed friend. Now, he's the one comforting me.

It gives me hope. If he can look past this, maybe we'll be all right, after all.

"I'm gonna do somethin', all right? And if it's not what you want, if things have changed for you, I'll get it. But I'm still gonna try."

I don't have time to figure out what the heck he's talking about before Easton's familiarly callused grip is circling around the back of my neck and pulling me forward.

In one instant, life is as it always has been. And, in the next, my friend's lips are against mine, and everything—*every-thing*—has changed.

PART IV: FINDING FOREVER

CHAPTER 26

Easton

I don't know why I waited so long to do this.

It's the very first thought I have.

Wyatt is motionless at first, and I worry I messed up. For all I know, his feelings for me, assuming Becca was right—a pretty safe assumption, seeing as Becca was always right—have already dried up. He might not want me still, after all this time.

But before I can make the decision of whether or not to back off, he makes this sound, like a dying animal that's finally found enough water to wet its thirst. Except *beautiful*. Just this quiet, tiny little hoarse whimper, so small, so filled with unexpected relief and yearning. Just one little sound, and yet it's monumental. It's a lifetime of *want*.

And then Wyatt moves.

His hands come around my head, and if I had enough hair, I'm sure he would be tugging it. He holds onto me tight, as if refusing to let me go an inch.

His lips are soft, yet surrounded by stubble, and the sensation is so different than what I've known. But a good different. Like finding out chocolate cake tastes even better with cherries in it.

My entire body lights up, something I haven't felt in so very long. Having someone I *want* in my arms, their lips against mine, it's only the second time it's happened. And it's been so long since the first. I want more, I want all of it.

I press as close as I can to Wyatt, which isn't nearly close enough, seeing as I'm still kneeling on the ground and there's a couch in my way. But I slot as close as I can manage, and I just keep tugging Wyatt until he gets the hint and inches his hips forward enough for his legs to bracket around me.

I go on instinct, kissing my friend as if it's the most natural thing in the world, and somehow, it is. We open to each other at the same time, and suddenly, I'm not the aggressor anymore. Wyatt is, taking over the kiss in a way that makes my toes curl against the inside of my boots.

I grunt when his teeth nip at my bottom lip hard, more in surprise than anything else, but it seems to be enough for Wyatt to back off. Suddenly, his hands are leaving my head, when all I want is for them to be back, there or elsewhere. Anywhere really, just *on* me.

He sits back, running his fingers through the long strands of his hair, pushing them away from his face. His eyes are wide, almost fearful, even as he refuses to drop my stare. His lips are slick and red, and it's giving me all sorts of ideas. If it weren't for the look in his eyes, I would've been very happy to entertain those. As it is, I can tell Wyatt is freaking out, and my stomach sinks.

"What're we doin'?" Wyatt asks, rubbing his hand over top of those lips and sounding a little dazed.

"We were kissin'," I reply, keeping my hands on his thighs, not quite ready to break our physical connection.

Wyatt looks down at me, his eyes casing my face, and I wonder what he sees there.

"Where'd this come from?" he asks, looking around the room like it might offer the answers. "What're we *doin*?"

"Wyatt," I say, getting my friend's attention as I squeeze his legs. "It recently came to my attention that I might not be as straight as I assumed I was."

"How recent?" he asks, eyes latched onto my face once more.

I shrug. "'Bout two years now." His eyes widen again, but I keep on, knowing I need to lay my cards on the table. "Remember that day in the barn, with Harrison?"

"Where you saw us—"

"Yeah," I say, not really needing him to rehash the details. "Couldn't stop starin' at you, and I was real jealous." Understatement.

"I..." Wyatt says, shaking his head, a look of wonderment on his face.

"Listen," I say. "What Becca said in that letter? I don't know if any of that was true for you, or still might be. But I know what I want, and I'm hopin' I'm not too late. Am I too late?"

"*Fuck*," he mutters, shoulders softening as his blunt nails scrape the hair on the sides of my head once more. I lean into his touch, wanting more of it. "Not too late," he says, pulling me forward. "Never too late." His mouth brushes against mine before he kisses me in earnest.

As quickly as it starts, it's over again. I try to chase after him, but Wyatt pulls back.

"Wait," he says. "Shouldn't we, I dunno, talk about this some more first?"

"Wyatt," I say, a big smile on my face. It feels like my friend and I have switched places. Him overthinking things, me being the impulsive one, even though this feels like a long time coming in a way. "I've wanted you for the past two years. And it sounds like you've wanted me a lot longer than that. So, what're we waitin' for?"

Those seem to be the magic words.

Wyatt follows me down onto the floor, like he suddenly can't stand there being any space between us. In my surprise, I end up on my ass. Our combined weight knocks the wooden coffee table out of the way, and I have a feeling that'll smart later, but right now, I don't even care. Because Wyatt is pushing me the rest of the way onto my back and blanketing me with his body, his hips straddling my own.

His lips come down on mine hard, almost like a challenge. Everything about his movements, the way he grabs at me with bruising force, the way he grinds his crotch over top of mine—and *Christ*, I can feel his erection against my own—and even the way he can't seem to settle in one place for any length of time, it's all laced with a sense of urgency. Like he's making up for lost time.

Like he feels like I might slip through his fingertips, and he isn't about to give me the chance.

I could tell him he has nothing to worry about, that I'm not going anywhere. But, instead, I just choose to show him. I grip him tighter, holding the hair at the back of his head and grabbing his ass, and I grind him down on me harder.

I have the very distinct impression I might not last long enough to get to anything else if we keep up at this rate and am about to say so, when the sound of the front door slamming shut breaks through my thoughts.

"Pop!" Will yells, stomping closer. "I saw your truck. You in here?"

Wyatt and I both freeze, but we don't have time to do a thing before Will is rounding the corner into the family room. He stops in an instant, almost tripping over his own feet in his haste to halt his movement. His eyes widen comically before his face breaks out into a massive grin.

I open my mouth. Wyatt does the same. We look at each other and back at Will.

I need to say *something*, but Will beats me to it.

"Yes! 'Bout time," he says, looking weirdly pleased about finding Wyatt and I in a compromising position. "Does this mean you're stayin'?" he asks Wyatt.

"Uh," is all Wyatt gets out before Will is waving his hand.

"Never mind. We'll talk later. I'm gonna head back to Gran and Gramps's for the night. I'll text you when I get there. All right, bye!"

And with a huge, cheeky smile on his face, he turns back the way he came from and leaves.

"Should we be concerned that our twelve-year-old son just gave us privacy to have sex?" Wyatt asks.

I snort because it's so ridiculous, the whole thing. Me and Wyatt after all this time. The fact that we've been together for so long, but not like this. The fact that we have a *son* together and yet had never so much as kissed before today. And yes, even our own son giving us his blessing, giving his *dads* his blessing, before running out of the house like his tail was on fire.

The snort turns into a full bout of laughter I can't seem to stop. Wyatt looks amused for all of five seconds before he joins in, dropping his head onto my chest as his body rumbles with laughter.

"At least he approves," I finally say when the shaking has stopped.

Wyatt lifts his head, and even though it's not the first time I've had this thought, I'm struck again by how beautiful he is. I don't know why it took me so long to figure it all out, but I'm damn well not about to waste any more time over it. I brush away some of Wyatt's hair, tucking it back behind his ear, and he closes his eyes, his gentle breath ruffling over my face as he leans into the touch.

When he opens them again, I realize I've never been quite this close before. Close enough to see the smattering of light freckles across the bridge of his nose. Close enough I can see all the little flecks and striations that make Wyatt's brown eyes uniquely his. Framed by those dark, overly thick lashes that could maybe be called feminine, except there's nothing feminine about Wyatt.

"We really doin' this?" he asks, his lips an inch away from mine.

"I sure hope so," I tell him sincerely. "Wyatt. Do you wanna come to my bed?"

A slow, knowing smirk spreads over Wyatt's face, making my stomach swoop. I've never seen Wyatt look at *me* like that before, and I find I really like it.

"Y'know," he says, "I've always wanted to hear you say those words."

Wyatt pops up, lifting his weight off my body in an instant and holding out his hand. He tugs me to my feet and immediately starts dragging me behind him, not stopping until we're in my bedroom. Then he turns us both around and shoves me onto the mattress none too gently, reaching down to pull off my boots.

"Ease up," he says after my boots hit the floor, giving me a little shove to move up the bed.

I drag myself towards the headboard until my legs are no longer dangling, and Wyatt springs up over my body, loosening my belt buckle with quick, efficient movements.

"Damn, you really don't waste any time, do you?" I say, chuckling, even as my insides go wild.

"Hey, now. You gave me the green light, so I'm goin' full speed ahead."

"Sounds like a mighty fine plan to me," I tell him, coming up on my elbows so I can better see.

Wyatt deftly pops the button on my jeans and lowers the fly. He taps my hip, so I lift up. In one rough movement, he tugs my pants and underwear down to my thighs, setting my erection free to slap against my stomach. Wyatt stops there, almost like he's frozen, still hanging on to the waistband of my clothes.

For however brief the moment lasts, I worry about why he stopped. Should I have done some maintenance down below? Is that the normal thing to do? Is that what Wyatt likes? Am I not what he expected?

But then, all at once, he sets into motion. With a muttered "*Christ*," he's burying his face against my crotch in a move so surprising, I can't help but gasp.

Wyatt looks up as he all but nuzzles against me, inhaling deeply. "Do you know how many times I've thought about this?"

I shake my head. I don't think I could even come up with a single word if I tried.

Wyatt turns his head, eyelashes fluttering closed as he places gentle kisses up the length of my erection. *Fuck.*

"So many times. I'm really gonna enjoy this," he says, opening his eyes and sucking my crown into his wet, warm mouth.

"*Fuck*," I curse out loud this time, hips coming up off the mattress. I can't even help it; it feels so good.

Wyatt doesn't miss a beat. He grabs me tight, holding me down with the weight of his body, as his tongue and lips and teeth take me apart in a barrage of sensations. He sucks me down, tongues my slit, bites my glans in a way that shouldn't feel good—at least, I wouldn't have thought so—but really, really does.

I can't keep up. I just stop thinking and let myself feel. I'm certain I'm about to come and am going to warn Wyatt, when he pulls off. I look down at him, and he looks back at me, a wild glint in his eye.

"Shit, I know we should probably take things slow," he says. "Maybe work up to it. I mean, there're handjobs and blowjobs and frotting and rimming and a whole bunch of other things we could do first, but I just really, *really* need you to fuck me."

My mind stutters, reels, and then reboots. There's a lot there to unpack, things I'll need to ask Wyatt about another time. But the last thing I understood crystal clear, and I'd be lying if I said I don't want that, too.

"All right," I say, squeezing my eyes shut, as well as the base of my dick. "But you gotta stop lookin' at me like that or we won't make it."

Wyatt's laughter is music to my ears.

CHAPTER 27

Wyatt

Easton looks like my wet dream come to life. In fact, I'm positive I've dreamt of him like this many times before: spread out naked on the bed, his broad body on display, dick glistening and hard and so fucking perfect I could weep.

And he's looking at me like I'm his dessert. I have no problem with that. He can eat me up anytime.

Right now, though, I need him inside of me.

"Please tell me you've got lube around here," I say, barely able to remove my eyes from Easton long enough to give the room a cursory glance. Not that it'd just be sitting out in plain sight.

"In the drawer," he says, reaching over and pulling it out of the nightstand.

"Thank Christ," I exhale, grabbing the bottle and flicking it open. I pour some into my hand and pause. "Condom?"

He shakes his head. "Don't have any. Do we need one?"

I squeeze my eyes shut. I didn't bring any with me from Harrison's, either. I've never gone without, but the idea of going bare with Easton is definitely appealing. So appealing it's hard to think straight. Easton hasn't had sex in a really long time, and he's always good about his doctor's visits. If he had anything to worry about, he would tell me.

"I had a physical a few months ago and was negative. Harrison and I always used 'em," I say, not wanting to dwell too long on that train of thought. "But I understand if you're not comfortable with that."

Easton just shakes his head. "I trust you, Wyatt. 'Course I do."

I exhale in relief. If we had needed to change direction tonight, of course I wouldn't have complained. But I'm so glad that's not the case. Easton's cock is right in front of me, waiting, and I want it something fierce.

"All right then," I say, pumping him a few times with my slick hand. Easton hisses, the sound setting my insides on fire. I've wanted this man for so long, and the fact that I finally get to bring him pleasure, that he *wants* this, wants me, is intoxicating. It's the biggest high I could imagine. "This one's gonna be fast. We can go slow next time if you want, but there's no way I can hold back tonight, all right?"

Easton swallows harshly and nods, watching with wide eyes as I prep myself quickly. And by quickly, I do mean it. Five seconds tops, just long enough to spread the lube with two fingers, and I'm scooting to the top of the bed and grabbing the headboard, ass out.

"You're up," I tell him.

Easton doesn't move. He just stares at me with those wide eyes. And shit. Maybe I'm freaking the guy out a little. This *is* pretty fast.

I let go of the headboard and slide back down the bed, straddling Easton's naked body. He has a serious expression on his face, jaw set, so I cup my hands there and run my thumbs along his cheeks gently, trying to soothe out the tension. "Is this too much?" I ask.

He shakes his head in a somewhat aborted way, like he's forgotten how basic motor functions work. Sensing he just needs a minute, I lean down and kiss him gently, coaxingly, until, finally, he relaxes against me.

"No," he says against my lips. "It's not too much. I'm just a tad overwhelmed. This is you."

Christ, this man.

He leans up to kiss me, harder this time, more urgent, like he's crossed whatever hurdle was holding him up. His hips start moving, too, chasing friction, and the smooth glide of his erection against my own has me leaking in no time.

Easton surprises me then by flipping our positions, rolling over top of me and propping himself up to look between our bodies as he grinds us together. I can't help but wonder if it's strange for him, seeing and feeling my erection next to his own. The very real evidence that I'm a male. Judging by the look in his eyes, he's enjoying it immensely.

Easton surprises me again when he sits back and uses those strong arms of his to lift my legs, causing my hips to tilt up.

"Can we do it like this?" he asks, running his eyes over my body and the way I'm now offered up, opened to him.

Oh Lord. This man is going to kill me.

I nod furiously, and Easton scoots himself closer.

"And I just..." He cuts off, but it's obvious to tell what he's thinking as he stares down at my asshole.

"Yes, you just stick it in there," I say, unable to stop the amusement that laces my tone.

Easton gives me an exasperated look, which just makes me smile wider.

"And you'll show me how to do that thing next time? Where you got ready with your fingers?"

Oh God.

"Yes. Yep," I say, nodding several times.

"All right."

Easton looks like he's giving this a monumental amount of thought, and I'm about to tease him about it again when he leans forward, holding the base of his dick as he notches himself against my entrance. All thoughts of humor die as I watch the man I love, who looks too goddamn sexy for his own good, press into me.

I gasp—I can't not. Not because it hurts, but because *holy shit*, this is happening.

Easton works himself forward in increments, being careful with me, and I'm too caught up simply staring at him to even care that this isn't turning out to be the fast and furious affair I had intended on earlier.

No, this is altogether different. And I find I don't mind that one bit.

Once Easton is fully seated, his hips pressed against my ass, he looks up at me in wonder. His lips are parted, his eyes wide, and with a blush staining his cheeks, he looks absolutely stunning. He blinks a couple times before saying, simply, "Wow."

Wow, indeed.

"All right?" he checks.

I nod quickly. "You can move now."

"Right."

He goes slow at first, pulling out and pressing back in in small, measured movements. Each drag is like torture, but not one I have any inclination of stopping. When he finally gives a full thrust, pulling nearly all the way out and then snapping his hips forward again, we groan in tandem. He stops and blows out a breath, eyeing me in wonder, and then he lets go, letting instinct guide his movements.

The smooth drag of his cock feels almost unbearably good as he moves in earnest, and I hold on tight, feeling like I might float away without a tether. My breath puffs out of me each time he slams home, and all coherent thought flees my brain. All I know is Easton. His feel, all hard muscle and the gentle bristling of his body hair. The way he still smells like hay and the sweat starting to glisten on his brow. The look in his sharp blue gaze as he holds me captive.

I've never felt anything quite so intense, and with anyone else, it would've scared me. But not with Easton. Never with Easton.

He drops down over my body, blanketing me with his weight as his lips claim mine, and it's all I can do not to cry. I've never been overly emotional during sex, but this isn't just sex.

This is...something I don't have words for.

Easton pulls back a hair, if that. Just enough to say, "I want you to come."

"I'm gonna," I tell him hoarsely, and it's the truth. I've been steadily climbing since the moment Easton got inside of me, and it won't take much to put me over the edge at this point. Probably a few choice words and the friction of Easton's stomach against my cock would do it.

Easton makes it even easier, however, sliding his hand between our bodies to roll his palm over the head of my penis.

I gasp out, back arching involuntarily.

"What else?" he asks.

I'm going to come in seconds one way or another, but I tell him, "Lift my hips higher."

He does, leaning back and using his free hand to shift me, and it's all over. On his next thrust, Easton pegs my prostate head on, and I hurtle into orgasm, coming into his fist so hard I lose my breath for a second. He keeps fucking me at the same angle, and each thrust sends an extra burst of sensation coursing through me, prolonging the pleasure until Easton himself is coming with a hoarse cry. His body bows over me, head dropping to the side of mine, as he stutters out a breath with the last of his release.

He doesn't move right away, just hovers, his hand still gently clasped around my softening dick and his cock still inside me. His breaths are rough against the side of my ear, and I smooth my hands over his back, not saying a word. Just feeling this world-shifting moment.

After a long while, Easton lifts his head enough to look me in the eye.

"Can we do that again later?" he asks. It's so unexpected I start laughing.

Easton groans as my muscles clench around him, and I attach like a monkey, my arms and legs wrapping around his body and holding tight. All of those heavy emotions from earlier settle into something that feels a lot like relief as Easton smiles, his gaze catching on my mouth.

"Most definitely," I tell him.

"Good." He leans down to brush his lips over mine. "Wow," he says again, dropping more of his weight onto me. I definitely don't mind. Easton can crush me anytime he likes. It's worth it to enjoy the feel of all that man and muscle pressed against me.

When he finally eases back, slipping from my body at last, I can feel his fluids leaking out down my crease. Easton looks down, presumably noticing the same thing.

"Why is that so hot?" he asks.

Much to my surprise, he presses two of his fingers against my slick rim, circling before he pushes them inside my body. I gasp, my dick twitching happily.

"Keep up with that and round two isn't gonna be later. It's gonna be now," I tell him, moaning as he twists his fingers inside of me, exploring.

"I'm good with that," he replies, dropping down onto his stomach to get a better view.

I have a feeling I'm really going to enjoy reaping the benefits of Easton's foray into gay sex. The man is clearly curious, and I'm not going to complain about that.

"What is frotting?" he asks, fingers still moving inside of me.

I bust out laughing, which turns into another moan as Easton crooks his fingers, unintentionally rubbing my prostate.

Oh yeah, I'm definitely going to enjoy this.

CHAPTER 28

Easton

"Dad?" Will shouts, running around the corner of the barn. He comes skidding to a halt when he sees me. "Is Pop back? Is he stayin'?"

I try to hide the blush on my face, but I'm pretty sure it's no use. I've been smiling and blushing the whole day through, thinking about Wyatt and what we did last night. Through most of the night, in fact. Again and again.

Christ.

I cough, clearing the images from my mind.

"I think so," I tell Will.

He grins. "So, you're like...*together* now? For real?"

"Think so," I say again.

Wyatt and I probably should've talked a little more about what we were going to tell Will. But to be honest, I think it slipped both of our minds. What with all the nakedness and various activities.

Will stomps his foot, giving me a faux-stern look. "Dad, c'mon! Now is not the time for vagueness."

"I don't have a whole lot to tell you yet. We haven't figured it all out."

He throws his hands up in the air. "You two, I swear. Leave it to me. Otherwise we'll be waitin' 'til I'm thirty."

He storms out of the barn in a flurry of dust, and I'm left wondering what just happened and what I have to look forward to. Checking my watch, I see it's near end of day, so I make my way over to Monty's field to bring him in for the night.

I click as I approach, and Monty's head swivels. He trots over to me from across his field, stepping right through the gate I opened up for him, and he doesn't stop moving until he finds me, laying his head over my shoulder as soon as he does.

"Hey, Monty boy."

I lean into his horse hug, and he accepts the scratches I give along his neck and shoulders. When I turn and give Monty's bridle a gentle tug, he follows, sticking right at my heel as I walk him in, chatting all the while.

"Got some news for you. Wyatt and I got together last night."

Monty huffs, his breath fanning across my ear. I chuckle, nodding, even though he can't see it.

"I know, 'bout time, huh. I'm gonna tell you this 'cause I know you won't tell a soul." I look around, making sure the coast is clear before I continue in a whisper. "It was real fuckin' good. I know it'd been a long time for me, but damn. There are so many things I wanna try with that man."

Monty huffs again as we enter the barn, losing the slight breeze.

"I know, probably more info than you needed. It's just real excitin', is all."

I lead Monty into his stall and give him a few more pets as he drinks some water.

"You're a good listener, Monty. I appreciate it."

"Talkin' to the horses again?" Wyatt asks.

I jump about a foot in the air, clutching my chest. "Startled me," I tell him unnecessarily.

"I can see that," he replies, and I can tell from his face he's trying his best not to laugh.

"Did you hear all that?" I ask, shutting Monty's stall and meeting Wyatt at the entrance to the barn.

"Not much, unfortunately. Just a bit about somethin' bein' excitin', and then you complimentin' the horse on his listenin' abilities."

I grunt. That's not so bad.

When I step up to Wyatt, my heart is already thumping hard. Maybe partly because of the adrenaline jump, but honestly, I think it's mostly this man. He reaches for me but hesitates.

"Can I kiss you?" he asks.

I scrunch my face in confusion. "You need to ask? 'Course you can kiss me."

He grins, tugging me close, our mouths colliding. His stubble abrades my face, and I don't know why I like that so much, but I sure do. His lips are soft and warm, and his tongue slides against mine in a way that makes me want to get him into bed pronto.

Except Will is home, and I suppose we'll have to be a little carcful about that so we don't unintentionally scar the kid.

The kiss lingers for a good long moment until Wyatt finally pulls back, knocking my hat back down into place from where it'd ridden up to accommodate his face being all up in mine.

"I wasn't sure of the rules," he says as we walk side by side toward the house.

"The rules?" I ask.

"Well, yeah. I was hopin' last night wasn't a one-off. I didn't think it was, but we didn't really clarify."

"Wyatt," I say, stopping and waiting for him to face me.

He does, head tilted a little in curiosity. "Yeah?"

"Definitely not a one-off," I say, making sure he hears each word.

He grins, nodding once. "Sounds good to me."

We finish our short trek to the house, but we don't make it more than a foot inside the door before Will comes around the corner with his hands on his hips.

"All right, Pop. What exactly are your intentions with Dad?"

Wyatt's eyes widen comically. "Uh, well, I think that's somethin' your dad and I should discuss..."

"Nope," Will says. "Y'all are too slow. Are you stayin' here again?"

Wyatt looks at me, and when I nod, he grins. "Guess I am."

"Good," Will nods. "Are y'all together now? Like a couple?"

Wyatt looks over at me again, and when I nod and shrug, a soft smile fills his face. "Yeah, kiddo, I guess we are."

"All right, then. Someone make supper, 'cause I'm real hungry."

With that, Will whirls out of the room like the little hurricane he is. Wyatt scrubs his hands over his face, looking amused and overwhelmed all at once. I know how he feels.

"Leave it to the kid," he says.

"Uh-huh. C'mon, help me make that chicken and rice thing with the paprika that tastes so good."

Wyatt grins, looping his arm through mine as he leads me into the kitchen. "The trick is with the herb butter," he says, launching into a detailed description of rubbing chicken that keeps my smile firmly planted on my face.

★

"Can I watch a movie before bed?" Will asks as we're cleaning up our plates. "I'm too excited to sleep yet."

Christ, that just melts my heart.

"Suppose so," I tell him. "But bed right after."

He nods vigorously.

As soon as the dishes are washed, Will rushes into the family room, vaulting over the back of the sofa and plopping down on the other side where I can't see him.

"So much energy," Wyatt chuckles.

"Always," I agree.

We follow our son, Wyatt and I sitting together on the shorter two-seater without discussing it. I guess we both just figured we'd want to be close.

"This is so cool," Will says with a smile.

"Y'know," Wyatt says around a chuckle, "it's not even that much different than before."

Except for the fucking, I think.

"Yeah, but now instead of just lookin' at one another, you're sittin' together and smilin'."

Gosh, was it really that obvious? Were my eyes always on Wyatt like that? Even before I started lusting after him? Was he pining for me, too?

Wyatt and I catch each other's gaze, a smile on both of our faces. He leans over and gives me a chaste kiss.

"And kissin'," Will adds, not at all sounding grossed out when he adds, "ew."

Wyatt's arm comes around me, and Will picks a movie. We snuggle close, and I realize how much I love this, too. This added affection with Wyatt. We've always had a stronger bond than most, but now it's something a little more. And I'm excited to see where that takes us.

I don't even realize I've fallen asleep until Wyatt is gently shaking me awake.

"C'mon now, bed."

I let him lead me to my room, *our* room soon, hopefully. My feet feel like lead, and my eyelids are half closed, but I trust Wyatt to get me there. Once inside, he pushes me gently into bed, and as soon as he joins me, I roll into him.

"Sorry I fell asleep before we could, you know," I mumble against his skin, eyes closed.

Wyatt just chuckles, his hand brushing gently across my forehead. "Don't you worry. There'll be plenty of time for that. Wore you out good last night, I can tell."

"Sleepy," I slur.

"Uh-huh," he says, voice full of laughter.

"Can I hold you again?" I ask. I loved being snuggled up to him last night, feeling his body in my arms.

"Any time you want," he replies softly.

With the last of my waning strength, I sling my arm over his body, holding on tight.

Chapter 29

Wyatt

"Wy, you awake?"

I open my eyes, but it's too dark to see anything.

"I am now. Somethin' wrong?"

I can feel Easton shift against me, the hair on his legs brushing mine. His hand runs along my torso, leaving a trail of warmth behind. And *oh*, there's a nice hard something poking my behind.

"No," he says.

"Is this a booty wakeup?" I ask, not at all displeased with that. In fact, I'm pretty sure I have a massive grin on my face because this is really happening. The day before wasn't a fever dream. It wasn't some midlife-crisis hallucination. It's real. At least in the dark, Easton can't see my ridiculous face.

"I just want..." he says, but he doesn't finish his sentence.

I roll over, aligning myself with Easton's front and running my fingers over his nicely toned arm. Mmm, muscles.

"It's all right, darlin'. I want you *all* the time. You won't find any complaints here."

Easton groans in this needy, exuberant way as he rolls on top of me. My eyes have adjusted enough that I can make out the outline of his body, but his features are still bathed in darkness. That's okay, though. I have them memorized by now.

Easton kisses me fiercely, hands running all over my body, not stopping on any one place for long, just exploring everywhere. His hard length occasionally bumps against my own erection, and I want more, but I also want to let Easton set the pace here.

"Can you show me how to touch you?" he asks, so earnestly, like all he wants to do is make me feel good. And *fuck*, that, in and of itself, makes me feel real good.

"Hold out your palm," I tell him, grabbing the lube we left on top of the nightstand. I squeeze some into his hand and set it aside.

Easton wraps his hand around me instantly, rubbing up and down and spreading the moisture. His thumb traces over my crown, and I bite my hand to avoid making much noise.

"That's good," I tell him. "A little firmer, and I like my glans played with."

Easton follows my direction, pumping harder, twisting his palm over the head between each stroke.

"Is that why you kinda bit me?" he asks. "'Cause you like more stimulation there?"

My mind flashes back to last night, and I grin. "Yeah. Did you like that?"

"Uh-huh. Surprised me."

I chuckle. "I like surprisin' you."

"I like it, too," he says, doubling down in his efforts.

"Shit, I'm not gonna last much longer," I tell him, my toes curling, muscles tensing.

Easton bends down, snagging one of my nipples with his teeth and tugging hard enough for a gasp to fly out of my mouth, at the same time tipping me over the edge.

"*Fuck, fuck*," I mutter, my release spilling onto my stomach and chest.

I think Easton already has my number.

"C'mere," I say, reaching for him in the dark.

"No need," he says. "Already came."

I still. "You were jackin' yourself, too? Damn, stud, shoulda turned the light on. I could've gotten a free show."

Easton chuckles, easing down next to me. I lift a corner of the sheet to wipe myself off, figuring that's good enough. With Easton at my side, I curl myself back towards him, and he immediately opens his arms to welcome me in. Mm, I like that.

But I also can't help but wonder how this isn't freaking Easton out.

"You're all right with all this? Bein' with a guy, I mean?" I ask.

"Yep," he says.

"Very enlightenin', thanks so much for that clarification," I joke, running my fingers over the length of his arm.

I can feel more than see Easton's shrug.

"You don't wanna take things slow?" I check.

"Wyatt, there's no one I know better than you. The way I look at it, we've done just about everythin' together except for this. If you wanna go on dates, I'll take you. I'd like that a whole lot, too. But this? No, I don't need to go slow with this."

"Well, all right then," I say, that massive smile back on my face.

"All right then," Easton agrees, and it's the last either of us says before falling into sleep.

"C'mon, you stubborn son of a bitch."

"Keep talkin' to it like that, and it's never gonna turn over for you," Hawthorne says, his lazy drawl making the words sound dirtier than I think he intended them to.

"Well, if he'd just submit already, we wouldn't be havin' this fight," I reply, grumbling under my breath.

"It's a four-wheeler, Wyatt. It's not tryin' to spite you."

I huff, dropping my hand away from the ignition. "This is why I prefer the horses."

"Need a ride back?" Hawthorne asks, canting his head behind him.

"Tryin' to make me your bitch?" I ask jokingly, hopping on up behind Hawthorne. His vehicle isn't meant for two, so it's a tight fit.

He just chuckles, shaking his head. I swear I hear him mumble "*Wrong brother*" under his breath.

We leave my troublesome four-wheeler behind for now, and Hawthorne drives us back to the main ranch building, where there's a break room for employees to eat lunch. I don't always use it. Sometimes it's easier to just bring my paper bag and stay out in the field.

Before we get inside, Hawthorne touches my arm lightly. "Hey, can I talk to you for a minute?"

"'Course," I tell him, stepping off to the side of the building with him.

"My guess is Easton already told you this long ago, but I've been makin' my rounds and wanted you to hear it from me, too."

I cock my head, unsure what he's talking about. I can't recall Easton giving me any news about his brother.

"Well, simple fact is I'm gay," Hawthorne says.

My head rocks back a little in surprise. "Oh," I say, a smile forming on my lips as I watch Hawthorne fidget with the brim of his hat. "Well, congratulations, man. Welcome to the club."

Hawthorne shakes his head at that, laughing and crossing his arms in a casual way.

"Do I have to pay membership dues?" he asks, deadpan.

I raise an eyebrow at that. "Pretty sure there are plenty of jokes I could make about jobs required, but I'll refrain. Thanks for tellin' me, Hawthy."

I had wondered a time or two, when I'd see Hawthorne's eyes linger a little too long on the back of some cowboy's jeans, but you never know. Nothing ever came of it, so I assumed my suspicions were wrong.

"That's not my name," he grumbles in response. "But 'course. You're basically family."

"Easton never told me," I add, so he knows his brother kept his secret.

"Hm," Hawthorne hums. "Figured he would've."

"Nope. I guess there are still some secrets between us," I say lightly. "C'mere," I add, pulling Hawthorne in for a hug.

He slaps my back, pulling away at the same time the word "*Faggots*" reaches our ears.

I turn around, and there's Shane fucking Merchant, one of the town's biggest homophobes, standing at the entrance to the building and giving us a sneer.

"Problem?" I ask, taking a step toward the man who's never made a secret of how much he hates me. Any time I see him around town, he drops a slur or snide comment before trudging off. I guess some folks just like being hateful. Most of the time, I ignore him, but I don't like the idea of him taking shots at Hawthorne, as well.

"Yeah, I got a problem, *pretty boy*. Now you're spreadin' your shit around, and it stinks."

Hawthorne sighs, stepping up next to me. "For fuck's sake, Shane, bein' gay isn't contagious. You should know. For how long you spend harassin' Wyatt here, you'd have caught it by now. Now grow some goddamn brain cells and shoo."

Hawthorne pushes past the man, holding the door open as my mouth drops open.

"Comin'?" he asks me.

I grin, the tension leaving my body as I follow Hawthorne inside and a tomato-faced Shane turns on his heel, stomping away. Once through the doors, I bump Hawthorne's elbow and wink.

"Hear him call me pretty, though?"

Hawthorne laughs as Clive pops his head out from the office wing of the building, which is down opposite corridors from the area Hawthorne and I were headed.

"You guys seen Shane? He was supposed to be here ten minutes ago to discuss distribution for that new market bein' built."

Hawthorne and I exchange a look.

"You mean the man droppin' homophobic bullshit right outside these doors? Nope, can't say I've seen him," Hawthorne says, nice and slow like a honey drip. "If I had, though, probably would've told him to get."

I hold in my laughter as Clive nods.

"Right. Guess I'll have to call and have a different representative sent over from now on, one who's a little more *reliable*," Clive answers, adding under his breath, "and not such an asshole."

"Sounds like a mighty fine plan," Hawthorne agrees.

"Glad we don't get folks like that 'round here," I say, heading off for lunch with a smile on my face. It's a good feeling, not being alone in this, knowing that there are allies here in Plum Valley. And that sometimes those other folks get their dues.

———————— ★ ————————

"Guess what I learned today," I call out, setting my boots on the mat to the side of the door.

Silence greets me.

"Easton? Will?"

When there's no response, I head through the house, but neither are anywhere to be found. I'm about to check the barn when I catch a glimpse of them through the window.

A smile lights my face, and I make my way out onto the deck.

"What're you doin' down there?" I shout.

Two heads swivel in my direction, twin grins in place on both father and son's faces.

"Plantin' plums," Will shouts up to me.

I stomp down the stairs and over to where a bunch of small, twig-looking trees are lined up on the ground, burlap encasing their roots.

"Been meanin' to do it," Easton says.

And I know why. Because Becca wanted an orchard here. Simple as that.

Without thinking much about it, I wrap my arms around Easton, squeezing him close before drawing his face toward me for a kiss. He smells a bit like the dirt they've been digging up, and I inhale it greedily, appreciating that no matter the scent, Easton smells like home.

Will whistles a tune as he turns around, making a show of giving us privacy, which makes Easton chuckle against my lips. When we pull apart, Will turns back around with a smile on his face.

"Can I help?" I ask.

Easton nods. "We still need to get this old one down. Figured we could all do the honors."

"Sounds great," I say.

Easton directs me and Will, and we methodically take down branches until the tree is just a tall stump. We dig around the tree to loosen the roots, and then Easton hooks chains to it, attaching them to his tractor. It doesn't take much, actually, to pull that tree out of the ground. Old as it is, it seemed half dead already. He tugs it away, and once we've cleared the area and flattened out the hole a bit, the three of us step back and look at the new trees that are waiting to be planted.

"Are we ready to usher in a new era of plums? To revitalize Plum Valley to its former glory?" I ask dramatically, placing a hand on each of their shoulders.

Easton looks over at me, and even though my tone was joking, I can see the emotion in his eyes. I can tell he's thinking about Becca and how he's finally fulfilling an unspoken promise.

"Can we get pizza after this?" Will asks, breaking the tender moment.

Easton and I share a glance. I laugh under my breath as Easton rolls his eyes, looking so much like his son that I take a mental snapshot of the moment.

"Pizza it is," he says to Will, who runs off to grab his shovel.

"Hey," I whisper to Easton. "You didn't tell me Hawthorne's news. Just heard it today."

Easton grunts. "Wasn't my place to say anythin'."

I rub my thumb over the back of his neck, reveling in the simple fact that I *can*. That I can touch Easton like this now, that he wants me to. Most of the time, it still feels like a dream. If it is one, I hope I never wake up.

"Any other secrets you're keepin' from me?" I ask Easton teasingly.

"Guess you'll just have to find that out for yourself," he replies, just about making me faint when he adds a wink. Yep, definitely dreaming.

"Oh, I certainly plan to," I say with a grin.

Challenge accepted.

CHAPTER 30

Easton

It feels like, these past few weeks, all Wyatt and I have done is frot like animals. Including actual frotting, as Wyatt told me it's called. I can't keep my hands off the man.

It's almost like I've come out of hibernation. When I was with Becca, we had lots of sex, too. Very enjoyable sex. I just didn't feel the need once she was gone. But now, with Wyatt, that drive is back big time, regardless of the fact that I'm a thirty-six-year-old man well past his teens or twenties.

There've been handjobs, blowjobs—and what a surprise it was to me to find out how much I enjoy being on the giving end—and said frotting. Plus, I've fucked Wyatt a handful of times. We haven't done the reverse yet, but I'm looking forward to that, too.

The other thing we haven't done is talk about what we're doing. Apart from agreeing it's a phenomenal plan, we haven't discussed what this truly means for us. I haven't had a chance to tell Wyatt my feelings, and he hasn't clarified one way or the other whether Becca was right about his feelings, either.

Maybe we're both avoiding it. Just trying to stay in this new and exciting bubble where potential problems remain on the outside.

I know we'll need to have a serious discussion soon, but it's hard to think rationally when Wyatt comes sauntering into my bedroom and drops his pants.

Or, like now, when he's dragging bags of feed into the barn. Shirtless.

It's early morning, but the sun is already baking the valley. We're meeting the family at my dad's later for a weekend barbeque, and, in fact, Will is already over there helping get everything set up. Wyatt and I will drive over later after we've finished the morning chores. And apparently, Wyatt's decided to torture me while we're at it.

Hence the shirtlessness.

"It's real hot today," he says in an obvious manner, dropping another bag down on the pile.

His torso is covered in sweat, as well as flecks of dust and straw, and, as I watch, he stretches his arms up above his head. I never knew I could find armpits sexy. And his obliques, hot damn.

He wipes his forehead and then turns back to look at me, waggling his eyebrows when he catches me staring.

"See somethin' you like?" he asks.

"Whole lotta somethin's," I tell him.

He beams, and I make a mental note to give him my words more often, to make sure he knows how he affects me.

"You gonna join me in the shower after this?" he asks, grabbing the last bag of feed from the back of his truck.

"I could help you out right now." I hold up the hose I was using to spray the buckets clean.

He eyes me slowly. "You wouldn't," he says, dropping the last bag on top of the pile.

"Wouldn't I?"

Wyatt narrows his eyes, apparently trying to decide whether or not I'm serious. Truth be told, Wyatt's the only one who's ever brought out the teasing side of me. He makes it easy to joke around and have fun. I don't have to overanalyze around him or second guess. I can just be.

I go back to spraying the buckets, which Wyatt must decide means he's safe. As soon as he turns his back, I aim the nozzle right at him, the water hitting him square in the back. His arms come out like he's bracing himself, but he doesn't even turn around. He just stands there in accepted defeat.

Once I stop the spray, lips pressed firmly together to hold back my laughter, Wyatt turns. Slowly. Dripping wet and looking raggedy as all get out. His hair is hanging in his face, but as he stands to his full height, he flips it up over his head in a move that sends water droplets shooting in an arc over the top of him.

My grin falls away as lust hits me straight in the gut.

Damn, that's sexy.

Wyatt comes towards me, stalking with purpose, eyes steely. I can tell he's intending to grab the hose for some revenge, seeing as his gaze flicks down to it, but as soon as he's within reach, I drop the hose and haul him against me, slamming my mouth against his.

He grunts in surprise but responds immediately, draping his soaking form around my body. He smells like sunshine and dirt and tastes like coffee and *mine*. He grabs my ass, something he seems to love doing, and I return the favor, rubbing myself against him.

It goes from zero to sixty in seconds, and when Wyatt pulls his face back, his honey-brown eyes are deepened with desire.

"C'mon, shower," he says, voice low and growly.

"Yessir." I swat his ass as he turns to walk away.

"Do that again in a minute," he huffs out around an aroused-sounding laugh. Wyatt does that a lot, I've noticed: that laugh when he's excited. It's quickly become one of my favorite sounds.

Wyatt tugs me after him toward the house, but we don't make it more than a foot inside the door before he spins and attacks.

"Fuck, I just wanna do this all the time," he says, dragging his lips along my jaw and down my throat. I know the feeling. "Let's just skip the barbeque, stay here, and fuck all day."

His hands slip under my t-shirt, and he moves his mouth away only long enough to drag the material over my head.

"Or," I say, breathing heavily as Wyatt goes to work on my jeans, "fuck now, go to the barbeque and fuel up, and then fuck again later."

Wyatt groans. "I like when you say *fuck*."

He whips away my belt and pushes my jeans and boxers down before coming back in to claim my mouth. I kick them off my feet as my hands find their way into Wyatt's hair. That was another surprise for me, finding out how much I love tugging the nearly shoulder-length strands. Case in point, I pull his head back enough to give me access to his neck and lick the skin there, tasting sweat and some remaining droplets of water.

Wyatt moans, the vibration of it tickling my lips.

"What d'you want?" I ask him, tugging his head back again so I can look into his eyes. They're half mast, lashes fluttering as he returns my stare.

"You know what I love about bein' with a man roughly my size?" he asks.

"Tell me."

"The *roughly* part." He grins a little ferally. "You don't have to be too careful. You can throw each other around, grapple a bit. Would you do that?" he asks, holding still in my grasp. "Would you toss me 'round a little?"

My dick twitches, apparently really liking that idea, and I swallow thickly. "Yeah?" I double check for some reason, maybe just to give me a moment to process what he's saying.

"Yeah," he says, managing half a nod in my grip.

"All right, cowboy."

In a quick move, I slip my arm under Wyatt's knee and pull up, bracing my other arm behind his neck to cushion his fall as I take him down to the floor. He lands on his back with a surprised gasp, and the momentum pulls me down over him, trapping my arm under his head.

Wyatt stares at me in barely refrained glee for all of two seconds before he twists his body, flipping his raised knee over me and reversing our positions. I end up on my back, and I reach up, grabbing his hair again, holding him in place, despite the fact that he's the one who has me pinned.

"You like this?" I ask, even though I can feel the evidence of Wyatt's erection through the denim of his jeans against my bare skin.

"Fuck, yes," he says, swinging his arms up to knock my hands away before grabbing my wrists and pinning them to the floor. He leans down and bites my chest hard, surely leaving a mark.

I buck up against him, both of us groaning as our dicks press together. I don't even care about the roughness of his pants against my skin, it feels that good. I use the distraction to flip us once more, and then I lean back so I can work on getting Wyatt's pants off. I tug them down, not stopping until I've thrown them free, and then I climb back up over his body, kissing him long and hard.

Wyatt's hand drops down to circle our erections, providing greater friction as we frot together on the entryway floor.

"Fuck me," Wyatt groans against my mouth, one hand reaching behind him to root around under the bench seat for the bottle of lube he'd hastily kicked under there a week ago when Will came home and almost found us together in the kitchen. He shoves it at my chest. "Here."

"*Shit*," I mutter, squeezing my eyes shut for a moment to rein myself in. Every time Wyatt asks me to fuck him, it's like a lightning bolt shoots straight down my dick.

Remembering Wyatt's request from earlier, I pull up enough to flip him onto his stomach. He grunts in surprise, looking over his shoulder as I bring my hand down hard on his ass cheek.

He gasps, his hips bucking off the ground as his mouth pops open. Then he drops his forehead onto the stone tile, groaning as I plump the pink skin.

"Oh, fuck. *Easton*," he pleads.

I slap the other side, soaking up the resounding moan that comes out of Wyatt's mouth. *Christ.* I flip open the lube and wet my fingers, and Wyatt cants up his hips without me having to ask. I stretch him quickly, the way he taught me, as he begs me to hurry. One finger, then two. A few passes along his prostate. Three.

Forgoing a condom, since we decided not to use them, I add some lube to my dick and line up, tugging Wyatt's hips up higher. He rises up on his hands and knees, one hand reaching out to grab the bench seat as I push inside his waiting entrance.

We moan in tandem, and I take a moment to enjoy the tight heat of his body, fitting me like a glove. My eyes roam the line of Wyatt's back, all the muscles and dirt there and the way his ribcage expands with each heavy breath.

"Easton," Wyatt complains.

"Hold your horses."

"I'm not one of your horses, babe. Stop pettin' me and—*oh fuck*," he groans as I pull back and slide home again.

I give it to him rough like he wants, my knees scrambling to find purchase against the smooth floor. The sound of my hips slapping his ass creates a dirty soundtrack that fills the room, and it has my entire body coiling tight.

"*Yes*, Easton," Wyatt moans.

I don't think I'll ever get used to this, being inside Wyatt, being connected in this way, hearing my name fall from his lips like a prayer. He's slick with lube, hot and tight, and moving against me urgently, rolling his hips in time with my thrusts in a way that has me mesmerized.

I don't want this moment to ever end. I want to memorize it. I want a thousand more just like it.

And, I realize, I need to tell Wyatt that. When we're not in the middle of fucking, we need to talk. I don't plan on ever giving this up, ever giving *Wyatt* up, and he needs to know that. I hope he's on the same page.

Neither of us lasts long. Wyatt strokes himself in time with my thrusts, his other hand on the bench keeping us in place. And I just hang onto him, one hand wrapped in his hair, the other leaving small indentations in the meat of his hip. Wyatt comes first, seizing around me as he spills over his fist. I follow him with a muttered curse, my entire body shaking for a long, blissful moment before I reluctantly pull out and drop my weight down onto the ground. Wyatt slides down onto his belly next to me, breathing hard.

We're both a mess, dirty and sweaty and covered in cum. And exhausted, too. I'd lie here all day if I could, on this hard tile floor next to Wyatt, two feet in front of the front door, basking in the afterglow.

But as Wyatt's phone rings, I realize we can't do that. We're probably running late for the barbeque as is, and now we have to clean up ourselves *and* the entryway floor.

Wyatt seems to come to the same conclusion as me, looking around and breaking into laughter. I grin, chuckling as he rolls onto his back.

"Probably should've waited 'til the shower," he comments, scrubbing his hand over his face.

Nah. That was perfect.

CHAPTER 31

Wyatt

"Geez," Will says, opening the front door before we're even up the porch stairs. "What took you guys so long?"

Easton and I exchange a knowing look but don't reply as we follow our son into Miller's house. It's all I can do to keep my feelings of jubilation hidden behind a secret smile. I'm still a little sore from our romp in the entryway, but it's the type of pain that's absolutely worth it.

In fact, I'd do it again in a heartbeat. Again and again.

Easton's family, I'm surprised to see, is congregated inside for once, instead of out back. Even the dining table is set up, food spread out along the top.

"We're not eatin' outside?" Easton asks no one in particular.

Autumn looks up and smiles. "Storm's comin' in."

"Good thing we left the horses inside," I note. Easton nods.

Autumn comes over and gives him a peck on the cheek, doing the same to me before she starts laying silverware. "Y'all could help with the barbeque. Miller should be finishin' up about now."

Easton nods and makes his way out the back door, but I stay inside, finding the other gals in the kitchen.

"Need any help?" I ask, accepting a hug from Aunt Perla and another kiss on my cheek from Christabell, whose eyes seem to linger on the beard burn that I'm guessing is still visible on the side of my neck.

"Here," Aunt Perla says, handing me a stack of linen napkins.

I pass Clive, who gives me a nod of greeting, on my way back to the table. And then I spend a few minutes folding the napkins into little lotuses, a trick I learned from Sadie. Thinking about my friend reminds me that I'm overdue to call her. Last I heard, she was happy and working at a yoga studio in Chicago.

The sound of the sliding door draws my attention, and the smell of barbeque quickly follows.

"Dang, that smells good," I say, sounding a little bit like Easton.

"Bet you have an appetite," the man himself says as he drops a plate of ribs off at the table, a little smirk on his lips.

Hawthorne furrows his brows, giving his brother an elongated stare before his eyes pan over to me. I can see his gears turning, but he doesn't say anything, which I'm glad for. I want Easton to be able to come out in his own time, not under pressure from me or by default due to his family's prying.

Not that Hawthorne is the type to pry. I get the feeling he's still keeping secrets of his own.

"Rain is startin'," Miller notes as he comes into the room, his shoulders dusted with droplets of water.

"That's good," Autumn says dutifully, taking a seat at the long dining table. "We can use it."

"Can always use more rain," Miller agrees, sitting down. I hold in my chuckle, though it's hard. I can't count the number of times I've heard folks around here praise the rain. I guess that's just par for the course when it comes to farmers and ranchers.

I slide into my seat at the table now that everything is ready, and it isn't long before the whole family is gathered. It feels a little strange being in here, instead of outside at the picnic table, but the smells and the faces are the same, and I suppose that means more than where we're sitting.

Aunt Perla starts off a short prayer, and, like usual, we bow our heads for a moment of silence. It's not something I ever do on my own, but I don't mind following the custom when I'm with Easton's family. We were both raised in the church—everybody around here, new generation withstanding, was—but neither of us are particularly religious anymore, and Will only goes to Mass on occasion with his grandparents.

My parents were always a little more doom and gloom, sticking to the letter of God, as they'd put it. Which meant they didn't—and still don't, I'm sure—approve of folks like me. I've made my peace with that and don't particularly find myself missing them anymore, only the memory of *what if*. What if I weren't gay? Would they have supported me more? Loved me better?

It's of no use contemplating now. I wouldn't change myself, and the past is in the past.

Easton's family, on the other hand, was always a little warmer when it came to practicing their religion. I never got the same vibes I'd get from my own family, apart from Miller's general dislike. But other than that, I've always been welcomed here. And, when they speak of God, it's love and patience and goodwill they preach.

By mutual agreement, our moment of silence ends, and conversation starts up as we pass dishes and plate up our food.

"How's business goin'?" Autumn asks Easton.

"Just fine," Easton replies, never one for tooting his own horn.

"Real great," I add. "He's even trainin' a thoroughbred from up in Kentucky."

"That right?" Hawthorne asks in interest, looking proud of his older brother.

Easton simply grunts.

"He's fast, that one. Agile, too. They'll probably wanna use him for barrel racing."

Easton looks at me curiously. "How d'you know all that?"

I shrug. "I've seen you workin' him, and you've talked about these things enough in the past. It isn't hard to take a guess."

I *have* seen Easton on that horse, and it's a sight. The two of them flying, the horse's legs moving so fast they're a blur, and Easton up top, so fluid and strong and at ease, looking like he was made for it. Damn near pop a boner every time I see it.

Easton reaches over like he's about to squeeze my arm, but at the last second, he pulls his hand back. I'm not sure why, seeing as he touches me all the time, and would've done something like that before we started *this*. This new thing together. But, for whatever reason, he stopped himself, and now he's looking guiltily into his plate.

Maybe he's worried about how it'll come across, that his family will figure it out. He's probably not ready for that.

"Well, that's awesome, brother," Hawthorne says, spearing a green bean.

"It's impressive for sure," Christabell puts in. "You've really made a name for yourself."

Easton looks mighty embarrassed, but I smile. Easton is self-taught when it comes to all things horses. And maybe folks in some spots wouldn't like that. But, around here, word of mouth is just as good, maybe better, than what some fancy piece of paper has to say. And Easton *is* good at what he does.

It makes me proud every day.

Conversation moves on to Aunt Perla's knitting circle, and I bump my knee into Easton's.

"All right?" I ask him quietly.

He nods, squeezing my knee, but I can still see the lines of frustration marring his face. I notice Will watching us, so I give him a little smile and a shrug. He looks at his dad in concern, but goes back to eating his pork ribs.

Kid is too observant for his own good.

Will hasn't made it a secret how much he approves of Easton and I together. Over the past couple weeks, anytime he's caught us standing too close or cuddling on the couch, he shoots us a smile and starts whistling. It makes me laugh every time. He's a good kid. Cheeky, but kind.

When it seems like just about everybody has finished their supper, Aunt Perla gets up to start clearing dishes, and I jump up to head her off. I can't stand seeing those sorts of tasks fall to the women. It reminds me of my childhood, watching my ma cook and clean and watching my pa keep to himself, content to do his own thing, so long as it didn't include chores.

"Perla, don't you dare. We got the dishes, isn't that right?" I say, pinning the men around the table with my gaze.

"That's right," Hawthorne replies, standing right up. He and Clive start collecting plates while Easton grabs the silverware.

When I give Easton a quiet "Thank you," he sends me a little smile, and I squeeze his shoulder in response, not prepared for him to tense up. But tense up he does. I let my hand fall away and move on, but I can see that Hawthorne is watching us again, brows furrowed.

Easton and his brothers walk back and forth between the kitchen and the table, stacking dishes near the sink, while I wash them in the big farmhouse-style basin. Before long, I hear Miller call his sons off for some family business, and then Aunt Perla appears, giving me a pat on the back.

"Thank you, hon," she says.

"Mhm," I hum back.

She pulls out the mixer and starts making whipped cream for dessert as I get lost in my thoughts. Easton and I should have a conversation soon. I have no plans to rush him; I just want to know where he's at. Being here today has shown me that he's clearly working through something. What with the aborted touches and tense body language, it's easy to tell he's uncomfortable with his family knowing about us.

I don't mind much. Sure, I'd love for Easton to claim me as his own, but we've only been at this for a few weeks. Even though we've known each other forever, *this* is new. It'll take some getting used to in regards to the outside world, especially for Easton. He's just discovering this side of himself, the one that's attracted to men.

Or maybe just one man. The thought makes me smile. I like the idea of Easton only looking at me like that. Which maybe isn't fair, considering I've looked at plenty of men in the past, but I guess I'm just a little possessive when it comes to Easton's affections.

Regardless, I understand that, for Easton, this is a lot to adjust to. I don't mind him taking his time. I'll be here, however long it takes.

I find myself humming a bit as I clean dishes. The rain is coming down in sheets outside, so heavy it's hard to see through. But, all of a sudden, a flicker of movement catches my eye.

I watch for a minute, and not seeing anything else, I'm ready to dismiss what I saw, when I see it again. A small animal, a dog, huddled against a post along the backyard fence. The thing looks scared, hunched over, making itself as small as possible. The poor thing is surely soaked and maybe injured.

"Perla," I say, setting down the dish I was working on and wiping off my hands. "I'm gonna hop outside for a minute. Looks like there's a stray out there that might be in some trouble."

Aunt Perla follows my gaze, frowning as she looks out the window. "All right, dear. I'll grab a towel."

"Thanks," I say, opening the slider and stepping out into the downpour.

CHAPTER 32

Easton

"Boys," my dad says, pushing away from the table. "A word?"

Hawthorne, Clive, and I exchange mutually confused looks, but since the table is cleared, we follow my dad down the hall. He goes into his study, taking a seat behind the big mahogany desk, and my brothers and I fan out along the couches and chairs in front of it.

"What's goin' on?" Clive asks.

"I've got some explainin' to do," he says, looking between us boys.

"All right," Clive says, nodding his head. "Go on."

Our dad takes a deep breath before speaking. "Our relationship has been tense these past couple years, ever since that day in my office." He looks between Hawthorne and me. "We didn't leave off in a good place, and that's my fault. I tried to apologize, but it was a right sorry one, and the way we've been walkin' on eggshells around one another ever since is not how I want us to be. So, I have some things I'd like to say, long overdue things, that apply to all y'all."

He leans back in his chair, hands folded over his belly. Clive glances between Hawthorne and me, silently communicating.

And I can practically hear the words. *I hope this is it, the apology you deserve.* Because our dad is right. He did apologize, but his "I'm sorry" wasn't worth much weight, and things haven't been quite the same since that day when I called him out and Hawthorne proclaimed his sexuality. Sure, our issues were there before, but airing them seemed to bring all of that turmoil into the open. And it's still there, coiling around us, that unrest and unease.

"I know I've been a hard man these past many years," Dad says. "I wasn't always this way with you boys. We used to laugh a lot more and have fun. Your mama always softened me, and without her around, it's hard to remember who that man, that father, was. Now, your mama was also good-natured and stubborn as a mule. She would've given me what's for if she saw the way I've been behavin'."

He sighs, running his fingers along the brass frame on his desk that contains a picture of him and Mama from years ago, when they were young. After a quiet moment, he looks back up at us boys.

"I was tryin' to do right by y'all. All of y'all. I know that's probably hard to believe, but it's the truth. I didn't want your lives to be any more difficult than necessary. It's not easy bein' gay 'round these parts," he says, a pointed look at Hawthorne and then me. "We all know that. Now, I got nothin' against it, I swear. But I can see now how my actions would've made you feel otherwise. I was in the wrong."

I don't think I've ever heard my dad give such a speech, and it leaves me feeling a little off balance. Admittedly, I can understand what he's saying, even though a part of me wants to stay mad. But I think about Wyatt and the fact that he would tell me to forgive the man. He's never been one to hold onto the bad.

"I appreciate that you're tryin' to make amends," Hawthorne says, slow and measured, "but I need you to understand that even though I didn't know I was gay back when we were kids, we all grew up in a town where that wasn't all right. And seein' the way you treated Wyatt on top of that...how you were never very nice, how you were always tryin' to push him and Easton further apart, it got to me, too. So when I figured it out, that I was just like Wyatt, it made me afraid. Not 'cause I cared what everybody else around here thinks, but because of *you*. I was afraid you'd start treatin' me the same way, and I didn't want to lose my dad."

"I know," Dad says with a sigh.

Clive nods, reaching over to squeeze Hawthorne's arm in support. "You've gotta do better," he says to our dad, who nods.

"I will."

Clive looks over at me then. "All right, brother? Anythin' you wanna add?"

I'd been picking at my fingernail, thinking about what my dad said and how *I'd* been behaving around Wyatt this afternoon. As soon as we arrived, I realized I had no clue if I could tell my family about Wyatt and me. We hadn't talked about it yet, and supper was underway so quickly, I didn't get a chance to pull him aside.

So I avoided his touch, acted aloof and unaffected, trying to make sure no one would notice that something more was going on between us.

But that's not who I want to be.

And the more I think about it, the more sure I am that Wyatt wouldn't want us to hide like that. I probably hurt his feelings, pulling away the way I did.

Shit.

Well, I can fix that, starting now.

"Yeah," I say, "I do have somethin'. Wyatt isn't just my friend anymore. We're together now."

There's a beat of silence, and then Hawthorne's face breaks into a smile. My dad nods, like he's not all that surprised by the news and had maybe prepared himself for it, and Clive comes over and squeezes my shoulder.

"'Bout time," he says.

"Really?" I question, looking around the room. "Did everybody see this comin' except for me?"

Hawthorne shrugs. "Pretty sure everybody thought there was somethin' goin' on long before now."

I shake my head, smiling a little.

"All right," Dad pipes up, probably having met his quotient of talk today. "Everyone get. Dessert'll be on soon." And even though we probably have a ways to go to mend this thing between us, it's a start. And it feels like a solid one.

We file out of Dad's study, and I fully intend on finding Wyatt and apologizing. But, when I get back to the dining room, he's not there. He's not in the kitchen either. Only Aunt Perla is standing there, in front of the kitchen window, a towel in her hand.

"Where's Wyatt?" I ask in concern.

"Out back," Aunt Perla replies.

"What?" My gut sinks. "What d'you mean he's out back? It's pourin' buckets out there."

He must be really upset, to have stormed outside while it's raining this hard. *Double shit.*

"Easton, hon," Aunt Perla says, laying a hand on my arm and looking confused as to why I'm so upset. "It's all right. He just—"

"No, it's not all right," I say, louder than intended before walking out of her grasp and opening the sliding door to make my own amends.

I look around, the storm drenching me in mere moments, and I finally spot Wyatt out near the back of the fence that encircles the yard. He's on his haunches, facing away from me.

"Wyatt," I call out, rushing over to him.

He turns his head, looking surprised to see me running at him. He stands up, turning in place.

"What..." he starts, but I don't let him get anything else out before I'm grabbing his shoulders and staring right into his eyes. Those lashes of his are covered in tiny droplets of water, and he blinks rapidly as I start my spiel.

"Let me be clear," I say, holding onto him tightly. "I love you, Wyatt James Montgomery. I am in love with you. I know *this*, my attraction to you, is new, but I have no doubt in my mind that you're it for me." I wipe one hand over my face to clear some of the rain, a useless endeavor, seeing as more takes its place instantly. "I know you better than anyone. I know you, and I know us, and I don't need time to question this or figure anythin' out. I love you, plain and simple. I want to be with you. And I really hope you feel the same, 'cause I'm not lettin' you go ever."

Wyatt blinks some more, but when he doesn't say anything, I soldier on.

"I told my dad and brothers. They know now, and I don't care if everybody knows. In fact, I want them to. I'm not ashamed of you, of us, all right? I'm sorry I wasn't actin' right back in there, but that's done. I'm not hidin'."

To make my point, I tug Wyatt forward, chasing his lips through the haze of the downpour. He opens to me immediately, tasting like sweet barbeque and rainwater, and our tongues dance together right there under the storm clouds. He pulls me close, arms coming around my shoulders. I can feel his smile against my mouth, and he gives me a couple more nips before pulling back gently.

He looks so beautiful. Even soaked down to his boots, he's the most perfect person I've ever seen, and I vow he'll always know that.

Assuming he forgives me.

CHAPTER 33

Wyatt

"Christ, you're a sight," Easton says, brushing my wet hair back off my face. "I'm sorry," he repeats, as if it needs to be said.

"I'm not mad," I tell him, now that he's letting me get a word in.

"What?" Easton asks. He's soaked to the bone, just like me, and I'd laugh if I weren't so utterly enchanted by the speech he just gave.

"What, did you think I came out here to wallow in my heartbreak, like some kinda bad country song?" I ask.

Easton just looks confused. I shake him slightly, feeling giddy.

"I'm not mad," I repeat. "I saw a dog."

I shift to the side so Easton can see the stray huddled up near the post. It's watching us warily but not moving away, which tells me it's probably more interested in getting warm and fed than it is in being scared of us.

Easton looks down at the dog, blinking. "A dog," he says slowly.

"Yes, a dog." I squeeze his shoulders and run my fingers down his arms until I'm lacing our hands together. "But let's back up just a bit and talk about that great big ol' declaration of yours," I say, my mouth widening into a huge smile there's no way I can contain. "That whole *I am in love with you, Wyatt James Montgomery* thing. I'm a fan of that part."

Easton relaxes, taking a step forward and squeezing my hands in the space between us.

"You are?" he asks around his own bashful smile.

"Big time. Easton, I love you," I tell him more seriously. "I'm madly in love with you, and I want nothin' more than to be yours, and for you to be mine, until we're dead and buried in the ground."

"You do," Easton says around a sigh of relief, not quite a question. "Got a little morbid at the end there, though," he jokes, tucking his arms around my waist.

"What can I say? You make me think all sorts of romantic thoughts."

Easton chuckles.

"Seems fittin' it would be like this," I muse. "I tried sayin' goodbye once in the rain, and now you're tellin' me I don't ever have to."

Easton's quiet like he's thinking, and I can see the moment realization comes to him. "When you left?"

I nod.

That night all those years ago, not terribly far from where we are now. It was pouring sheets of rain, just like tonight, and Easton stood before me as I told him I had to go.

"Was that 'cause of me?" he asks softly.

"We can talk about that later," I tell him, squeezing him close, not ever wanting to let go. "But right now, we have a stray to bring inside and a family of window-gawkers to address."

Easton looks over his shoulder, taking in the faces of his family, who're watching us through the rain. Christabell waves, a huge smile on her face. Will is grinning from ear to ear, bouncing on his toes.

"All right, then," he says, giving my lips one more prolonged peck before he drops his arms.

I reluctantly step out of his grasp and bend back down, holding my hand out toward the bedraggled stray. It's hard to tell much about it, other than it's small, maybe brownish, and isn't wearing a collar or anything identifying.

I click my tongue, trying to lure it forward, but it doesn't budge. It just stares at me with its sad, little eyes. Easton crouches down, too, and when the dog makes no move to back away, Easton simply plucks it up off the ground and tucks it into his body. The dog shivers but doesn't even try to wiggle away.

"All right, animal whisperer," I chuckle. "Let's get this little lady or lad inside."

Easton and I head back towards the house. Will opens the door before we even get there, and Aunt Perla holds out the towel she gathered. Easton wraps it around the shaking bundle of fur and dirt, and we both stand inside the door, dripping onto the tile.

"Here," Autumn says, passing a few more towels over.

Easton and I do our best to dry off, but it's honestly no use. We're soaked through. But at least we can stand on the towels and avoid dragging water everywhere.

Will examines the dog, who stays curled in its little blanket nest. The dog sniffs his hand, and Clive comes back with a package of hot dogs. He hands one to Will, who breaks off little pieces and starts feeding the mutt. It gobbles them down excitedly, looking perkier immediately.

"So," Hawthorne drawls out slowly, a grin on his face. "You two."

Everyone's eyes swing our way, varying levels of amusement on their faces.

"Us two," confirms Easton with a nod. I swear my heart kicks up extra hard in my chest.

Christabell squeals. "This is so excitin'."

Miller doesn't look up from his position near the kitchen, but he also doesn't say anything negative, which I think is about the best I could've hoped for. I can see Easton shoot his dad a glance, but he doesn't push it.

"I thought you two were a thing back in high school," Clive comments, handing Will another hot dog.

"Really?" I ask in surprise.

"Well, sure. Y'all hung out *all* the time."

Autumn nods. "I thought for sure once Wyatt stayed here in Plum Valley after, you know," she says, not saying Becca's name, but we all know what she's talking about.

Aunt Perla just sighs from the kitchen entryway. "It warms my heart to see two people in love."

I can't help but be a tad surprised by her words. It's not that I thought she'd have a problem with us, but out of all the family, her and Miller are of the generation where being gay is even less accepted. So I figured she might not be as vocally supportive about it.

"You're really all right with it?" I find myself asking.

"Wyatt, dear," she says, coming close to pat my cheek, "you've always been family. Now it's just a little more official."

Christ.

I swallow around the lump in my throat. "Thank you. All y'all."

Easton squeezes my arm, sending me a little wink.

"Have I told you guys how much I love this?" Will pipes up from down on the ground, his smile a mile wide.

"Many, many times," I reply, sighing happily.

"We're gonna have to name it. Any ideas?" I ask Will.

"Her," he corrects me, stroking the small dog's now-clean fur. The dog, who we think is only a year or two old, is lying on his lap, content as can be. "And I dunno. Maybe after Mom?"

I smile. "I think that's a great idea."

Easton is watching us fondly, and at the mention of Becca, his eyes soften even more. "She liked daisies," he puts in.

Will's head pops up, eyes glistening. "Daisy. Yeah, that's perfect."

Easton's gaze locks onto me, and I can see a world of emotion behind his eyes.

"We'll bring her to Doc Hanson tomorrow for a checkup," he says. "And we'll have to scan for a microchip, make sure she doesn't belong to anybody already."

Ever the practical thinker, but I understand why he's saying it. He doesn't want Will to get too attached yet, on the off-chance the dog is spoken for. I don't think that's likely, though. She's skinny, ribs visible even under all that fur. She's clearly been on the loose for quite a while, and I haven't heard a peep from town about a missing dog.

"Can she sleep in my room?" Will asks.

"Sure can," Easton nods. "You'll listen for her, in case she needs to go outside?"

Will nods, taking the responsibility seriously. "And I'll get some of the extra blankets outta the closet for her to sleep on. I'll feed her in the mornin', too."

He's already off, Daisy in his arms. Easton cants his head down the hall, and I smile, following him into our bedroom. We strip down, scooting together under the lightweight covers, and I ask the question that's been on my mind the whole night.

"You sure you're all right with all this?"

"'Course," Easton says, tucking me closer against his solid body. I lay my head on his chest, and he threads his fingers through my hair, tugging gently.

"How d'you feel about folks knowin' you're bisexual? Well actually," I pause, "would you consider yourself bi? I guess I should've asked."

I can feel Easton's slow nod. "I suppose so. I haven't thought much about it, to tell you the truth, but that makes the most sense."

"And you're all right with it?"

"Wyatt, folks have been thinkin' I'm gay for years. I didn't care then, and I don't care now that it's true. Or half true."

"You make it all seem so easy," I tell him. I'm not complaining because I'll admit it feels wonderful to be seen, to know Easton is mine and he's not afraid to show it. But it still shocks me a little, how easy it's been, falling into this relationship.

"It is easy," he says simply.

And I guess, to Easton, that's true.

CHAPTER 34

Easton

I wake up to Wyatt nuzzling against my chest. One of his legs is thrown over mine, and he's rubbing his morning wood against my thigh.

"Mmm," I hum my approval.

Wyatt drags his blunt fingernails down my torso, sliding his hand underneath my boxers to circle my erection.

"Seems like somebody is up this mornin'," he says, stroking me slowly.

"Part of me, at least," I agree.

"Turn over," Wyatt says. "Wanna show you somethin'."

I don't know what he has to show me that involves me face down on the bed, but I do as he says, rolling onto my stomach. Wyatt scoots his body lower on the mattress, taking the sheet down with him. He pushes my legs apart and slots between them, and before I have a chance to ask what he's doing, he spreads my ass cheeks with his hands and blows across my pucker.

The sensation is wholly unexpected, and I'm sure my grunt tells him so. But I trust Wyatt. He chuckles and, a moment later, licks a broad stripe across the same spot. I buck up in surprise, but Wyatt grabs my hips and holds me still as he drags his tongue over and around my hole.

Rimming, that's what he called this.

I just didn't know it'd feel so *good*.

He keeps at it as I rub myself on the sheet below, seeking friction. I can't help it, can't stay still. This is so unlike anything I've ever experienced, and I *like* it. A lot. It feels amazing, like all these nerve endings I never knew I had are lighting up for the first time. I'm hard and leaking and just want more.

Wyatt must be able to tell because he replaces his tongue with a finger, running it around the rim of my hole before adding pressure. It slips inside, and he holds it there, moving it around slightly but not going any deeper.

"All right?" he asks.

I nod my head. It's different and new, but not bad.

He retreats and pushes further, and he must've added extra lube or spit or something, because he glides right in. *Christ.* I moan into my pillow, and he repeats the movement, sinking in and out and, occasionally, adding a flick of his tongue that drives me wild. The inside of my head is just a litany of curses.

He pulls his finger out, and then there's some added pressure, like he's using two. The invasion is a little more jarring this time, but before I can even wonder if it's too much, Wyatt is shoving a hand underneath me to grab my erection. I lift my hips to give him access, and he tugs me hard with a slick fist, simultaneously stroking his fingers inside of me.

Any trepidation I had is long gone. It feels like fireworks are going off inside my body, and I sink into it, letting Wyatt light me up in this new way.

Just as I'm wondering how much more I can take, he crooks his fingers, hitting this place inside of me that feels like I'm being electrocuted in the best sort of way. I'm coming before I even register it. Pretty sure I shout. Might even lose consciousness for a moment. Once I'm capable of managing coherent thought processes again, I register Wyatt's hand on my back, stroking me gently.

"That my prostate?" I ask.

"Oh yeah," Wyatt replies, voice smug. He comes up next to me, dragging his stubbled face across my shoulder, smudging little kisses across my skin.

"Can't wait for you to fuck me," I admit, still catching my breath. Dang, that felt good.

Wyatt's head pops up, his eyes wide. "I can't believe I'm hearin' those words outta your mouth after all this time," he says, chuckling and shaking his head. "You're one smooth talker, stud."

My brain stutters over the implication of what he just said. *After all this time.*

Wyatt made a comment yesterday about saying goodbye in the rain. That was sixteen years ago. Is it true what Becca implied in her letter, that he's loved me since way back then?

"Is that why you left?" I ask, picking up on our conversation from yesterday.

Wyatt seems to understand what I'm asking. He scoots up, sitting against the headboard. I lay my head over his thigh, looking up at him and tracing my hand absentmindedly across his hip bone as Wyatt takes a deep breath. He exhales it out through his mouth before answering. "Yeah, it is."

"'Cause of Becca and me."

He nods.

"Christ, Wyatt, I'm sorry," I say, my very heart hurting at how hard that must've been for him. Watching me get serious about someone else. Watching me *marry* them.

He looks down at me. "Don't be. That was life. And you were happy."

Still missed him like hell, though.

"And you?" I ask. "Were you happy?"

"I found my moments," he says. "And look at us now." He winks, trying to lighten the mood. "I'd say things turned out a-okay."

I turn my head, kissing the top of his leg. "When did you know?" I ask, continuing to run my fingers over his skin.

Again, Wyatt understands what I'm asking. "Mm," he hums, absentmindedly scratching his forehead. "For sure when we were seventeen. But, I dunno, maybe before then, too."

Seventeen?

"That was nearly twenty years ago," I say sadly, unable to stop my feelings from bleeding through into my tone.

Wyatt *has* loved me, all this time, for our entire adult lives. From before we graduated high school. While I was with Becca. When I got married and had a child. The entire time he helped raise Will. When he was with Harrison.

He loved me through it all, and I had no idea.

I wish I could say a part of me knew, but I guess I just wasn't ever that smart. I knew Wyatt loved me, in a way, because no one would stick with me all that time otherwise. But I didn't know he was *in* love with me. And thinking about that one-sided love, over all those years, it breaks my heart.

"I'm so sorry," I say, voice catching.

"No, don't," Wyatt replies, running his hand over my shoulder and giving me a firm squeeze. "There's nothin' to be sorry 'bout. I was the fool who couldn't ever get over you."

I turn my face against his thigh again, closing my eyes tightly and inhaling his scent. Man and home, that's what Wyatt smells like to me. How didn't I see it until recently?

"I can't imagine," I start, but Wyatt cuts me off, running a hand over my short hair.

"It was my life, Easton, and I chose to live it how I wanted. I wouldn't change a thing."

I look up, seeing the truth of it in his eyes, the steely determination not to make me feel badly about all the years we can't rewrite. Even if Wyatt says he wouldn't change a thing, I'm not so sure. If I could go back in time and have Wyatt like this, have Wyatt be mine for longer, I think I would take it.

And yet I know there's no use in wishful thinking. The past can never change.

"Thank that heart of yours for me," I tell him. "I'm glad it never let go."

Wyatt smiles, a lopsided thing that lights up his whole face, reminding me so much of the teenager I spent my days with out on the ranch. Carefree and young, tender-hearted, our whole lives ahead of us. Wyatt may have more lines in his face now, but it's the same young boy inside, the one who just gets me and always did. The one who loves me.

I'm a lucky bastard that he chose me at all. That he's still choosing me.

"I'm sorry," I say again, can't help it.

"Don't." Wyatt shakes his head.

I place a tender kiss against his thigh before rising up on my knees and scooting forward. I bracket Wyatt's face between my hands, running my thumbs over his cheekbones. His eyes ping back and forth between mine, those thick lashes fluttering each time he blinks.

"I love you," I whisper instead.

Wyatt's eyes fall closed, a hitch in his breath telling me *those* are the words he wants to hear instead. I press my lips, featherlight, against one eyelid.

"I'm in love with you," I say again, kissing the other.

Wyatt's hands come up, gripping my wrists tightly, not pulling or pushing, simply tethering himself to me and me to him. I keep going, making sure that in no uncertain terms, he understands and believes me. I can't give us a different history, but I can give him now and forever.

"I love you." A kiss to his nose.

"I love you." The corner of his mouth.

"I love you." The edge of his jaw.

The pulse point in his neck. "Baby, I love you. So much," I say, nuzzling against his skin.

Wyatt inhales sharply, and I bring my eyes back up to his face. He's watching me, a world of emotions in those wet eyes. I drag my thumbs under his lids, catching the moisture there and kissing it away.

"Thank you for lovin' me," I tell him again.

"Easiest thing I ever did," he replies, voice hoarse but true.

I don't stop thanking him. I show him, over and over, with soft kisses and gentle touch. I tell him. That I love him, that I always will, that he's the most beautiful person in the world.

I map every expanse of his rugged, muscled body. Every ridge, every valley, I explore with my mouth and my fingers. The rough hair over his chest, the trail down below.

And when I finally close my mouth over his straining erection, the contented sigh that greets my ears is the most satisfying sound I think I've ever heard.

———————————⭐———————————

Late morning, we bring Daisy to Doc Hanson for her checkup. I called ahead, but he was able to fit us into his schedule without a problem.

"No microchip," he proclaims.

Will's eyes light up, and he bounces in the corner.

"We'll go ahead and do all her vaccinations, since we don't know what she does or doesn't have," the vet says. "She needs a little bulkin' up, but don't overdo it. And you'll need to get her license set up."

I nod. "Thanks, Doc. Appreciate it."

Doctor Hanson nods, and as we're getting ready to leave, Wyatt approaches the man.

"Is Harrison around?" he asks, smiling apologetically.

The doc just shakes his head. "Harrison moved on," he says, much to my, and Wyatt's, surprise. "Got a job several counties over."

"Well shit," Wyatt says, grimacing as he glances over his shoulder to make sure Will didn't hear him swear. "I hope I didn't create any problems for you."

The vet shrugs, looking nonplussed. "Life is messy, no gettin' around that. It's not your fault I can't seem to hold down an employee."

"Need one?" Wyatt asks.

Doc Hanson nods. "Eventually. These old bones won't keep goin' forever."

Wyatt chuckles. "You're hardly old, Jake."

"Older than you," he says, clapping Wyatt on the shoulder. "Take care now," he adds a little louder so Will can hear. "Daisy is real lucky to have y'all."

Will beams, swinging Daisy carefully into his arms. The little dog is already taken with him, never far away and following along on his heel wherever he goes. The four of us, Daisy included, make our way outside and into the truck.

Turning over the ignition, I think out loud, "We should stop by the feed store and get her supplies."

Will nods, listing off things we'll need. "Bowls, food, a collar and leash, some toys, a dog bed..."

I chuckle, sparing a glance at Wyatt as I drive, but he's lost in thought, staring out the window.

We all pile out at the feed store. It's primarily geared toward livestock, but it does have a small pet section. Will carries Daisy in, and the first thing we do is pick out a collar and a leash, so she can be let down safely. As Wyatt and I follow behind Will, who's examining all the available toys and dog bedding, I twist my fingers with his.

"Everythin' all right?" I ask.

He looks over at me, blinking slowly before sighing. "Yeah, I just feel bad for how things went with Harrison. I never wanted to hurt him."

"I know." I squeeze the back of his neck and rub along the tendons there with my thumb. I wish I could make him feel better, but I don't think there's anything else I can say to lessen Wyatt's guilt. The only thing I know how to do is be there beside him as he works through it.

Wyatt leans into my touch, his shoulders relaxing marginally. He gives me a grateful smile and loops his arm around my waist, tugging me against him right there in the middle of the feed store. I kiss the side of his head, not caring one bit about being in public, and am rewarded with Wyatt's gentle sigh.

When we pull apart slightly, I notice Stephy Martinez, a woman about our age who works at the market, standing further down the aisle. She notices us, too. Her eyes drag over Wyatt and me, and even though she turns her gaze away relatively quickly, I can see a little smile tugging at her lips. It makes me smile, too.

Will, having finished picking out bowls and toys for Daisy, drags us into the food aisle next. Wyatt helps him pick out a good formula for her, and on our way to the checkout, a man I don't recognize bumps into Wyatt's shoulder hard. I reach out to steady him, and the man's eyes drop to my hand with a sneer.

Well, shit. That didn't take long.

"Gotta problem?" Will asks loudly, placing his hands on his hips. Daisy stands next to him, looking like a little sidekick, as Will's eyes spit fire at the stranger. I instinctively move my hand to my son's shoulder, not sure whether I'm holding Will back or getting ready to block him from the stranger's sights.

The man barely spares Will a glance, however. He just shakes his head disapprovingly and walks away. My shoulders lose their tension, and Will huffs at his retreating form.

"Who was that?" I ask, pivoting my attention back to Wyatt.

He sighs. "No one important. Just an alfalfa farmer from next town over who's never taken kindly to me." He turns his sights on Will. "Thought you were about to go to war," Wyatt says, raising an eyebrow. "I appreciate the thought, kiddo, but don't you get yourself into trouble on my account. I can fight my own battles."

Will rolls his eyes, looking put out. "What, was he gonna punch a twelve-year-old?"

"Almost thirteen-year-old," I say, to which Will smiles, his body finally deflating. "Probably not, but you still need to be a little more careful, Will. Now c'mon, let's get this little lady home and settled."

As we're loading everything at the register, Wyatt leans over. "Sure you're ready for this? That sorta thing might happen more now."

I grip Wyatt's arm, pulling him around to face me. "Worth it," I tell him, making sure he sees the conviction in my eyes. "Besides," I say, pulling out my wallet to pay for Daisy's haul, "it's not all bad. Times are changin'."

"I hope you're right." A quirk of a smile touches Wyatt's face.

I know I'm right.

It's not the first time I've experienced something like that. Folks in this town have been assuming things about me for a long time now. And maybe I'm lucky because being a bigger, white male, and straight-passing, as Wyatt has told me, means I probably don't have it as bad. I know Wyatt has always had it much worse, and I think the difference is because he's been openly gay for quite a while.

The thing is now I can hold Wyatt's hand, stand beside him proudly and show Plum Valley or the world that I'm on his side. That I don't care what they think. And, for me, that makes me feel like less of a bystander in this battle and more like an active partner, like I'm fighting this with Wyatt.

And it *isn't* all bad. There are supporters out there, even silent ones, who'll look at us and smile, like Stephy. And there are champions, like Will, who'll be a whole lot louder about their support.

Love is love. And I love this man.

As long as he's happy and Will's happy—not to mention Monty and Daisy now, too—then I'm happy. That's all I need.

CHAPTER 35

Wyatt, age 38

"It's not fair! I'm *fourteen* now, dad, I'm not a kid anymore."

"I don't care. You're still too darn young to be goin' 'round San Antonio on your own," Easton says.

"I won't be alone. There'll be a whole group of us," Will says sulkily.

"Yeah, a group of other teenagers. You're not adults, and that city is different than Plum Valley. Gramps or Gran stays with you the whole time. That's final."

Will grumbles, turning on his heel and storming off, Daisy right behind him.

"What's this?" I ask, coming fully into the kitchen where I stumbled upon the scene playing out between father and son.

Easton sighs. "Will thinks he's hot stuff these days. He's meetin' with the LGBT club in the city tomorrow, and they're gettin' food and goin' to a movie or somethin' afterward. I told him he's not goin' off on his own while he's there, and he doesn't wanna hear it. There's no way he'll be the only one with a chaperone. Most of 'em are still too young to drive," Easton says, taking a breath after he concludes his rant.

"Easy there," I laugh. "You'll strain somethin'."

Easton walks over, tucking his face into my neck. "He's gettin' older."

"Yeah, he is. But he's a smart kid. He'll be all right."

Easton sighs. "Doesn't mean I have to like it."

"Suppose not. But, just think. In a few short years, when he goes off to some hotshot college, we'll have the house all to ourselves." I press my hips firmly against him.

"Stop distractin' me," Easton grumbles, even though he pulls me closer.

"Is it workin'?" I ask, grinning.

He pulls back, but his hands remain on my hips. "Li'l bit. D'you think..." He doesn't finish his sentence.

"What?" I ask.

"Well, he joined that group last year, but he's never said anythin' to us about *himself*. Do you think he's gay or somethin' other than straight?"

"I think it's entirely possible," I say, having wondered the same thing over the years.

"Should we say somethin'?"

I think about it for a moment but shake my head. "No. If Will isn't straight, he'll come out in his own time in his own way. He knows we support him unconditionally. We should let it be his choice."

Easton nods, fingers flexing against my hips. "You're right. Sometimes it just helps to hear someone else say it."

"Glad I can be your Jiminy Cricket," I say, smudging a kiss against his cheek.

"What does that make me, your puppet?" Easton asks.

I laugh. "Well, you do have nice wood. I can even make it grow longer." My laughter ramps up at my own corny joke.

Easton rolls his eyes and pushes me away playfully. "C'mon, we have to drive him to the Thompsons' for the weekend, and then we're goin' out."

"Oh, we are, are we?" I ask. That's news to me.

"Yep, so get yourself in gear."

"Oh, bossy, I like it," I joke, earning a swat on my bum.

After we drop Will off at his grandparents'—with a "Goodbye, Dad" and "Goodbye, Pop" letting us know all is forgiven by the moody teen—Easton drives us over to his dad's. I look over at him curiously, since my idea of a date doesn't generally include going to another family member's home, but Easton keeps his eyes straight forward.

When we get out of the car, he comes around to my side and slides his hand into mine.

"Where're you takin' me?" I ask, keeping my fingers around Easton's as he leads us around his family home.

The house looks dark, so I'm assuming Miller is either gone or asleep. And even though I know we're always welcome here, it feels a little bit like we're trespassing.

"You remember what day it is, right?" Easton asks.

I scoff. "'Course. It's the Fourth of July."

"Mhm," Easton hums, not really giving me anything new to go on.

As we approach the backyard, where Easton's treehouse still stands, a bit worse for wear, I notice a blanket spread on the ground.

"What's this?" I ask.

"You really can't let your curiosity rest, can you?"

"Uh, you do know me, right?" I joke.

"I'd like to think I do," he says, tugging me down with him to the ground.

"We're watchin' fireworks?" I guess.

Easton taps the tip of his nose with his finger. *Bingo*.

I hum my approval, slotting myself between Easton's legs so I can lean back against his chest. His arms come around me, and we sit there, enjoying the night sky, the stars, and the peaceful quiet.

I can't believe it's been over two years of this. Of me and Easton. Being boyfriends, although that word doesn't feel like enough. And it sounds particularly strange to use as a nearly forty-year-old. Easton doesn't enjoy when I remind him how old we are, but I don't mind aging. Especially now that I snagged the man of my dreams. These years have been some of my favorite.

Without preamble, the fireworks begin overhead. Every year, they're shot off on the highest peak surrounding Plum Valley so that most everyone who lives here can view them.

It's nice, sitting here with Easton now, watching them like we did so many years ago.

I remember one year, when we were little, I imagined myself as a firework. I wondered if the pain of the blast would be worth it to make people happy. It seems like such an odd thing for a child to think, and yet I can't help but recall that moment with perfect clarity. The question reminds me, in a way, of all the years I spent by this man's side, wanting, first and foremost, for him to be happy.

So, if I could go back in time and tell myself the answer, I'd say yes. Yes, it's worth it for the people you love.

And sometimes, when the stars align or, heck, maybe just by chance, that happiness will come back at you tenfold.

I snuggle closer into Easton's arms, a big, goofy smile on my face as I watch the display of color overhead. The crackles, hisses, and booms are muted where we are, but they're still there, a chorus with the crickets and katydids.

"Y'know, gay marriage has been legal in Texas now for a couple years," Easton says, his breath ghosting over my ear.

My heart kicks up.

I turn my head and peer up at Easton. I know that, of course, but my mind is currently mush. Muddled, anxious, excited, hopeful mush. So all I answer with is, "Yeah?"

"Mhm."

And then, nothing.

I try to be patient. But I'm only human, and when Easton doesn't say anything else, I flip in his arms, looking in confusion at the face of the man I love. Every time a firework explodes overhead, his face is lit up a little with light. It shouldn't make him even more beautiful, and yet, somehow, it does.

"That's it?" I say, a little indignantly. Maybe a lot indignantly.

There's humor flashing in Easton's eyes, and even though I don't think I could ever be truly mad at the man, I scowl and give his shoulder a shove. He doesn't budge much.

"What the hell, Easton," I grouse.

"Stand up," he says.

"What?"

"You heard me," he repeats, looking cool as a cucumber on a hot Texas day. "Stand up."

After a quick stare down, and upon deciding he's serious, I push up off the ground. I hold my arms out, twirling around in place.

"All right, I'm standing," I declare. "What n—"

The *now* dies on my tongue as I complete my circle. Because there, in front of me, is Easton, up on one knee, holding a simple gold band between his fingertips.

"*Shit*," I whisper.

"Wyatt," Easton says, face flickering in the firework light. "I have known you for my entire life, as far back as my memories

go. You're in most of 'em, from that very first day of kinder-
garten when they lined us up alphabetically, Montgomery next
to Moore, and we decided, right then, we'd be best friends.
I've seen your face for more days than I haven't. I've loved you
for as long as I can remember. I've always wanted to be with
you. To talk, to touch, to be in your life and have you in mine.
And I still don't understand how, knowin' all that, I was such
a fool for so long."

I cover my mouth with the back of my hand, but it doesn't
do much to block my embarrassing whimper.

"Hush now, or I'll never get through it," he says, a crooked
smile on his face.

I blink my eyes a couple times and nod at him to continue.

"You told me once that *you* were the fool. But that's just not
true—I was. I can't change the past. And I could tell you how
sorry I am for the missed time, for all those extra moments
we could've had, but I know you don't wanna hear it. So I'll
just tell you this. I love you, Wyatt James Montgomery. Like,
really dang love you. I'm so stupid in love with you, and I don't
ever wanna let a day go by where I have any regrets where it
concerns you. And I'd regret it if I didn't ask you to marry me
right this instant. So will you? Will you be my husband so our
two fool hearts can love each other for the rest of their days?"

Fuck.

I drop to my knees on the blanket in front of him, hands
shaking slightly. "As if I could ever say no to you," I croak out.

"Is that a yes?" he asks, smile wide, eyes bright and beautiful.

"That's a heck yeah, Easton William Moore," I say, letting
Easton slip the ring onto my finger. "You'll never be rid of me
now."

"Countin' on it." He tugs me in and seals his lips over mine
like a promise.

CHAPTER 36

Easton, age 40

"Tomorrow's the day?" Sadie asks.

Wyatt starts cracking up, and I smile from my location in the kitchen where I'm grabbing a bottle of wine. Even though I barely drink the stuff, it was a special request from Wyatt for Sadie, so we stocked up. I swipe some glasses, as well, and snacks.

"You said the same thing last time," Wyatt replies. He adds something else after that, but I can't quite hear it.

As I pad up to the archway between the kitchen and family room, my hands full, their voices fall to a hush. I stop outside the room, not wanting to intrude if they're having a private moment.

"You rewrote your story."

"What d'you mean?" Wyatt asks.

"This Wyatt got his Easton after all," Sadie says, sounding fond.

"Yeah, Sades, he did."

I smile, even as my heart aches a bit. I have a feeling whatever they're talking about has to do with the years where I was oblivious to Wyatt's feelings. But, as Wyatt himself likes to remind me, we can't change the past. And even though we didn't start our romantic relationship until recently, almost four years ago now, we sure did have a great friendship before then. Still do, really. That's never changed.

"Are you ready to get married?" Sadie asks.

"I've been ready to marry that man for a good long while," Wyatt replies, making my heart skip a beat.

"I'm so happy for you."

I take that as my cue and step into the family room, declaring, "Good stuff has arrived."

Wyatt looks me over, raking his gaze from head to toe. "Mm, sure has."

Sadie laughs, but I just shake my head. He sure does love to try to embarrass me.

"Ahh," Sadie sighs, clutching her chest. "You two are goals. Easton, you have two brothers, right?"

Wyatt laughs and smacks Sadie's arm lightly. "One is gay, and the other is in a relationship now."

"Well, crap," Sadie says, deflating against the couch. "All right, gimme that wine, then."

I hand it over, and Sadie pops the top, pouring us three glasses. I sit down next to Wyatt, and he immediately leans into me.

Sadie looks over. "And I even lost my snuggle buddy? What is this nonsense?"

"Nah, get over here, darlin'," Wyatt says, motioning her over.

She grins and squeezes against his other side. I was so glad to finally meet Sadie after all these years. She was this concept in my head every time Wyatt talked about her, but the reality of her is even better. She's vibrant and funny, just like Wyatt himself. Her hair is a riot of black, afro curls, she wears eyeliner that makes her look like a cat, and her smile is mischievous and warm.

I liked her instantly, and I'll forever be grateful that Sadie was there for Wyatt when I was not.

"So, explain this to me," she says, taking a sip of her wine. "Why is it called Plum Valley if you don't have any plums?"

Wyatt laughs. "Well, we used to. This whole valley used to be plum orchards. But then they brought in beef production, and most of the plums were either pulled up or left to die."

Sadie frowns. "That's so sad. You two have plums, though, don't you? I thought I saw some trees when we were pulling in."

Wyatt looks over at me and smiles. "Yeah, we do. Just got our first plums this season, too. Becca's plums," he adds softly.

Sadie glances at me, a small, understanding smile on her face. I clear my throat and kiss the side of Wyatt's head, breathing in his comforting scent. It meant a lot to me when Will and Wyatt helped me start that orchard in Becca's memory. I still go out there to talk with her. Will does, too.

The three of us stay up much later than I'm used to. At around midnight, Sadie finally pushes off the couch. "I may be a night owl, but I'm sure you two could use some sleep before the big day. Show me to my room, and I'll get out of your hair."

Wyatt helps Sadie get settled in the guest room, which used to be Wyatt's room, and I clean up the mess we left behind. As I'm getting ready for bed, I check to make sure I have everything ready for tomorrow. My suit, tie, cufflinks. The rings stashed in my dresser drawer. Underneath them is the letter I pulled out last week when I got to thinking about marriage and love. It's the letter Becca wrote to me while she was pregnant. The one I received after she passed.

I didn't fully understand her message at the time, but as I read it again this past week, it clicked.

"What's that?" Wyatt asks, coming into our room and closing the door.

"My letter from Becca. Like the one she gave you."

Wyatt's eyes soften. "I forgot that you mentioned she wrote you one, too."

I nod, then hold it out to him. "Here, I wanted you to see it."

Wyatt's brows furrow, but he takes the envelope, gently removing the letter from within and unfolding it. I know exactly what he's reading, having read it myself so many times that I have it memorized.

Easton,

Hey baby. I hope you never have to read this. But since we decided to get our affairs in order before the baby comes, I couldn't get this idea out of my head. It was keeping me up at night because I didn't want anything left unsaid.

I love you. You know that. And I know you love me, too. I can only hope we'll love each other for a long time to come. And, maybe, this letter will never reach you. Maybe you'll go first, when you're old and gray and have lived a full life. That's my hope, that we'll reach that point.

But if we don't, and if I'm the one who's not long for this world, I need you to make me a promise. Don't close your heart or your mind. I don't want you to be alone, Easton, and I'm afraid you might be content to be just that. I know you don't see the world quite the same as others do, and that's not a bad thing, not at all. But you have a lot of love in your heart. It's already there. Trust in that. Listen to it.

I want you to know I'm so honored that you chose me. You've made me so happy, darling. But there are many paths we can wander in our lives, so please—please—don't make camp just yet.

I love you always,

Becca

Wyatt's gaze lifts to me, a tender look in his eyes. He puffs out a breath before saying, "At the end, she was talkin' about me. About us."

"Yeah," I say, "I think she was. I didn't understand her choice of words back then. But she knew I loved you, too. I guess she really wanted us to get together." I chuckle.

Wyatt smiles. "She was shippin' us before it was a thing."

"Huh?"

"Nothin'," he replies around a laugh. He folds the letter up carefully and hands it back to me. "I think she'll be watchin' us tomorrow."

"Yeah," I agree, voice a little hoarse. "I reckon she will."

———————— ✱ ————————

In the morning, Wyatt and I make our way over to my dad's. We debated where to have our small, private ceremony, but it seemed fitting to both of us to have it where we spent so much of our beginning together. At the ranch.

We spend most of the day getting everything set up in the High Hill pasture, on one of the flatter portions of the hill. My dad agreed to shift the herd for our ceremony, so the area is clear, apart from a wooden arch covered in daisies and a handful of white chairs for our guests. Dad also agreed to allow the use of his many four-wheelers, so our guests won't have to make the trek by foot.

Aunt Perla offered, or more appropriately insisted, that she be in charge of food for the reception, which we'll have back at my dad's house, and Autumn and Christabell surprised us by setting up decorations. They hung twinkle lights in the backyard and put out vases of daisies, and I know it'll look even more beautiful at night.

The ceremony itself is set to be held at sunset, when the sun will cast that beautiful yellow glow over the pasture. The one that makes everything feel a bit cozy and warm. As time approaches, Wyatt and I finish getting ready. We shower, get dressed, help one another out with our ties and cufflinks, and spend a good portion of time just kissing. It's something I never get sick of with Wyatt. Kissing him feels like home.

"Ready for this?" he asks, smoothing my lapel one more time.

He looks so handsome. His suit is black, like mine, and his hair is back in a half pony. He's been wearing it up more often lately—something Will calls his hipster look, whatever that means—and I like it, just as much as I like when it's falling loose around his face. I think I just like Wyatt any and every way.

"I'm more than ready," I tell him.

The ceremony site is already filled with our small group of guests—my family, Will's grandparents, and Sadie—when Wyatt and I arrive via horse, not caring one bit about hair on our suits. There's a fleet of four-wheelers off to the side, and that's where we tie our horses. Wyatt grabs my hand, squeezing lightly, as we turn and face our family, both biological and found, and it hits me that this is it.

This is our wedding.

It may not be a big affair, but we didn't want that anyway. All we needed was us, the folks we love, a few words, and the pastor who'll make it all official.

It's quiet as we walk side by side up toward the arch. Faces smile at us as we go. Will gives a wink, and Daisy wags her tail excitedly.

We take our places in front of the arch, and the silence that rings out sounds anticipatory. Like the world is waiting, for just a moment, with bated breath. The sun is low in the sky, nearly to the peak of the highest hill, and it lights the flowers along the wooden arch, making them glow golden. Wyatt keeps his hands firmly clasped in mine as we stand across from one another, close enough that we don't have to let go. I stare into his eyes, into the gaze of the man who has been such an integral part of my life for so long. His eyes glow golden, too, the lighter flecks picking up the sunlight as it shines down on us.

The silence is broken as the pastor starts us off, thanking our friends and family for being here to celebrate our union, saying a few words about love and marriage. But I only have eyes for Wyatt. I can't seem to stop staring at him, and when he opens his mouth to recite his vows, I'm almost startled. I didn't realize it was time.

"Easton," he says, sighing around my name like it's his very favorite word. "I thought long and hard about what I wanted to say here today. I wrote and rewrote these vows a hundred times or more, wantin' my words to be just perfect. I wanted them to be the best representation of us, of what I feel for you. But I realized that no words are gonna capture that right. The way I love you," he shakes his head slightly, "it's just a part of me, of my very makeup. <u>You're in my atoms. My bones. My head and my heart.</u> I wish I could show you. I wish I could hold it in my hands, so you could see just how brightly that love shines. But I can't do that. What I can do is promise that my love for you will never go away. It won't fade. It won't falter. It won't die. I will love you, Easton William Moore, for all my days and on into the night sky."

I inhale a shaky breath, puffing it out through my mouth. "Christ, Wy, you're gonna make me cry," I mutter, shaking my head.

Wyatt wipes his thumb under my eye, catching the tear that's already escaped, a tender smile on his face. My gaze sweeps over him and the little freckles on his nose. I take another deep breath.

"Believe it or not," I say, "our vows kinda go together."

Wyatt tilts his head in confusion, but I just give him a little smile and say the words I memorized for him today.

"When I was a child, I liked to think about the stars and how, just maybe, we became one whcn we died. It's a notion I've never quite been able to get rid of. And maybe that's just my idea of Heaven. Spendin' eternity up in the sky, starin' down at the folks we left behind, watchin' over them. Now, I know talkin' 'bout death maybe isn't the most romantic thing to be doin' at a wedding." Wyatt snickers at that, and I wonder if he's remembering the time he told me he'd love me until we're dead and buried. "But I also remember, even as a child, thinkin' of you up there with me. I had this idea that we'd be side by side, shinin' brightly enough that someone could point up at the sky and pick us out."

I take a breath, letting the warmth of Wyatt's gaze saturate me as I go a bit off book.

"You said the way you love me is just a part of you. And I feel the same. Even before I understood it, my heart knew yours, and yours knew mine. I always had this idea we'd be together in the end, and I count my lucky stars every day that you didn't give up on us. I love you, Wyatt James Montgomery, with all of my heart, now and on into the night sky," I say with conviction, matching his words to me.

Wyatt squeezes my hands tightly, his eyes glistening, and I have to blink to clear some of the moisture from my own eyes.

Love you, Wyatt mouths at me. I do the same.

We exchange our simple gold rings, and before I know it, the pastor is pronouncing us husband and husband.

"You may now kiss," she says, voice joyful.

Wyatt tugs me in, not giving a damn about where we are or who we're in front of. He kisses me hard, with all the love stored up in him, and I kiss him right back with the same. It feels like hardly any time at all has passed since those teenage years we spent here on this hill. And I know, in another twenty years, we'll be right where we are now. Husbands. Best friends. Partners in life, and now love. There's clapping from our family, a few whistles, and even a cat call, but to me, there's only Wyatt and the feel of him in my arms. The feel of home.

CHAPTER 37

Wyatt

Husband.

It's the first word that filters into my head when I wake up and stretch against the long expanse of Easton's body.

We're *married* now. Ho-ly cow. I smile because how could I not?

"Mornin', husband," Easton says, his voice rumbling through me.

I grin wider, rolling my head up to take in Easton's sleepy face and blinking eyes. His body is like the warmest pillow, and I nuzzle my face back against his chest, soaking it up. "Mornin' to you, too," I say, giving his pec a lick. For some reason, I have a thing about licking Easton's skin and tasting the clean sweat there.

He chuckles, running his hand up my arm. I can feel the ring on his finger catching on my skin, and it pulls memories of last night to the forefront of my mind.

Easton and the way he looked, so handsome, so mine. Hearing the words "I do" come from his mouth. Exchanging vows under the setting sun, in front of an arch of daisies as an ode to Becca, one of our most unlikely supporters.

And then there were our family and friends, sitting in white chairs and watching us get married, and then celebrating with us back at Miller's.

Even Miller himself was there. Easton is still upset his dad has never given me an apology, saying he owes me one. But I don't mind. Miller Moore was never a man of words; he's a man of action. And seeing him there, supporting us quietly, tells me everything I need to know.

I slip my leg over Easton's, letting my hand trail down his body, filthy images of what I could do to my husband flooding my mind. I don't get a chance to enact any of my fantasies, however, because there's a sudden and loud knock at the door.

"I hear you up," Will calls out. "No hanky-panky this mornin'. We have a brunch to get to. Get your asses outta bed."

"Do we need to scold him for sayin' asses?" Easton mumbles jokingly.

"Nah, let him have his fun. C'mon, husband." I give Easton's chest a little slap as I push out of bed. "We've got a brunch to get to."

Brunch is at Aunt Perla's, a quiet and content affair with the same lot that joined us for the wedding. I wasn't sure why, exactly, we needed to do brunch, but Will insisted it was a necessity.

It isn't until after it's over that I start getting suspicious. Will keeps checking his phone, and after the millionth time, I call him out on it.

"What's goin' on?" I ask him quietly. We're the only ones left at Aunt Perla's, just Easton, Will, and me. Everybody else has already left, but Will kept holding us back.

"Nothin'," he says cheerfully. "C'mon, there's one last thing we needa do."

I assume he's up to something, but I shrug and go along with it. Knowing Will, it wouldn't be anything dangerous or bad. He leads us out to Easton's truck, getting into the driver's seat—something he's been a big fan of lately, ever since getting his license—and the three of us head back out onto the road toward town. Easton shoots me a curious look, but I shrug.

As Will makes the turn into town, my eyes go wide. Main Street is full of people. Like, chock full. And covered in a rainbow of colors. There are banners hanging across shop fronts, colorful flags everywhere, even balloons. And folks are dressed in all manner of things, from colorful mismatched clothes, to rainbow t-shirts, to a few bare chests covered in body paint.

"What's all this?" Easton asks as Will pulls the truck into an open spot just outside of the town square. He sounds just as baffled as I feel.

"Well," Will starts, turning off the truck but not quite facing us. "It's Pride Month. And I asked the school if we could have a festival of sorts. But they said no, so I went to the township board instead."

I can't stop the grin that takes over my face. The kid is relentless.

"The board said I needed at least a fifty percent approval to host a public event."

For just a moment, my stomach sinks. That seems like an impossible number for a Pride-related event in Plum Valley. And yet, looking over the road that's decorated and filled with people, it's obvious to me that Will succeeded.

"How many did you get?" I ask quietly.

"335."

"Holy shit," Easton whispers.

"That's a lot," I say in wonder.

"Sure is. 56.2 percent to be exact. So this," Will says proudly, gesturing grandly with his arm, "is the new annual Plum Valley Pride Parade."

Shit. I can't believe it.

"I had no idea," I say, not quite sure how to articulate what I'm thinking. Sure, there have been more and more friendly faces in town lately and even folks who've been downright happy to see Easton and I together after all these years, but I didn't realize *so* many people were supportive. Seeing it like this, laid out before me, brings to light exactly how much has changed since I was Will's age over two decades ago.

"I think some folks just needed a little nudge to see they weren't the only ones who believed in what's right. The more we speak up, the more others will, too. There are a lot of allies here who are more willin' to do that now," Will points out.

"Will," Easton says, voice choking up, "I'm so proud of you. For a million things, but also for this. For bein' that voice and for doin' this for me and your pop."

"Well," Will says, clearing his throat. "You're welcome, but it wasn't just for you. I'm queer. Surprise." He flourishes his hands a little. "So this was for you, and me, and all the other folks in town like us. We all deserve it." He gestures over near the post office, where Bobby Merchant, Shane Merchant's son and one of Will's biggest opponents back in middle school, is wearing a rainbow t-shirt.

I guess some folks are just full of surprises.

Will hops out of the truck before either Easton or I can say anything about his little reveal. For as outspoken as he is, Will has never particularly liked being the center of attention. Well, he should know better than to assume we'd just let that go.

I hop out after him, immediately rounding the truck and pulling Will into a hug.

"So proud of you," I echo Easton's words from earlier.

Easton joins in not a moment later, smushing Will and I in his arms, and for several seconds, the three of us just stand there amidst the background noise of happy chatter and kazoo whistles. Our little wonderful queer family.

"All right," Will finally says, trying to nudge us off. "You're gonna crush me to death."

I reluctantly let go.

"Did you know?" he asks, toeing at the ground in a nervous gesture. It's not hard to figure out what he's asking. Did we know he's queer?

Easton and I glance at each other over Will's shoulder.

"Had a feelin'," I admit.

"And we love you no matter what," Easton adds.

"Yeah, yeah," Will says, rolling his eyes before muttering a quiet, "thanks."

Easton squeezes his son's shoulder. "I can't believe you pulled this off," he muses.

"It wasn't just me," Will says, turning and leading us into the fray. "Had a whole buncha help, includin'... Where did Hawthorne and his friend get off to? Oh, there."

Will points, and I follow the direction of his finger to Hawthorne, who's standing to the side of the closed-off road, wearing a glittery pink crown and handing out colorful lollipops. Next to him is...*no way*.

"Is that..." I trail off.

"Yep," Will says, popping the "p."

I whip my head around to him. "And how d'you know who that is?" I ask, refusing to think of my baby boy as a teenager, well on his way to adulthood.

"Pop, c'mon. I'm sixteen and queer."

"Ah, nope nope nope," I say, covering my ears.

Will laughs, shaking his head.

Easton gently pulls my arms down. "Who is it? I'm missin' somethin'."

"That," I say, looking over at the man known as Silver, "is a really famous...performer."

"Porn star," Will clarifies bluntly.

Easton's eyes widen, and I see the moment he catches on, a cringe flashing across his face as he has the same realization I did that his son recognized a porn star.

"Wait just a minute," he says. "How does my brother know a porn star?"

That *is* the question, isn't it?

Before we have the chance to figure it out, there's a big cheer from the crowd. It takes me a moment to realize folks are cheering for *us*. All of a sudden, several people come over to congratulate Easton and I on our wedding, including Melinda Baker, who gives me a big ol' cherry-red smooch on the cheek, and Nash from the bar. Cindy Davenport is there, and her son, Jeffrey. Even Lou-Anna Smith-Travers. It astounds me, yet again, the sheer number of folks here, giving us a word of support or pat on the back. I'd always hoped Plum Valley would be like this one day, and it took my son setting up this Pride Parade to make me realize it already was.

All these folks, these Plum Vallians, are allies. That's clear as day. And maybe Will was right, that they needed to see they weren't the only ones to be a little more outspoken about their support. It makes me wonder what this town will be capable of in another five years, or ten, with a generation like Will's that's pushing for change. Maybe we'll find out there are more queer folks here than any of us knew. I hope, someday, they won't have to hide. I hope they'll see they're welcome.

I can, and that's a remarkable feeling. To be seen and loved and welcomed in my own community. To join these folks and to celebrate being queer. It gives me hope. For the future, for now.

I see Sadie up ahead, chatting animatedly with Christabell, and I wonder if there might be something more there. They seemed to hit it off at the wedding, and I could tell Sadie was interested in Easton's cousin. Maybe she'll get her country happily ever after, after all.

I see Hawthorne, bumping elbows with Silver, and Clive in his rainbow shirt, his new girlfriend Gracie by his side. I see Autumn passing out stickers to a couple kids, whose parents look happy to be here.

I see Will, looking so grown up already, and I'm proud of the man I know he will become. The person he already is.

And I see Easton, staring right back at me, so much love in his eyes. This man I've always felt attached to, who I can now call my own.

A few years ago, I wouldn't have seen myself here, forty and married to my best friend. Being loved by him, the way I'd always hoped for.

I reckon, sometimes, hope is worth holding onto.

Epilogue

Two Years Later

Easton, age 42

My very favorite way to wake up is any way that involves Wyatt next to me.

Or, in the case of this morning, inside of me as he spoons me from behind, fucking me slowly.

I love when we have time for morning sex.

His stubble scrapes the back of my neck as he lays kisses across my skin, and I hold onto his arm tight, cocooning it against my chest. I'm half on my side, half on my stomach, with my leg thrown forward. I could easily confuse this angle for sleeping if it weren't for Wyatt's hips slapping softly against my ass every time he hits home and the feel of him inside me.

I don't know what it is about that feeling, whether fast and hard or slow, like now, but I love it. Maybe it reminds me of how close we are. Maybe I just like having Wyatt there, knowing he's the only person with that right.

Whatever it is, it makes me feel secure, and a little bit dirty.

"Mmm," Wyatt hums. "Love wakin' up like this."

Wyatt always sounds a little more country when he's sleepy, horny, or mad. Right now, he's two of the three.

I huff out my agreement as his cock slides over my prostate. One of my other very favorite things.

"Love you," I tell him, voice muffled by my pillow.

"You say the sweetest things," he croons.

Suddenly, he draws back, and I grunt out my protest as his thick length leaves my body.

"On your back, darlin'," he says, slapping my ass hard enough for me to feel the sting.

Wyatt enjoys the tender moments, but he also has a rough streak a mile wide. I can't say I have a problem with that. In fact, I very much appreciate both of those qualities and the way Wyatt can somehow mix them together when I least expect it.

I roll onto my back, morning erection stiff and leaking. Wyatt's gaze rakes over my body, making me feel even more on display. He grabs the lube from beside the bed and rolls a healthy dollop down my cock. In one quick movement, he straddles me and slides down, impaling himself fluidly.

I hiss, the sensation overwhelming in the best way.

Wyatt just gives me a cheeky grin, winking one of those mischievous brown eyes, before he starts riding me. My hands fly to his thighs, needing something to hold onto.

"Christ," I mutter, back bowing.

"Y'know what that song says, somethin' about savin' a horse and ridin' a cowboy." Wyatt's voice is breathy with his exertion.

"What horse we savin'?" I ask.

Wyatt laughs.

"How're you this energetic at six in the mornin'?" I want to know. "We were supposed to sleep in today, y'know."

"Are you complainin'?" he asks, bouncing up and down. "Besides, you know there's no sleepin' in for folks like us. We're hardwired to wake up before the sun."

"Hmm, well, I appreciate your mornin' vigor," I admit.

"Less talkin' now," Wyatt says, rolling his hips in a way that makes my eyes cross.

Wyatt doesn't let up until he's practically panting. I take his erection in my hand, pumping in time to his strokes. He calls out, and then he's coming, spine arched and head thrown back, his hair falling messily around his face. The image gets seared into my brain, and I know it's one I'm not likely to ever forget.

I follow him over the edge as his body grips me like a vise, nearly vibrating with my release. I slump when it's over, feeling utterly wrung out.

Wyatt grabs my hand from his cock, bringing it to his mouth and licking his own juices off my fingers. If I weren't a forty-two-year-old man, I'm sure that would be enough to make me rally. As is, my dick merely twitches at the sight, making a valiant effort.

"Y'know," Wyatt says, slipping off of me and rolling against my side, "I thought I couldn't get any hornier than when I was a teenager, or maybe in my early twenties. But this takes the cake. It just keeps gettin' better, and I only want you more and more."

I squeeze my husband to my side, running my hand through his tangled hair.

"You have me," I tell him. "Always."

"Well, that's good 'cause I want another forty years of this. When we're in our eighties, old and gray, it'll still be you and me. We'll be so stupid in love, we'll embarrass all the young folks in town 'cause we won't be able to keep our hands off one another."

It's true that things in town are a lot different than they were when *we* were kids. Way back then, I couldn't imagine seeing two men holding hands in public, let alone kissing. And yet now, that's not something I have to worry about. Sure, Wyatt and I aren't going around making out like teenagers, but we hold hands sometimes, and I can lean over and kiss his lips whenever I want to. There are still a few folks who keep their distance or shoot us snide looks, but most are friendly and supportive. Nash even has a rainbow flag hanging in his restaurant's window now.

Here, in Plum Valley, we take our beef and our Pride seriously.

"Nah, they won't be embarrassed," I tell him. "They'll be jealous."

"Of our wrinkly skin? Whatever you say, Gramps."

"I like your wrinkly skin," I say, pressing my lips together to stop from laughing as I run my finger over Wyatt's face.

"Excuse me?" He pushes away from me. "I meant when I'm *eighty*. I don't have wrinkles."

I can't hold back my laughter any longer because we both know that's not true, and Wyatt's face breaks into a smile as he joins me, ducking his head against my chest and chuckling.

"Sounds like a perfect life," I tell him seriously.

Wyatt sighs, rubbing his cheek against my skin. I bet he can hear my heart beating, and I wonder what it sounds like to him. If he can pick out the notes that are just for him.

"We should prob'ly get movin'," Wyatt finally says. "I bet Will is already pacin' the house, checkin' to make sure he's got everythin' packed."

"I can't believe we're sendin' our little boy off to college," I admit.

He's eighteen now. It's hard to believe that it's been so long since those days when Wyatt and I would rock him to sleep.

When I'd carry him outside because the country noise seemed to settle him. When Wyatt would sing to him.

Suddenly, a flash of memory hits me so hard it feels like it's happening in real time. It's Wyatt, singing that song, "I Say a Little Prayer," walking Will around the deck, crooning him to sleep. I smile at the image in my head, and I can hear the words he sang. I remember them vividly and how, in that moment, my heart felt so full. It felt like Wyatt was singing to me, too, saying he'd love me forever and ever, asking me to answer his prayer. And now I wonder if maybe he was.

"Don't let Will hear you call him little," Wyatt says, "or you'll incur his wrath." When I don't answer, Wyatt looks up at me, his brow crinkled. "What's that smile for?"

"You," I say simply. "Just thinkin' 'bout you."

"Well, Easton William Moore," Wyatt says, humor dancing in his golden brown eyes. "You look like a fool."

"A fool in love," I tell him.

Wyatt lifts his hand, tracing my lower lip, before he rests his palm over my heart, right where he belongs. "Makes two of us."

———————— ✦ ————————

The End

About the Author

Information about Emmy Sanders and her complete list of works can be found on her website. Subscribe to her newsletter, join her Facebook reader group, Emmy's Enclave, and connect via email or social media:

www.emmysanders.com

Find online:
www.facebook.com/emmysandersmm
www.instagram.com/emmysandersmm

Printed in Great Britain
by Amazon